# MISSION 37

*A Novel*

MICHAEL A BERK

# Dedication -

*To my wife Wendy and the kids-*

*Elizabeth, Grant, Jennifer and Drew*

*ISBN : 979-8-3507-3687-8*

# CAST OF CHARACTERS

*Jack Monroe MD - Army Air Corps Flight Surgeon*

*Sgt. Kemp - Monroe's Aide*

*Colonel Kleet - Military Intelligence*

*Major Clifford. - Aide to General Bedell Smith*

*Dionne - Canadian Relief Worker*

*Bernie - Dionne's father*

*Morty Gruber - Dionne's uncle*

*Harry Gruber - Dionne's cousin, British 8th Army*

*Sammy - Dionne's boyfriend*

*Avrum - Israeli operative*

*Simon - Israeli operative*

*Guy St. Germaine - French physician*

*Geoffrey Menzies-Smith - British physician*

*Georgi Dugasvili - Russian physician*

Peter Monod - Swiss physician

James Watson - British Intelligence (MI5)

Dimitri -Russian operative

Cosette - Simon's sister

Michel - Cosette's husband

Conrad Monod - Swiss banker, brother of Peter,

Fr. Giuseppe Lordo -Vatican priest

Marie - Lordo's lover

Captain Antonio Civelli - freighter Captain

Mr. Abadi - a hawalder

## Historical Characters

Martin Bormann - head of the Nazi Party Chancellery, Personal Secretary and close associate of Adolf Hitler

Adolf Hitler - Nazi leader of Germany 1933-1945

General Walter Bedell Smith - Chief of Staff to General Eisenhower. Later head of CIA

General Dwight "Ike" Eisenhower  Commander -in-Chief SHAEF, later President of the United States

Winston S. Churchill - Former Prime Minister of England, Painter

Desmond Morton - British Civil Servant

Chaim Weizmann - Russian-born biochemist, Zionist, friend of Churchill and later First President of the State of Israel

Haj Amin al-Husseini - Grand Mufti of Jerusalem

Menachem Begin - Irgun member, later Prime Minister of Israel

## Terms

S.H.A.E.F - Supreme Headquarters Allied Expeditionary Forces - headquarters of the Commander of Allied forces in northwest Europe from 1943 until the end of the war

Irgun - a Zionist paramilitary organization that was linked to acts of terrorism in the Palestine Mandate

SA - Sturmabteilung - Storm troops also known as the Brown Shirts. Nazi paramilitary group that aided in Hitler's rise to power. Later purged by Hitler

# PROLOGUE

June 22, 1941- The Kremlin

The Red Army general stood ramrod straight. His voice quavered, "Comrade Stalin, it is as the British warned. Hitler has attacked. Three German armies have crossed the border. Your orders?"

Stalin appeared an ashen old man, his small stature more evident without his usual air of authority. Certainly he was not the revolutionary Man of Steel, his Bolshevik nom de guerre. He did not speak for several minutes. The officers present stood still, none of them willing to break their leader's revery, look away, or appear at all nervous.

When he looked up, Stalin's face had no expression. "That is impossible. One of your young officers has panicked." He looked as if he was trying to convince himself.

"We...we have aerial photos, sir. We can show you."
"Leave them. You are dismissed. Send in Comrade Beria."

The officers backed out of the office, making no further comment. In Stalin's USSR, it was not good to be a bearer of bad news.

A rotund man in an ill fitting suit entered. Leverenti Beria was one of Stalin's closest confidants. Among the Soviet Union's ruling elite, only Stalin himself was more feared.

"You are aware, Leverenti?"
"Yes, Comrade Stalin."

"It wasn't supposed to be this way. *We were supposed to spring the trap.* The NKVD failed me. You will take care of those responsible."
"Yes, Comrade."

"And those bearers of bad news as well. "

"Yes, comrade. If I may, comrade, we have to activate all our military and espionage assets immediately. Shall I have Molotov reach out to the English?"

Stalin slowly rose from his chair. "I am going to my apartment. You have your orders."

Stalin would speak to no one or issue any orders for three days. His military, fearing him as much as the Germans, did not take any initiative. As a result, thousands of Soviets perished in those early days, and millions more would until Berlin fell four years later. He and Beria were the only ones who knew the entire story of the final victory. In their minds, only when enemies of the state from within and without were eliminated would they be truly victorious.

# PART I

## 1

The war in Europe had ended in May. The Japanese surrendered in August. The ward was actually quiet. He hadn't really noticed it before, but the constant drone of aircraft and, thankfully, the screeching of ambulance sirens were gone. He only heard a few groans and snores of the patients as he made his way to his tiny office. Tonight was the last night shift for this week. He had never quite gotten used to working nights, but it was part of the drill. He had already written his orders. Most were automatic, almost reflexive. The night nurses, most of whom liked working alone without interference from anyone else, would take those orders off and add their own interpretation as to when and how they would be executed. By morning they would have everything done. He went to his office with a cup of coffee, loosened his tie, and began completing charts.

Jack Monroe had been a flight surgeon for a little over four years. He joined the army in early 1941 after finishing his medical training. He had accepted a position in a hospital in St. Louis to begin after his year of military service was to be completed in 1942. It was a remarkable stroke of poor timing. December 7 and the bombing of Pearl Harbor came, and soon after he was transferred to the Army Air Corps. Even that had been delayed by an investigation into his background.

James "Jack" Monroe had been born Yacov Moskowitz in southern Russia. He had come to the United States when he was two with his widowed mother and older sister. A customs officer at Ellis Island with a twisted sense of history had given him his new name. He often wondered whether former fifth President would be amused or appalled that his namesake's mother called him Jackie with her thick Jewish accent. He grew up in the Bronx and later enrolled at the University of South Carolina. He joined the track team running the 100 yard dash. Based on his grades, his mother thought he was having way too much fun running track and chasing girls rather than studying. She shipped him off to St Louis figuring that anything out on the Mississippi must be so boring he would be forced to work harder at college.

For some reason, G2 had decided because of his Russian birth that he might be a Russian mole and delayed his transfer to the Air Corps. Fortunately, the Army is run by clerks. Jack was able to persuade a clerk needing a medical excuse for a couple of days leave to expedite his clearance, something a real spy probably would have done.

He came to England in 1943 and was made Flight Surgeon for the 68th Squadron after D-Day. He had been with them for 36 of their 50 missions. The surviving airmen would be rotating home in a week. Many of the squadron's personnel from 1943 were dead or missing. He had treated or sent home most of the wounded. No transfer orders had come for him yet.

A Hoosier twang interrupted his thoughts, "Doc, there's a guy to see you. Says it's some kinda 'official' business. Looks like a headquarters weenie."

"Thank you Sergeant Kemp, but let's leave the appraisals to the medical experts. Bring him in." They both laughed. Kemp, who had been his aide and unofficial, often unsolicited, advisor for over a year rolled his eyes and walked out. He still limped as a result of the 'ack-ack' wound he had suffered soon after Monroe's arrival. He had refused to be transferred home. He told Monroe at the time, "It's just not right not to finish this up." Monroe had been able to wrangle an aide position for him. Kemp had become a loyal friend and confidant.

Jack stood to his full six feet four inches, ran his hand through his curly brown hair, and pulled on his white coat. "Might as well play the busy doctor part for this guy," he mused.

The stocky Kemp ushered in an officer who handed Kemp his soaking wet rain coat and hat. The officer's uniform was starched and parade ground perfect, like a thousand other professional soldiers. He was average height, slim with brown hair starting to grey, clean shaven and crew cut. His expression was all business, his dark eyes riveted on whomever he spoke to. "Thank you, sergeant. And it's 'Colonel Weenie' to you."

"Yes, sir."

"Dismissed, Sergeant Kemp," said Monroe. Kemp saluted and was quickly out the door.

The colonel turned to Jack. "As your guard dog is likely within ear shot Captain, I will ask you to read these orders so we can be on our way." He handed Jack an envelope and remained standing.

Jack decided he wasn't going to be rushed by this officious character. He had dealt with too many of these types among his medical professors "Coffee, Colonel...?"

"It's Kleet. No thank you. We need to move along."

Jack sat behind his desk and opened the envelope.

Captain Jack Monroe:

You will accompany the officer presenting these orders to SHAEF Headquarters by order of General Walter Beedle Smith.

"I'll take those back now, Captain. Please grab a bag. I am told you will be away several days."

"If you'll pardon me, Colonel. I've just come off a 12 hour shift and need a meal and a shower. I also need to speak to my chief about coverage."

"Your chief has been notified. You can sleep in the car There will be time to clean up and eat before your meeting. And Captain, bring a clean uniform. There will be big brass at this one, and they won't be impressed by your MD or a white coat."

"Yes, sir. I'll get my gear."

Kemp snapped to attention, eyes forward, as they walked by his desk. "The boss will be letting you know who's covering, Sergeant. I'll be leaving with the Colonel." Kemp stood there for a moment wondering what the hell was going on. Monroe had been his friend and protector. Kemp decided he would check the scuttlebutt on Colonel "Weenie." Monroe was a good doctor, but Kemp thought he might need some protection from this guy from someone who understood the army way of doing things like he did.

It was obvious to Monroe that Colonel Whoever He was not interested in any conversation. The Colonel gazed straight ahead while Monroe looked out the car window at the overcast, wet countryside. Maybe the phrase should have been, "There will always be a 'wet' England." They had passed through one small village after another. They all looked the same to Monroe. Yes, they were charming, but he noticed the weariness on the villagers' faces. He had seen that look in the mirror recently as well.

The driver, a three striper, was built more like a linebacker than a chauffeur, but seemed to have some skill in steering around the roads clogged with military traffic and the odd civilian vehicles without ever resorting to the horn or digital gestures. He was finally defeated by a farmer leading his sheep across the road.

While they were stalled, Kleet turned to Monroe. "Headquarters isn't far. My driver will escort you to Bedell Smith's aide who will take you to the general. I would advise you not to offer any opinions unless asked directly by the general." Kleet smiled for the first time. "He's not exactly the most open minded person you will ever meet."

"I appreciate the Colonel's candor+," said Monroe.

"It wasn't a favor, more of a warning. Whatever they want you for, it isn't fixing Eisenhower's hemorrhoids, so shut up and listen. I don't have the time or interest to go driving all over England finding another medic that pleases them."

Kleet didn't strike Monroe as a fool blindly running around England without having some inkling of what his mission was about. "I will try not to inconvenience the Colonel any further, sir."

"That's what I mean. A nod or a 'Yes, sir' will suffice over your feeble attempts at humor." The last sheep was finally across the road, and the car started moving. There was no further conversation the rest of the way.

# 2

SHAEF Headquarters was in an old manor house surrounded by outbuildings and trailers for the staff. There were a few cottages on the property that were obviously set aside for the brass. They had passed a golf course conveniently close enough for a quick round. Kleet's car was waived through security with barely a glance at his ID and a perfunctory salute by the MPs. When they pulled up to the entrance to the manor, an MP opened Monroe's door and snapped to attention. "Welcome Captain Monroe. Please, follow me sir." He about-faced and briskly walked toward the front door. Monroe turned to salute Kleet, but his car was already pulling away. "I definitely need to speak to his doctor about a personality graft," thought Monroe, and followed the MP in.

They walked through the main hallway, exited the rear of the building and walked toward a small house. Monroe wondered how many of the people hustling around were actually important, and how many just thought they were. He was ushered into a sparsely furnished ante room, just a couple of chairs and a table with the obligate ash tray.

General Bedell Smith's aide casually returned his salute, barely looking up. "Welcome Captain or doctor. Which do you prefer?"

"Well, since the 'Captain' is likely temporary as the war's over, doctor is fine if it pleases the Major."

"Thank you, doctor, and it's Major Clifford. Nice to meet you. If you will follow me, the general is waiting for you. I would remind you he is quite busy."

Monroe had never met a headquarters officer who wasn't "busy". Kemp would say that meeting *two* weenies in one day might be a warning of an impending shit storm.

# 3

Monroe had expected to see Bedell Smith alone for some reason. He was surprised to see the back of a tall General in a short jacket, talking to Smith, who could only be Eisenhower. When "Ike" turned around, Monroe assumed his most military bearing and snapped to attention. Eisenhower returned the salute with the famous smile.

"Sit, doctor. Oh, and don't worry, you're not making a house call. The last doctor I saw cleared me back into the States after Normandy. I think the general here had a word with him. Shortest exam in my life. General Smith will brief you on a mission we want you to consider. Bedell, go ahead."

Smith's expression left no doubt that there would be any "considering " involved. His grave expression was enhanced by his round spectacles. The ease that Eisenhower's greeting had brought dissipated instantly. Monroe felt like he was in the principal's office.

"Captain, we have an errand for you that will require your medical expertise more than your military skills. You come highly recommended and your ability to be discreet has been vouched for. This conversation is classified, and there will be no record of it. Should you not wish to proceed, tell us now and you will be escorted to your unit. Your commander already thinks you're here on some bureaucratic bullshit anyway."

Kemp would say not to volunteer and get the hell out of Dodge. Fortunately or unfortunately, Monroe was far more curious than Kemp. Monroe looked at Eisenhower, whose smile had been replaced by a look of expectation that Monroe *would* be on board. He was beginning to understand why this guy was so successful at bending people to his will.

" I understand, sir. Please go ahead."

Eisenhower stood and looked directly at Monroe. "Captain, General Smith is my trusted associate, and I have the utmost faith in his judgement, as I hope I will in yours." A smile, a salute, and Eisenhower was gone before Monroe could stand.

Smith polished his glasses and placed them deliberately on his head. "Well, Captain, I hope you have a good memory."

"The Allies occupy Germany but do not really control it. Even the Russians are having problems in their zone. The British are worn out and the French, well, they're having enough trouble trying reclaim their own country. It is imperative that we get some stability and go home. It's hard enough to find Germans without a Nazi past somewhere in the closet even to pick up garbage or drive a bus. We have to assure that there is nothing left of the Nazi big shots or any new ones coming. So, it is paramount that we find and punish the ones living and make sure as hell the ones that are supposed to be dead are dead. Hell, there are still people saying Hitler is hiding in the mountains in Bavaria." He paused for a moment and Monroe, ignoring Kleet's warning, felt a need to fill the void.

"Yes sir. I understand. I'm not sure where I fit in."

"I am getting to that *Captain*," Smith said, clearly not wanting any further comment.

"A body was recovered in Berlin that is supposedly one of Hitler's inner circle. Someone who, if alive, could make the pacification of Germany more difficult; and if dead, well, one less Nazi to worry about. The Russians, in a surprisingly cooperative act, have asked us to help with the identification of the remains. Frankly, I don't trust those bastards as far as I can throw 'em, but General Eisenhower is under orders from President Truman to grab at every opportunity to keep things moving ahead diplomatically. So, you Captain, are going to help us. You are going to Germany to attend an autopsy as a representative expert of the United States Occupying Forces along with our British, French, and Russian allies. You will get the details from Colonel Kleet who you have already met. Questions?"

"Yes, sir, a couple."

"Make it brief."

"Yes, sir. First, who recommended and vouched for me, and second, who is this Nazi?"

"Senator Stapleton endorsed you. Don't know how or why it's any of his business. He sits on the Intelligence Committee, which is how he got wind of this; and we got wind of you. I understand you know him. He certainly knows you. The Nazi in question is Martin Bormann. Now, *with your permission,* Captain, I have other matters to attend to. Colonel Kleet will be waiting for you. You are dismissed."

Major Clifford told Monroe to make himself comfortable, that Kleet would be back to get him soon enough and went back to appearing to be busy.

# 4

Monroe had no idea who Martin Bormann was but was well acquainted with Senator Stapleton. They had first met at a restaurant in New York. At that time, Stapleton was a Congressman, but more importantly, he was Monroe's future father-in-law. Monroe had met Kathy Stapleton in St. Louis at a Washington University mixer. She was aggressive, smart, and had the good looks and social background that set her in the crosshairs of the wealthy frat boys. Monroe had never quite understood what had made Kathy pursue him, and looking back, she was definitely the pursuer. Not that Monroe had objected. They began dating Junior year, and by Monroe's second year in medical school were engaged with a society wedding in the offing.

Their relationship, never truly passionate, began to fall apart when Monroe began looking for an internship. He had always wanted to be an internist who, along with surgeons, had the toughest training. He had the grades and recommendations to get a good position even with most programs having Jewish quotas, which were basically "Jews not welcome here." Kathy wanted him to come east and go into dermatology. Her father had the influence to get him into a program of his choice. She said dermatology would fit into their future life the best. "Nobody gets sick, and nobody gets better. My dad could get us into his club, our kids could go to great schools, and we could vacation whenever we wanted to." Monroe wondered how they had spent so much time together and had not had a common vision of the future.  Their relationship just ended - no fireworks, no passion.

Monroe had met Stapleton on numerous occasions.  He had always been friendly but not warm.  Monroe knew he loved his daughter, who was his only family, his wife having passed away a year or so before Monroe and Kathy met.  He hadn't seen the Senator or heard from him in nearly 5 years.

# 5

*Fall, 1940*

Monroe had just finished his resident's clinic when the nurse told him he had a call, from a Congressman no less.  Her look suggested that the caller must be mistaken asking for Jack, that it must be some other Dr. Monroe.  Monroe knew immediately who it was.  He and Kathy had lost contact after their breakup.  Through a mutual friend he had found out she was dating an attorney at a Manhattan "white shoe" law firm.  Certainly someone who would fit her mold.  So what the hell did her dad want?

Stapleton was pleasant but curt.  "Jack, I'm here in St. Louis meeting with some party people and donors.  I'm bored

22

to tears.  I was wondering if you and I could get a drink somewhere."

"Sure, Congressman."

"I'm at the Chase Park Plaza.   Meet me at 6 in the bar. And, it's Tom."

"See you at 6, sir, er Tom."

Monroe lived just a few blocks from the Chase.   He was able to get changed and make it to the hotel with a few minutes to spare.  Thomas Stapleton was sitting at a table looking out over Forest Park.   When Monroe had visited Stapleton's Manhattan home, he had informed the native New Yorker that Forest Park was the largest city park in the country, bigger than Central Park across the street. Stapleton, who believed that nothing of much value existed west of the Hudson River, politely nodded.   Today, he was dressed in a tailored, charcoal grey, three piece pin stripe suit that offset his steel grey hair, looking every bit the scion of Manhattan's elite that he was.  Monroe wondered if people like Stapleton took "patrician lessons" at Harvard.   He stood and ushered Monroe to sit.

"I'd shake your hand but that's all I've been doing since my Senate campaign got started.  Gets sore at the end of the day. Nothing personal.   What can I get you? Beer? That's all anybody drinks in this town."

"Gin and tonic.   House brand is fine."

They made small talk until the drinks arrived.

"Jack, my purpose here is not totally social." Monroe was not surprised. Stapleton always had an agenda.

"As you know, I hope to be the next Senator from New York. My opponents are trying to stir up some bullshit about me being an anti-Semite because of the break up between you and Kathy. They're saying I encouraged it because I didn't want a Jew, especially a Russian one, in my family. I will admit that I didn't think it would work. I know my daughter. When you derailed her life plan by pursuing your career choice, you were done. I want you to know that I always liked you and had nothing to do with your breakup. But, I do have a favor to ask. You may get calls from newspaper people asking you about me and maybe about any role I played in your breakup with Kathy. You answer them the way you want, but I hope the worst you can say is 'No comment.'"

"Thanks, Tom. I appreciate your candor (if politicians can have candor, Monroe thought). I will tell you that my folks were wary of me getting involved with someone of Kathy's pedigree as well, that I would never be one of you and all that (Monroe's mother had only grudgingly accepted her). You always treated me well, and I have no hard feelings toward Kathy or you. You will have no issues with me and reporters."

"Thanks, Jack. Just out of curiosity, everything going OK with you?"

"My training is over and I've joined up to get that out of the way. Planning on coming back here after discharge."

"If I'm not being too personal, anyone to come back for, a future Mrs.Monroe?"

Jack knew that Stapleton probably hoped there was a "future Mrs. Monroe." It would make things politically more tidy. He also suspected Stapleton knew the answer to his own question. He was never surprised. "No. Had a few flings but nobody serious since Kathy."

"Well, good luck. I've got to go meet Harry Truman. Son-of-a-bitch owned a clothing store and ended up a Senator. Hard to believe. Only in America, as they say. If I can ever help, you let me know."

"Thank you, Tom."

# 6

Major Clifford interrupted Monroe's thoughts. "Captain, Colonel Kleet is here. He'll meet you where he dropped you."

Jack returned his focus to the present. "Thank you Major Clifford.

"Well, I see you survived your meeting. Get in the car. We have a quick ride to take. I'll brief you when we arrive."

"Yes, sir, I guess I did," said Monroe, not sure if Kleet was paying him a back-handed compliment. That notion was soon disabused.

"Captain Monroe," Kleet said with some irritation, " there will be no more 'guessing'. You have your orders to complete a sensitive mission. For some reason, the brass think that you have the smarts to get this done right. If you 'guess' wrong, they will be embarrassed. If they are embarrassed, I will be embarrassed. *I* really hate being embarrassed but *you* will hate it even more. Do I make myself abundantly clear?"

"Yes, sir. I will not embarrass you."

Monroe wondered what Kleet's blood pressure was. They drove a short distance to a quonset hut at the edge of the base. There was another round of ID flashing before they were allowed in. The room was furnished in the usual military fashion. There were two desks, one inhabited by a staff sergeant, an empty one that Monroe presumed was Kleet's, and a table with a folder on it.

"Sergeant, why don't you take a break and write a letter home. Make it a long letter," ordered Kleet.

As soon as the sergeant left, an MP who could have been Kleet's driver's twin closed the door, barring any entry.

Kleet pointed to the folder on the table. "Captain, you are to read and memorize the documents in that folder. I will then go over the mission with you in detail and answer any questions that you have that I think are relevant. The file will not be leaving here. Take all the time you need. You have one hour." Kleet left, saying something to the MP as he did so. Clearly, Monroe wasn't leaving for one hour.

He opened the folder and found a dossier on one Martin Bormann. It was not particularly thick, especially by the bureaucratic standards of the army. Monroe went into the same "cram mode" that he used to memorize anatomy his first year at med school.

Bormann was born in 1900 and had been one of the early members of the Nazi Party. The dossier noted that he had been secretary to Deputy Führer Rudolf Hess for eight years before Hess had flown to England to recruit Nazi sympathizers to force peace with Germany. That misguided attempt has led to his capture and imprisonment. Apparently, Bormann had somehow managed to avoid the disgrace that his boss had suffered and ended up being Chief of the Nazi Party Chancellery and eventually Hitler's Private Secretary. "Must have been a slippery SOB to survive in that crowd. Unfortunately, the same types exist everywhere," thought Monroe. The file had little else in it. Bormann was rarely noted in any domestic or foreign press or seen with Hitler publicly. There were a few photos taken by Eva Braun at Hitler's Bavarian retreat at Berchtesgarten with Bormann in the background talking to some Nazi big shot. "Why do they care about this guy?" Monroe wondered.

# 7

Landesburg Prison, 1925

Martin Bormann waited for Hess in the back seat of an old Mercedes outside the prison gates. Hess was visiting Adolf Hitler, the prison's most famous inmate. Two SA brown shirts stood outside the car to ward off any attempts by guards to make them move. Hitler had been sent to prison after a failed attempt to take over the Bavarian government. Coverage of his trial had given him a platform and a national audience for his message. His incarceration was more of a house arrest than a prison sentence. He was treated more like a guest than a prisoner.

Hess had been with Hitler for over an hour going over proofs for *Mein Kampf*, Hitler's holy writ for the Nazi Party. Bormann had transcribed some of Hitler's notes himself. The original notes were to be destroyed after Hitler reviewed the manuscript. As it was Bormann's duty to destroy the originals, no one suspected that he had kept certain key handwritten notes for potential profit should Hitler and the movement succeed. Personal security and advancement were always his mission. He did not require notoriety, only direct access to influence power for his own purposes. Hitler, Goering, and Hess adored the flashbulbs. Bormann avoided the limelight scrupulously, viewing his own privacy as protection from potential enemies known and unknown.

Bormann had first met Hitler at a Nazi Party meeting in Munich after World War I. Bormann had always kept his political views quiet. He had voted for several different parties in the many elections that occurred in the Weimar Republic created after the Great War. He had never actually joined a political party. Better not to be on a list. He had heard about Hitler from his employer who advised him that Hitler was a rising force who was drawing together a coalition of diverse political interests in Bavaria including war veterans, socialists, ultra-nationalists, anti-Semites, and business interests. Hitler spoke to all of them. They heard what they wanted to hear while ignoring or quietly endorsing the uglier, darker side of his rantings.

At that small rally, Bormann saw the power of Hitler's oratory. He started quietly. As his voice grew louder, he became more animated. The crowd gained energy along with him. By the end of the speech, they were drunk with enthusiasm (and no small amount of alcohol). Bormann saw the potential for Hitler to rise in the precarious political world that was Germany at the time. He also saw the potential havoc such a man could wreak if not controlled. His curiosity peaked, he decided he needed to learn more about Hitler.

Bormann had to join the Party in order to meet Hitler. As there were more followers than dues paying members,

Bormann was easily able to secure membership and was invited to meet the Nazi party leaders at a party picnic.

He was greeted by Hess, who extolled to him of the virtues of National Socialism and Adolf Hitler. Hess clearly idolized Hitler and was honored to serve as his acolyte. Bormann appraised Hess as ambitious but not particularly politically savvy, clearly a follower who could be influenced as long as he felt he was serving the cause and Hitler.

When Bormann met Hitler, he was not particularly impressed. The man he met was not the spellbinder he had seen at the rally. He was physically unimpressive, not particularly energetic, and was more than content doing the bidding and letting others do the work, concerned only about the outcome, not the method. It was the Hitler of the beer hall that was rising in Germany, not this social Bohemian he met here.

Bormann quickly realized that he could not break into the inner circle that also included Goering, Himmler, and Goebbels. Hess was the way in. Bormann would be to Hess what Hess was to Hitler. He volunteered to be Hess' secretary and quickly made himself Hess' constant companion. Where Hitler went, Hess often followed. Always a step behind Hess was Bormann.

As Bormann waited for Hess, he contemplated his future. Hitler would be released soon and the Nazi party was putting up candidates for the next parliamentary elections. He suspected that they might win a few seats but not enough to influence the current government coalition. It might be a good time to seek other allegiances. Bormann had always been patient. He would wait until after the voting. If circumstances changed for the worse, he would move on. No one outside of the party really had any idea of who he was or what he did. He would be a Nazi a little bit longer.

# 8

*Berlin, May, 1941*

Bormann was truly frightened. He had always been aware of events around him. He made decisions that always allowed him a way out without danger if things did not go his way. He had stayed with the Nazis in the early '30s when they appeared to be on the wan. Even then, he was in the background, virtually unknown. Had the Party failed to attain power, he would have gone back to some bureaucratic position somewhere, working for a former Nazi sympathizer in industry most likely. The Nazis had been victorious, and now the new Germany controlled the continent. He had risen along with Hess, who had become Deputy Führer. He exercised critical influence over Hess, or so he thought.

He hadn't seen Hess for a few days. Hess had told him that he had some personal business, which Bormann assumed to be a rendezvous with a bar maid or, worse for Bormann, some Party member's wife. Another Hess mess to clean up.

That had been his only concern until the SS had arrived that morning. Bormann was instructed to come with them.

Bormann's anxiety became worse as they proceeded through Berlin. They were headed toward the government offices.

Now he was sitting outside Hitler's office. Had Bormann been accused of something by a Party rival, something all too common in the Nazi hierarchy? Had someone gotten to Hess or, worse, to Hitler? While Hess depended on Bormann, he would not remain loyal to Bormann if his own position were threatened. Goebbels hated Hess. Maybe he was behind this, or Himmler, another master intriguer.

The door opened and Admiral Canaris, head of the Abwehr, German military intelligence, walked out. What was he doing here?

"Bormann, the Fuhrer would like to speak with you. We have some questions," said Canaris in a clipped tone.

Bormann snapped to attention and tried to appear unruffled as he walked into Hitler's office.

Hitler's office was the size of a banquet hall. Bormann imagined he had copied some of the opulent decor from Versailles. Hitler sat at the far end behind an enormous desk that was as grandiose as its surroundings. The desk was on a raised platform so that Hitler could look down upon his guests, making him appear more intimidating.

Hitler was not alone. Also present were Goebbels and Himmler. Everyone's expressions were grim. Bormann saluted with the expected "Heil, Hitler!" Hitler barely looked up. He motioned Bormann to sit.

Canaris spoke first. "When did you last see Hess?"

Bormann noted that Hess's rank was left out. He decided to answer truthfully, as he did not know anything anyway and suspected that they all knew a lot more. "A few days ago, Admiral."

"Be more precise."

Bormann knew his next answers would likely seal his fate, whatever he was accused of. "Three days ago, in the morning. He told me that he had personal business to attend to and that he would call me on his return."

"And where was this personal business?"

"He did not tell me. Sometimes he does that."

"And what did you think the business was, being his personal secretary?"

Bormann hesitated. "I thought he was with a woman. I did not know who." He stole a glance at Goebbels, a notorious womanizer. Did he see a glint of acknowledgment in his expression?

Canaris looked directly at Bormann. "Our intelligence has learned that Hess used his authority to commandeer a single engine aircraft and fly to England."

Bormann did not have to fake his astonishment. " I knew nothing of this...Admiral." Now he was pleading. "Nothing."

Himmler now spoke. "We have investigated the matter. I have been through documents recovered from his home. We have thoroughly interrogated his staff and the personnel at the airfield. You are the last."

Bormann knew better than to interrupt. He knew that interrogation by Himmler's thugs always got answers, some of which were suggested by the interrogator to suit Himmler's selfish purposes.

"He left a letter behind. I would like you to read it."

The letter was clearly in Hess's handwriting. It was one page long and addressed to Hitler.

"Mein Fuhrer,

I am leaving you tonight on a mission to make peace with the British. I know that there are sympathizers to our great cause in England. I believe if I can make contact with them and assure them of our commitment not to destroy the British empire, that they will overthrow Churchill and his gang. We will then be able to build our new Reich and finish off the Bolsheviks and Jews in the east. Even though I do this without your order, I know that you will support my efforts.

No one knows of my mission, not even Bormann, whom I have always trusted. I know he would have tried to talk me out of it because of his loyalty to me and to you.

Your servant,

Rudolf Hess"

Bormann looked up at Himmler, waiting for him to speak. Himmler looked directly at Bormann. "We consider him a traitor," he said with finality.

" And will proclaim it to the world," Goebbels interjected stridently.

Now Bormann was terrified. He was the "traitor's" confidant. Himmler was certainly not one to trust someone's word unless it suited his purpose.

No one spoke. Hitler motioned for the letter, read it, and looked at Bormann. They all waited for his response.

"Indeed, Hess is a traitor," Hitler affirmed. "Canaris will use our agents in England to find out what the British have done with Hess. Himmler will continue his investigation here to root out further traitors in our midst. Dr. Goebbels will say nothing public for now." Goebbels started to speak but thought better of it. "You may now go to your duties. Bormann will stay behind with me."

After they left, Hitler stood and began to pace back and forth. The two SS guards remaining in the room stood a few feet away from his desk.

Hitler shook his head. "I do not know what possessed Hess. I thought him loyal. I was deceived. When we achieve our victory, I will deal with Hess. Now, Bormann, I must deal with you." Bormann stole a glance a the guards, waiting for the blow to come.

"You were Hess's right hand. Now I want you to become mine. Don't look so surprised. You know how things work, you shielded Hess from bureaucratic machinations and did so while remaining unknown to the public. The only person you could not protect Hess from was himself. You will not have that problem with me. I *am* Germany. You will help me to continue my efforts without getting caught up in the mundane. Well?"

"It is my honor, Mein Führer," Bormann barely uttered. He had gone from a dead man walking to the highest of insiders. His mind was racing. It was difficult to maintain his usual business-like expression. He decided to probe Hitler a bit more. "Will I answer directly to you?"

"You will work for me, here, just next to this office. You will make yourself available at all times and be present at most of my appointments. I will expect absolute loyalty.

You have no sponsor but me. Remember, neither Himmler nor Goebbels trust you and will be quick to point out anything that could be perceived as disloyalty. That is the legacy that Hess left you."

Bormann stood at attention. "Then Mein Führer, with your permission, I will begin my duties immediately. Heil Hitler."

Hitler waved him out dismissively. He was escorted by an aide to his new office. His papers and files were already being moved there. It was a large and elegant office, fitting for the Fuhrer's private Secretary. He asked to be left alone. He was now at the summit. Hitler was right; the vultures would be after him. He knew he needed to make himself indispensable to Hitler and had no doubt he would succeed.

# 9

Monroe was done reading the Bormann dossier in 15 minutes. It took another ten to commit it to memory. He figured Kleet would return at exactly the one hour mark, leaving him plenty of time to analyze his situation. His assignment was to observe an autopsy, with several other unlikely volunteers, on a minor player, or so it seemed, in the Nazi hierarchy. He was not a pathologist nor even a high ranking medical officer, yet he had just been given orders by the highest of the brass. There was his "connection" to Senator Stapleton, but was Stapleton really keeping that close an eye on Jack? And, why the hell was Stapleton involved with missions like this? He had always been a big picture guy. Jack hadn't seen or spoken to him or his daughter since before the war. He had not followed Stapleton's Senatorial career except for a cursory read when he saw his name in Stars and Stripes. He never was mentioned as one of Truman's inner circle, so where did the clout to influence Ike come from? Probably the intelligence committee. Maybe this was just some kind of political move. Maybe Stapleton was like this Bormann guy, a minor player, but on the inside. It still kept coming back to "Why this and why me?" Monroe would put aside the questions for now and wait for answers to come. His military experience told him that further questions were not a good idea. His medical training and his otherwise innate curiosity told him not to be satisfied until all questions were resolved.

Kleet came back at exactly one hour, as Monroe had expected. "Well, Doctor, what's our subject's diagnosis?"

"Not much to go on, sir. He seems to be an upper level Party functionary who lived in the shadows. There was only one picture of him, in the background with a bunch of Nazi big shots. No personal or medical information. Not sure why anybody is interested in him."

"You mean like the headquarters types at the Pentagon."

Monroe thought this was Kleet's attempt at humor, so he smiled - briefly. He thought he saw a hint of appreciation in Kleet's eyes. "Above our pay grade."

Monroe knew it was above his pay grade. He wasn't so sure about Kleet's.

"I suspect a smart boy like you learned that folder in about 15 minutes. I won't quiz you on it. That would waste your time and mine."

"Thank you, sir."

"Save the thanks for more genteel types. If I had to guess, you spent the rest of your time trying to figure out what the hell you are doing here. Am I close?"

"Yes, sir. I thought you might enlighten me," said Monroe, knowing full well that enlightenment was not in Kleet's job description.

"Well Captain, the brass sought not to enlighten me, so I will tell you what I have been ordered to do, which I know will disappoint you. In this man's army, curiosity is not relevant and best kept to oneself."

"We will be leaving in forty-five minutes and flying to a base near Berlin. You will be driven to Potsdam outside of Berlin where you will be housed in suitable accommodations for your rank and mission. You will meet your medical colleagues for dinner at 1900 hours. As you were told, they are all selected representatives of Allied powers.  I will give you their particulars on the plane.  The autopsy commences at 0800 the next morning and should last no more than two hours.  You will then meet together to compile your opinions, which will  be submitted to the respective government superiors.  I will meet you after that for a personal debriefing.  The next morning we will return here, and you will be driven back to your base to resume your previous duties.  That will be the end of your mission.  As it is classified, you will tell anyone who cares to ask that you were at a medical conference on rebuilding German health facilities.  Clear?"

"Completely, sir."

"Let's get at it.  Sergeant, the jeep."

# 10

It was a short drive to a small airfield on the base.  There was only one runway.  It didn't look like the base got a lot of traffic.  Monroe saw a few P-51's parked alongside the runway.  There were too few of them for any serious combat missions.  He guessed they were there to fly escort for the VIPs.  The jeep parked near a C-47 with the engines running.  Monroe, Kleet, and the driver boarded.  Monroe had decided in his own mind that "linebacker" was a better title for the driver.  He didn't think either Kleet or his aide would find the nickname amusing, however accurate.  They were the only passengers.

"You must be more important than I thought," said Kleet. "We have ourselves a general's ride."  The plane was equipped with leather armchairs and trimmed with wood.  A steward waited to attend to any passenger requests.  The plane was airborne  within minutes.

"May I help you, sirs?"

"I'll have a bourbon, neat. Captain? Enjoy it now.  You'll be working the next couple of days."

"I'll have the same, Private.  Thank you," answered Monroe.

"Wouldn't have pegged you for a whiskey guy, Captain," said Kleet.

" I wasn't before the war.  Our CO is from Kentucky.  I developed a taste.  When I get home, the first thing I'm going to drink is Coke over ice with an order of toasted ravioli."

"What the hell is that?" asked Kleet.

"It's a St. Louis  thing.   Basically fried ravioli. Supposedly invented at the 1904 World's Fair.  They serve it on the Hill, the Italian neighborhood," explained Monroe. "It's an acquired taste."

"I was stationed at Jefferson Barracks once. Went to a place called Steak and Shake for hamburgers. About all we could afford then," said Kleet in an uncharacteristically nostalgic tone.

The steward brought their bourbon. Kleet took a sip and opened his briefcase. Time to get down to business again. Kleet opened a folder that was thicker than the one Monroe had memorized about Bormann. It was marked "Top Secret" Monroe was beginning to think that everything that had to do with Kleet was Top Secret. "These are the other doctors that will be present on your mission. Familiarize yourself on what background we have on them. As you can imagine, there isn't much on the Russky. He and the Brit were in combat theaters like you. The Frog was in the French Underground, but these days all French say they were in the Underground." Monroe wondered how Kleet would have fared in an occupied country.

"I don't know how much time it will take for you four to reach a conclusion. The bosses want a single, unified report with all four doctors in agreement, so be on your best behavior and get it done." Kleet handed Monroe the folder.

Monroe wondered what the other doctors were reading about him. He figured his Jewish background would be included. He had been a good student, getting Honors in courses that interested him and high passes in the others. He was more interested in clinical medicine than courses like anatomy, which was ironic since he was going to an autopsy. He remembered when he had participated in a psychological test during his psychiatry rotation for a study one of the professors was doing. He got paid $20. When they went over the results, the prof looked at him and said, "I'm not sure how you ever chose medicine. Your profile is more like that of an artist or a philosopher." Monroe had mumbled something about looking at the world in different ways. Mainly he wanted to get done and get paid. He wondered if that was in his file, and if there was any truth to it.

Monroe decided to start with the British doctor whose dossier was the most extensive.

Major Geoffrey
Menzies-Smythe

Educated at Cambridge and Guy's Hospital in London.

General Surgeon. Offices on Harley Street before the war. "The correct pedigree to take care of the upper crust," he thought. Served at Dunkirk. With the Eighth Army in North Africa and European campaigns as a combat surgeon. Several commendations for bravery. There was a notation that he was "not particularly known to be discrete, which had kept him at his current rank." Monroe wondered why they would pick a guy with a big mouth. Aunt was Lady-in-Waiting to the Queen in the last war. Likes trout fishing and bird watching. "Great to have connections, I suppose. Hopefully, the brains will match the pedigree."

The French doctor was next, Guy Saint-Germaine. Born in Morocco to a French diplomat serving there. Returned to

France to be educated at the Sorbonne. Was studying to be a pediatrician when the war came. Avid cyclist. Served in the Battle of France and was evacuated with the British at Dunkirk. Remained in the Free French and was present at the North African and Normandy landings. Was serving at De Gaulle's headquarters as a staff physician when the war ended. "Probably someone Le Grand Charles trusts," thought Monroe.

The last dossier belonged to the Soviet doctor, Georgi Dugasvili. It was one page long. Born in Tiflis. Educated in Moscow. Served in The Great Patriotic War. Party member. "Concise as only the Soviets can be," thought Monroe. "I bet his secret police file is a lot larger. He comes from Georgia like both Stalin and Beria so there's probably more there than meets the eye. Maybe the son of an old comrade."

Monroe closed the last folder and looked up.

"Questions," asked Kleet, not expecting any.

"Just one."

"Only one? I guess we're making progress. Go ahead."

"There's nothing here about the doctor who is actually performing the autopsy. I assume he's a pathologist, as none of the others appear to be one, and it wasn't my best subject in med school."

Kleet thought for a minute. He looked like he was trying to decide how much he could tell Monroe. "All I can tell you is that he is Swiss and has a French sounding last name. I've been told he's an expert."

"So is he Red Cross?"

"That's two questions. You can size him up soon enough."

"Just seems odd using someone from a neutral country in a war matter."

" A warning. Just because he's Swiss doesn't mean he's neutral. You may want to catch a nap," said Kleet and turned toward the window. Monroe knew Kleet was done talking . He closed his eyes and tried to get some sleep before landing.

# 11

It was late afternoon when they touched down in Berlin. The airfield was busy, mostly with cargo traffic. They taxied to a shed away from the air traffic. Two MPs with a car were waiting. Without any word from Kleet, the driver set off. They passed through the outskirts of Berlin, or what was left of it. Monroe reflected that some of "my guys" could have done the damage. They were in many of the thousand plane raids over Berlin, Americans by day and Brits by night.

"It still amazes me that the Germans accepted that bastard, Hitler. Many did it enthusiastically, even the ones who should have known better," said Monroe.

"Don't be amazed, Captain. Every country in Europe had authoritarian parties. There were American and British Nazis. Commies, too. Even docs like you. Hell, if the Germans or the Japanese had set foot on our soil, some of those assholes would have crawled out of the woodwork. Crying for 'Peace at any Price.' And, they would have had a lot more listeners than you would think. People choose security over uncertainty."

Monroe decided to change the subject to one less depressing. "Where are we headed?"

"We're going to a resort the Nazi big shots used to use. It wasn't that heavily damaged and is more secure than Berlin. The brass wanted to use a non-military site to assure better secrecy. It's called Wannsee."

# 12

Bormann sat just to the right and behind the lectern. It was the proper place for Hitler's secretary. Bormann preferred the back of the room, better to observe. He had been instructed to attend by Hitler.

"You are to be my eyes and ears at the meeting, Bormann. You are not to mention my name. Please note if anyone else does. Heydrich and the others have their orders from me, but not officially from me, if you understand me. It will become clear to you once the meeting starts."

Bormann would indeed pay attention. This type of information would be useful to him at some point, especially if things went bad for Germany.

Reinhard Heydrich, one of Himmler's top officers, and Heinrich Mueller, head of the Gestapo, were at the center of the table. Adolf Eichmann sat to the right of Heydrich. Some called him "Heydrich's Bormann." Bormann saw him as a pure bureaucrat. He would do no more or less than he was ordered to do. The room was otherwise filled with about 25 people from the other departments of the government.

There were no aides. Notably absent was anyone from the army. This was not a military matter. The army preferred to avoid the matters to be discussed.

Heydrich strode toward the lectern. He was the recruiting poster image of the SS officer, ramrod straight, blond, blue eyed - the perfect Aryan. One could not help but see utter ruthlessness in those eyes.

"Before I begin I order all participants not to take any personal notes. You will be provided orders specific to you.

My comrades, today we have before us a mighty task. As our brothers in arms conquer the Bolshevik armies that topple the Communist scourge, they leave behind them the refuse of humanity: Jews, gypsies, Slavs, and Communists. This is the problem that we must solve. We must rid the Reich and the world of these parasites, money grabbers, and saboteurs.

So far we have isolated them from Germans and forced them to labor for the good of the Reich. The men work in factories and their women are field whores for the army, which is all they are worth. Now as we go forward to build a new German Reich we must rid ourselves of those who are of no use to us."

Bormann suspected what was coming as he recalled Hitler's instructions. Now, the absence of Nazi big shots and the army now made sense.

Heydrich continued.

"We plan to make the East, Jew free. We will use the Gestapo and the SS to find the undesirables and move them to labor-extermination camps. Others will be eliminated by special squads -Einzatsgruppen. Yes gentleman, we are going to exterminate these vermin now and forever. The army has agreed not to interfere but will not be actively participating. We also expect some help from those in the occupied areas who have welcomed us as liberators.

Top priority will be given to construction of the camps and to transportation. Colonel Eichmann will coordinate transport scheduling. Those requisitions have precedence over all others, including the army.

This task must be completed as soon as is possible. Slackers will be punished.

Colonel Eichmann will brief you individually. None of this leaves this room until you are given detailed instructions. Heil Hitler!"

Heydrich approached Bormann outside near their vehicles. "Well Bormann, I trust you found the events satisfactory."

"As an observer only, I can only say that if successful, this Final Solution will change the world. But then, I will have no direct involvement.

Heydrich smiled. "Of course. Only those here are responsible for the execution, both figuratively and literally." He laughed at his black humor.

Bormann got into his car and ordered the driver back to Berlin. "We have time to stop at my quarters, then I will see the Führer. Please go there and wait for me."

Bormann went directly to the table in his quarters and made notes of Heydrich's remarks as well as listing who was present at the meeting. He took out a small Leica camera and photographed them. He then burned his notes in the sink and returned the camera and film to a small compartment in his closet. "These could be a weapon but certainly will be insurance," he mused.

Bormann reported to Hitler as ordered. They were the only ones in Hitler's office. The usual SS security waited outside. Hitler left orders that they were not to be disturbed under any circumstances.

"Well, Bormann, how was Heydrich's performance?"

"The performance was professional, the program breathtaking, Mein Führer."

"And I was not mentioned?"

"Your inspiration and spirit were present, though no mention of your name occurred. There will be no blame attached to you."

"Of course there won't," said Hitler, his voice rising, "because we will be victorious.  But we must be careful of intrigue within.  We don't want to give a propaganda victory to our enemies by a leak or worse from a lackey who does not have faith in our victory."

"Faith may have nothing to do with it, more likely Russian tanks," thought Bormann.

"Go now.  We will speak no more of this meeting. Himmler and Mueller will keep me informed of progress in this venture.  I need you to watch them and that clerk, Eichmann.  General Jodl is waiting.  The generals are trying to convince me to consolidate our position in Russia and not advance any further now."

"Surely not Mein Führer.  We must go on to victory."

"Unfortunately, Bormann, everyone does not have your faith."

Bormann left Hitler's office.  Jodl and two other staff officers were ushered in with Hitler's SS guards.  "Hitler will continue the offensive.  Most satisfactory," thought Bormann.

# 13

*Berlin, present day*

As Kleet and Monroe left the Berlin area, the scenery became more pastoral. Signs of war were present but rare, serving as occasional reminders of recent conflict. As they approached the resort, Kleet turned to Monroe.

"After they take you to your room, you are to meet with your colleagues for a dinner to get to know each other. Only discuss professional matters beyond the usual chit-chat, especially around the Russian. I will be elsewhere in the hotel. Contact me if you see or hear anything unusual."

" In case you haven't gotten it yet, I am not an intelligence operative, so I'm not sure what that means," replied Monroe.

"You are certainly not an operative, but you are both intelligent and skeptical. In another time, you might have been an operative. So don't sell your self short."

Monroe could not resist asking, "Was that a compliment, sir?"

"Let's just call it an appraisal by a superior officer, Captain."

Banter over. The car pulled up to the hotel. Monroe was taken to a spacious room with a well equipped bar. There was a large bed with enough pillows for five people. The marble bathroom was bigger than his room at base. The bellman told him that dinner would be at 7 in the dining room downstairs. Monroe walked around the room studying the furniture and the pictures. He realized he was looking for microphones. "This is getting too strange. I am not a spy," he thought and began getting ready for dinner.

Monroe was the last to enter the dining room. It had the feeling of a hunting lodge including the appropriate taxidermy. He recognized his three colleagues near the back of the otherwise empty room. They were easy to identify based on their uniforms. A waiter approached and asked if he wanted something to drink. Maybe Kleet had spooked him, but he thought it better to forego his usual cocktail. "Just water - bubbles."

"Yes, sir, sparkling water." It struck Monroe that the waiter looked too young and fit for his job. Most of the waiters he had seen in England were too old to have fought in the war or had clear evidence of having been a casualty. He figured it would have been even worse in Germany.

Monroe could not place the waiter's accent. It was not German, British or American. Russian? He didn't think so. "Maybe a drink would have calmed me down," he wondered.

The Brit approached him, hand extended. "Dr. Monroe, is it? Geoffrey Menzies-Smythe, please call me Smythe. Come join us."

"Please call me Jack," said Monroe as he shook hands with the Brit. The waiter arrived with his water, and he followed Smythe toward the others.

Monroe shook hands with everyone. The Frenchman was to be called Guy. He was friendly but aloof. "No wonder De Gaulle likes him," thought Monroe.

The Russian, Georgi, was surprisingly buoyant. He spied Monroe's drink and said, "Come, come you must have something stronger, my friend."

"Maybe wine with dinner," said Monroe.

"At least champagne," laughed Georgi.   Monroe couldn't help but like the guy.

"Our Swiss colleague will not be joining us," said Guy. "He said he has to make some further preparations and review documents."

"I hope he has more than I do," Smythe said." Know more about you fellows than this Bormann chap. Though I suppose things may go quicker that way.  Get back to London sooner."

"I hope you are correct," said Guy.  "I want to spend as little time in Germany as possible.  I have had enough of them the past 5 years."

"Maybe they are wasting time on another dead Fascist pig. But we just do as ordered," Georgi echoed.

Monroe remained quiet but nodded in agreement. The way these guys were talking, he'd be back at base in a day or so. Surely, that would make Kleet happy.

Dinner was sumptuous, the best meal Monroe had had since coming to Europe. The waiter was never far away but didn't appear to be close enough to hear anything. Georgi switched to vodka about halfway through dinner and became more and more festive. Smythe chuckled at his antics. There was plenty of champagne, but Monroe limited himself to two glasses. Even Guy warmed up a bit. Talk was mostly of home, wives, mistresses by Guy and Georgi. There were a few medical school stories, mostly gallows humor. They all kidded Monroe about not having someone in his life. Georgi told him he must be too particular and too romantic.

Georgi then became serious. "My wife was a peasant girl. She was raped and killed by the Germans. I loved her but have learned to love again, maybe not so much as before. In Russia, it can be easy to lose someone." He swallowed the rest of his vodka.

Monroe thought that there was more to this guy than the garrulous persona he projected.

Guy and Smythe spent a good deal of time debating the greatness of Paris versus London. Monroe was sucked in as the final arbiter and sided with the Frenchman. He thought Smythe probably agreed but had to defend King and Country.

There was not talk of their mission until dessert and brandy. Monroe declined the latter but did have coffee.

"I say we let this Swiss fellow do most of the talking. If we agree with his findings, we can meet over lunch and put our findings to paper. My superior has assured me there will be someone to quickly transcribe our findings and prepare a formal report," said Smythe.

"We have our own Russian secretary who will prepare a Russian version. She is fluent in English, and very easy on the eyes," added Georgi.

Guy just nodded as did Monroe. He wondered if Kleet had already checked out the secretaries. Probably.

The waiter followed as they left. "I hope you enjoyed the meal," he said to them all, but looked directly at Monroe.

Monroe went back to his room. He tried to get his head around the dinner. He thought he had a pretty good impression of the others. All seemed to have been given the same instructions. They were all friendly or maybe more collegial but were otherwise superficial about the mission. Maybe they would be more forthcoming tomorrow. He didn't know what to make of the waiter. He seemed to be staring at Monroe, but for what reason? "Maybe I'm just paranoid," he thought.

He was about to get in bed when there was a knock at his door. He heard Kleet in a muffled tone, "Open up, Captain."

Kleet entered quickly and quietly closed the door. He sat in the only chair in the room. Monroe went to the bed and also sat.

"Well doc, tell me about your dinner companions."

"Why the interest?"

"Let's just say I have certain curiosity about people who could affect my mission. I don't think the files tell a whole lot. I hate surprises."

Monroe paused to get his thoughts organized, like he was presenting a patient. He decided to start easy.

"The Brit seems to be a typical British public school guy. I suspect well connected. I think he enjoys the "secret mission" aspect of the case but probably won't quibble with the details.

The Frenchman has that air of superiority which only a Frenchman can assume. Though I think that's his official face. He became much more relaxed when he was talking of his wife and girlfriend and kidding me about my lack of either.

The Russian is a little more complicated. On the one hand, he is the two fisted vodka drinking peasant. On the other he has deep seated emotions. He has a visceral hate of the Germans as well as a deep sadness over the loss of his wife. I can't get a sense of his duty to the Party or to Mother Russia.

This may sound ridiculous, but the one that bothered me the most was the waiter. I couldn't peg his nationality by his accent, and he seemed to have looked directly at me for just a bit too long a couple of times. A Sergeant Kemp would say, "His eyes were too damn close together."

Kleet had taken in Monroe's appraisals without saying a word. He said nothing for a minute or so.

"I had dinner myself with my allied colleagues as well. Nobody said much, as I expected. Shop talk mostly. Nobody stood out as hiding anything more than anyone else.

You're probably right about the Brit and the Frenchman. The Brits love to make things neat and tidy. Dot every 'i'. Don't ask too many questions or rock the boat.

The Frenchman's superior officer was very much a De Gaulle loyalist. I think he felt it was his duty to convince us that France was an equal partner in all of this and would not be dictated to by the rest of us.

The Russian doctor is likely not what he seems. His last name is the same as Stalin's and he is from Georgia. That's about all we know now. Stalin places great value in his old family friends and relatives."

"Why would Stalin care that much about a bureaucrat like Bormann?"

"Good question, but not for you to worry about." Monroe wondered if Kleet really knew the answer himself or just wanted to cut off a discussion where he was just as much in the dark.

"I'm more curious about the waiter. He was added at the last minute when the one we had checked out already got sick. It wouldn't surprise me if the Russians put in a ringer. Or he could be a Nazi. Word of this may have leaked out."

"Or one of Kleet's guys to watch me," thought Monroe.

"Well, he won't be there tomorrow. Just watch the Russian."

"Anything on the Swiss doc?"

"Nothing. The Swiss are specialists in anonymity."

Kleet got up and headed for the door. "Get some sleep, Doc. You gotta be sharp tomorrow."

Monroe lay in bed thinking, "First it's a routine bullshit mission. Now it appears to be something a little more. Maybe things will be more clear tomorrow." Somehow he doubted that.

# 14

He was awakened by a waiter with a breakfast of eggs, sausage, pastry and coffee. He got no special looks from this one. Monroe had learned as an intern to eat everything when you can because you might not get to eat again for hours. He put on his uniform. They must have scrubs in the path lab. Better to show up official and military.

They all met in the lobby and were taken to what looked like a pavilion that someone would use for a wedding. Georgi looked a little worse for wear but managed a weak smile. They were told to take off their jackets and given surgical gowns. Once they were changed they were ushered to an ante room.

A tall, grey haired man entered the room. His wire rimmed spectacles added to his professorial air. "Colleagues, allow me to introduce myself. I am Dr. Peter Monod from Zürich. I am a medical examiner in the city of Zürich and will be conducting today's examination. I was asked by my government at the request of yours and have provided them with my credentials. If you have any questions about those, please address them to your superiors. As we have a tight schedule I suggest we begin." He turned and left the room.

The others looked at each other, shrugged their shoulders and followed. Monroe was somewhat amused by Dr. Monod's officious manner and wondered if he was from a family of Swiss bankers.

The room they entered had obviously been set up just for this procedure. There was a gurney with temporary lights around it, a portable suction device, basins, refuse containers and a tray table with instruments on it. The body was draped in a green tarp. There was no one else in the room.

Monod removed the tarp. The corpse was a male, somewhat obese with obvious external wounds. Monod started at the head and moved down the length of the body. He spoke in a clipped economical manner.

"The victim is a Caucasian male who appears to be in his 40's. He is overweight but is otherwise well developed."

Monroe interrupted, "Is anyone going to transcribe this?"

"I will dictate the report to the stenographer furnished by your government when we are finished here. I will need no notes."

Monroe knew he had been dismissed.

Monod went on, "There are multiple lacerations and wounds consistent with shrapnel involving the head, neck and torso. The extremities show superficial abrasions from falling or being forced to the ground. There is a large deformity at the base of the skull, which likely caused herniation of the brain and death. I will confirm this when we look at the brain. These findings correlate with witness statements."

Monroe spoke up again, feeling like he was the only one who had questions. "There was a witness? Can we see any testimony so we can corroborate things on our own?"

'The witness statement was taken by Russian intelligence, I am told."

Monroe looked at Dugashveli. "Georgi?"

"The witness has been interrogated by the NKVD. They are very thorough and have assured me that his statement is true. He is unavailable."

"How convenient. Who was he?"

"We have verified that he was Bormann's dentist. He was with Bormann when he died. Dr. Monod will confirm his contribution to the case."

Monod sighed. His expression showed that he did not appreciate Monroe's questions. "The dentist was Dr. Hugo Blaschke. He attended Bormann and his family before and during the war. Your Russian colleague has assured me that his dental verification of Herr Bormann is accurate. So we know who he is and should be able to confirm the cause of death once we open his skull and torso. May I proceed?"

Monroe was not done. "Let me get this straight. We now find out about a witness we should have already known about, who we cannot interview or speak to, and are dependent on the word of Russian military intelligence as to the accuracy of his statements?"

"The Russians are your allies. Your colleague has verified the NKVD role in this case. I think you will also find that your superiors will confirm the witness as well. Now, if you don't mind, we will carry on."

"Fine," said Monroe. He would have a word with Kleet later. Neither Guy nor Smythe seemed to be upset and even looked a little put out by Monroe's interruptions.

The autopsy then proceeded without interruption. Head trauma was confirmed as the likely cause of death. Monod told them they would have his report to them in an hour. "Likely to the minute," thought Monroe. Orderlies came for the body.

"Where are you taking it?" asked Monroe.

"We have orders to cremate," answered the orderly.

"Of course you do," sighed Monroe. They were scheduled to meet later in the afternoon to discuss and finalize their reports. Monroe decided to try and find Kleet. While he wasn't totally surprised at the way things had gone so far, he wasn't satisfied with the answers he had gotten.

# 15

Monroe went to Kleet's room. There was no answer to his knock. After a couple of minutes, he headed to the lobby. He saw Kleet in the bar at a table facing the entrance. An attractive dark haired barmaid had just delivered a drink to him. As Monroe sat down, she returned.

"May I get something for you, Mein Herr?" She didn't sound German, almost like the waiter the night before but a lot better looking. Her hair was jet black, her eyes were hazel, almost blue. Her gaze, directed at him, made him wish he was at a bar in St. Louis rather than on a mission in Germany.

"No, thank you," was all he could manage.

"My associate won't be staying long, but I'll have another whiskey," said Kleet.

She walked toward the bar, where last night's waiter was also working. When she was out of earshot, Kleet turned to Monroe. He was clearly not happy. He kept his voice low. "What the hell are you doing here? Aren't you supposed to be meeting with your doctor buddies?"

Monroe answered in a near whisper. "We just finished the autopsy. It was perfunctory at best. I had what I thought were some reasonable medical questions that a fourth year medical student might have asked that were basically dismissed. Then I find out there was a witness to all this, who the Russians have interrogated, but who we cannot question. We have to take their word for it, and now they are cremating the body so we can't have anything reexamined."

"Your point?"

"My point is that I think you knew about the witness and that this so called inquest was to be a formality. Why all the show for a so called Nazi bureaucrat? How can I sign on to this report when my very simple questions can't or won't be answered?"

"Dr. Monroe, I cannot answer all your questions. It is above your pay grade. I will admit that they are not unreasonable. I will tell you that there is not a hope in hell of getting access to the witness. The Russians simply won't allow it, and our bosses seem to be OK with that. What I can tell you is that raising too big a stink and not signing that report could adversely affect your career, even after you leave the service. Frankly, I don't think this Nazi bastard is worth that, do you?"

Monroe tried to keep his temper. Kleet was not someone to fool with, and who knew how his superiors would react if Monroe made waves. "Is that some kind of warning, sir?" He thought threat would have been a better choice of words.

"No, Captain, as your superior officer, I would call it good career advice. Now don't you have a meeting to get to?"

Just as Kleet finished, the waitress arrived with his drink. Monroe stood and saluted, knowing that Kleet would get the not so respectful message. As he turned, he was looking the waitress right in the eye. She stared back for just a second then averted her gaze a little too quickly. Monroe headed for the restaurant and his "working lunch."

Again, the dining room was empty. A large table had been arranged for them. They all sat across from each other around it. Monroe was opposite the Frenchman. The waiter from last night approached. "Gentleman, we will be serving sausage with sauerkraut and boiled potatoes for your meal. I would suggest some local beer to accompany." They all nodded in assent. Again, he appeared to look at Monroe a little longer than the others.

"Between this guy and the waitress, I must be getting paranoid, though those eyes of hers were something to remember," he thought.

Four women in the uniform of each doctor's country entered and gave them each a typewritten report of the autopsy in their own language already signed by Monod. One, who Monroe guessed, was the appointed leader said, "Dr. Monod expresses his regrets, but he was called back to Zürich. He trusts that his findings are clear and that you will have no issues with his report. Should you have any questions about the accuracy of translation, please address them to me later. Thank you." As she left, the waiter returned with two large pitchers of beer. Two others brought the food. They closed the door behind them.

Smythe looked at Monroe. "Two reports in English. I guess whoever was in charge believed Mr Bernard-Shaw that we are two peoples separated by a common language." He laughed, very proud of his witticism. Monroe acknowledged with a smile. They ate quietly and read their reports. Georgi's hangover had obviously improved as he consumed two steins of beer quickly.

The reports were an accurate summary of the autopsy as Monod had performed it. Monroe had to admit that his memory was as he said. There appeared to be no details left out. There was a place for each of them to sign under Monod's own signature. Monroe noticed that Georgi signed after only a cursory review.

Smythe spoke first, "Nothing new here. Wasn't much to begin with. Pretty open and shut I would say."

"Don't you guys see anything funny here?" asked Monroe. "We're basing the identification on the word of a witness that we can neither talk to nor even verify exists."

Georgi responded in an irritated tone. "My government has assured me that the witness's identity and testimony is reliable. We have been over this."

"No offense, Georgi, but the word of some government official isn't good enough for me."

"I suppose the government officials in your country are not as truthful as in mine," Georgi said sarcastically.

As Monroe was about to answer, Smythe intervened, "Now gentleman, I would say the point, while possibly having some validity, is moot. Based on the medical evidence we have, I think we must attest to the accuracy of this report. I, for one, want to get done and get back to London."

Monroe looked at Guy, "Your opinion, doctor?"

The Frenchman was clearly hesitant in his answer. "In France, we certainly would have been more forthcoming with witnesses and would have left nothing to doubt. Alas, we are not in France. I sympathize with my American friend. I, too, have some questions. I also know they will not be answered and further delay will not get those answers. We are soldiers now under orders and must answer to our superiors. I will sign the report."

"His superiors sound like Kleet," thought Monroe. He also thought about Kleet's not-so-veiled warning, really more of a threat. What the hell, why should he rock the boat for a dead Nazi? "Well gentleman, it appears I am in the minority. In the interest of being a good ally and getting the hell out of here, as Smythe put it more eloquently, I will sign as well." There was clearly resignation in his voice.

After they all signed each others' copies, the secretaries returned to pick them up and take them to their superiors, where they would be stamped "classified" and placed in a file cabinet, never to be seen again.

"All neat and tidy. Kleet will be relieved, thought Monroe. They finished lunch, wished each other well, and headed back to their rooms.

# 16

Kleet was waiting when Monroe got back to his room. "I'd ask you how you got in here, but I'm not sure I really care anymore."

Kleet shrugged. "Get packed. A plane is waiting to take us back. We'll discuss the meeting on the way back. I'll be out front in five minutes."

Monroe packed the few things he had brought along into his duffle. For some reason, he had packed his stethoscope. "Back to reality," he sighed. For all the secrecy, he realized he had sort of enjoyed the past couple of days. Maybe a secret war story to tell his kids someday.

Kleet was his usual silent self on the way to the airfield. After the plane took off and he was settled in with his bourbon, he turned to Monroe. "Doc, tell me about lunch."

"The report, which I suspect you already read, had no surprises. I signed it."

"That's it? You had no reservations?"

"I expressed the same concerns at the meeting that I had to you, and still have, by the way."

"What about the others?"

"Dugashveli was right along  party lines. I think he knows not to question anything. Smythe just wanted to go home. The Frenchman had questions and doubts. I had  some hope he might side with me, but in the end it was 'C'est la vie.' I knew I was out voted and thought about your earlier sage advice and signed."

" A prudent decision on your part. We will get you back to base where you can resume your duties. You will stick to the story I gave your boss, if asked. Otherwise say nothing. You only have a few months left over here. Make them quiet and routine."

Monroe decided to voice his suspicions about the waiter and waitress but guessed that Kleet would dismiss them as the product of an amateur's overactive imagination. "Colonel, I was ill at ease about the way that waiter at dinner and lunch and the waitress at the bar paid a little too much attention to the goings on and to me. I don't know if they were just curious or had other motives."

"The waiter was probably just a busy body. All these foreigners in his restaurant. As for the girl, maybe you were just hoping that a pretty girl was giving you the eye. Yes, I noticed her eyes, too. I think you should quit being concerned. There is nothing there."

Exactly as Monroe expected. He wasn't sure he would ever forget those eyes.

# 17

The hotel restaurant had closed. Most of the staff had gone home. The waiter and waitress stood at the bar, he with a beer, she with a glass of red wine.

"I was able to hear most of what they said through the window I left cracked open. Unfortunately, things went as expected. They all followed orders," he said.

"I thought you said the American had objections."

"He and the Frenchman. I think the Yank would have pushed harder if the Frenchman had backed him. Once the Frenchman signed, he did as well. He didn't sound happy."

"Do you think he suspected that we were watching him?"

"I don't. He's not a professional."

"True, but he is a Jew, and after all that has happened, he might be a little more vigilant."

"He was born and raised in America. I suspect his parents wanted him to be more American than Jewish. He was engaged to a shiksa. I doubt it is in his nature to be vigilant."

She remembered how the American had held her gaze and wasn't so sure her associate was correct. "Doctors are curious by nature. He may not give up. Let's see if he might be useful."

"And I think we should go back to Paris. We are finished here. I don't think we can spare someone to follow the American. I'll go back through the American sector here. You go back through the French sector, since your fluency will help you if you get into any trouble. See you in Paris in a few days. "Auf Wiedersehen, Dionne."

"Au revoir, Simon."

Dionne boarded a train that took her through the Russian Occupation Zone and into the French Zone. Her papers showed her to be a Canadian Red Cross worker from Quebec. Her papers were not checked again until she entered France. She would travel to Aix-en-Provence, spend the night there, then go on to Paris. Once Simon got out of Germany, he would be taken by car to Paris. Since French was her first language, no one paid her any attention. Her Canadian papers would explain her Quebecois accent should anyone be curious. She stopped in a café on the way to the station in

Aix for a croissant and coffee. There were three men at a table discussing the events of the day, one interrupting the other with no one really appearing to be listening. "Just like home," she thought.

# 18

*Montreal, 1944 -*

Dionne was upstairs dressing to go out with her boyfriend, Sammy. She looked at herself in the mirror. An attractive woman with deep blue eyes and a striking smile looked back. She wore her curly black hair short. Her new dress was flattering to her petite figure. "Not bad at all," she thought and added lipstick to complete the picture.

She could hear her father and her uncle having one of their current events and war strategy discussions. True to form, they took opposite positions. "By the end they'll each end up taking the other's position as usual," she laughed to herself. Her cousin Harry was serving in the Eighth Army with the British, so her uncle tended to be more pro-British. Her mother had lost her eldest brother at Vimy Ridge in the last war. He had been her father's good friend and introduced the two of them. Her father was cynical when it came to Britain. "British generals will fight to the last Canadian," he would say.

Dionne knew her father was worried about his nephew. Her mother said the boy had reminded her of her own late brother. Whenever she said that, her father would just laugh to himself with a nostalgic look on his face. "He was always the fearless one," he would say.

Dionne and Harry grew up together and were very close. Like his late uncle, Harry was indeed an adventurer. He had even tried to volunteer for the Lincoln Brigade in the Spanish Civil War. His Canadian accent made the American recruiter suspicious, but it was more the fact that he looked too young that had kept him out. In fact he was barely sixteen at the time. He had one more year at McGill when the war was declared. She was not quite sure how he had ever ended up in the Eighth Army rather than a regular Canadian unit but was not surprised. He could talk his way in or out of almost any situation. Her uncle always said he could sell ice to Eskimos. She worried about him but never doubted he would come home.

She went downstairs and stuck her head into the kitchen to say good-bye. "I'm going to meet Sammy. We're going to the movies."

Her mother frowned. "Mom, I know you don't like Sammy, but he's a great guy. Uncle Morty knows him from schule. Tell her Uncle Morty."

Her Uncle paused for a moment. "He's a nice boy. I'm just not sure he'll amount to much." Dionne knew that put Sammy somewhere just above pond scum in her uncle's eyes.

Her father tried to soften the blow. "Your Uncle is a good judge of character, but so are you."

She decided that there was no point in further debate. She kissed them all and left. As she was walking toward the theater to meet Sammy, she wondered what it was that made her Uncle feel the way he did. She knew he loved her almost as much as he loved Harry and was probably trying to protect her. She was like Harry in a way. She didn't need protecting.

It was less than a kilometer to the theater. She wore a long beaver coat with a matching hat and muff for her hands to protect her from the cold as the theater was nowhere near the Montreal underground. As she neared the theater the sidewalks became more crowded. The talk was mostly in English in this part of town. She heard some French and even a little Yiddish. Montreal was different than any other big city in Canada, more European. She imagined that Paris must be the same way. It was what she loved about the city.

She heard Sammy calling her. He was standing in front of the theater waiving their tickets. He was slim, almost slight, a little over five-eight, barely taller than Dionne. She never wore her highest heels when they were on a date. He had a warm, toothy smile and curly black hair. His thick glasses made him look like the Hebrew scholar he was trying to become. His yarmulke completed the picture. He was always serious.

She kissed him on the cheek and they went inside. The movie, a John Wayne western, was preceded by newsreels about the war. Montgomery was shown in his beret with riding crop in hand, first riding in a tank then inspecting the troops. Next came film of guns firing and tanks moving into battle. The news reel concluded with German prisoners being marched into captivity. Dionne always looked for Harry just hoping to see that he was all right. Sammy held her hand, more interested in her than the news. "More propaganda," he whispered.

The film was the usual Hollywood western. The good guys were really good and the bad guys really bad. Wayne predictably beat the bad guy and got the girl.

After, they went to a café that they frequented. It was cozy; everybody was friendly, and it fit their budget. Dionne ordered coffee and chocolate cake, Sammy just coffee. They talked about friends, family and other personal events. Sammy was talkative as usual. Like others, they began a lot of sentences with " After the war…" Sammy framed most of his conversation with "we." They had been going together around a year, but Dionne never really thought much about a future with Sammy one way or the other.

After they split the bill, he offered to walk her halfway home. She thought to herself that they were always splitting things in half. She said half way would be good enough as he lived in the opposite direction. After they parted, she decided to go a couple of blocks out of the way to look in the window of her favorite dress shop. As she was crossing the street she happened to look in one of the local taverns. She saw her father sitting with some men that she did not recognize. Her father rarely went to taverns. When he did, it was with her uncle, who she did not see. She kept on walking but was very curious and a little bit suspicious. She would see what she could learn tomorrow.

Dionne worked for her father's import-export business. It was located in an old warehouse on the St. Lawrence River that opened onto a dark, narrow street. Her mother always warned her to be careful when she left for work. Her father would not allow her to go home unescorted during the short winter days, but she was accustomed to the catcalls from the dockworkers that came in several languages.

She hung up her coat on a hook by the door and went to her desk not far from her father's office. He spent most of the day on the phone with customers, only emerging when there was a problem or a visitor. Her uncle had an office in the back. He kept the books and handled the money. Dionne worked mainly for her father, at first answering the phone and typing. Her father had been giving her more responsibility over the past several months. She now handled a few accounts on her own. He would tell her that she would manage the office when he went on vacation, which he never did. Her mother viewed the situation as temporary since she was supposed to marry and raise children. At present she had no interest in either.

She was doing paperwork but mainly thinking about last night's events when her uncle stuck his head in. "I'll be gone about an hour. I have some business at customs." After he left, Dionne decided she would ask her father about what he had been doing at the café. She picked up some papers that he would need to sign and went to his office.

He was on the phone at his old metal desk. There were pictures of Dionne and her mother on it. He always said that they were keeping an eye on him. The desk was otherwise a mess of papers. Dionne would arrange them at the end of each day only to have the chaos return within minutes of her father's arrival at work.

He motioned her to one of the two chairs in the room. The office had a small bookshelf, but was otherwise plain. The white walls had turned light tan from years of his cigar smoke. He hung up the phone, pulled a pencil from behind his ear, scribbled something on a stray piece of paper that he folded and put in his shirt pocket. "So have you brought me papers from Uncle Morty?"

"Just a few. He just went to Customs so I suspect that there will be more when he comes back." She handed him the documents. He pulled out the fountain pen that his father had given him and quickly signed them.

"Everything in triplicate," he mumbled and gave them back. When she didn't get up right away, he leaned back in his chair and arched his eyebrows. "So, nu?"

She thought for a second. This really wasn't her business, but it was also not typical of her father. I need to ask you something.  "Sammy walked me part of the way home last night."

"Your mother will be happy."

"No, it's not about Sammy."

"Then your uncle will be happy."

"I saw you in the tavern with some men I didn't recognize, and I was wondering who they were."

Her father had a tell when they played cards.  He would lick his lower lip when he was bluffing.  He did that now.

"They are business associates.  We were discussing some opportunities that would be beneficial to all of us."

"Do I know them?  Is Uncle Morty part of it?"

Another lick.  "I haven't said anything because it may never happen.  You know Uncle Morty, he'll get all wound up then be disappointed if it doesn't work.  Let's keep it to ourselves."

"Can I ask what it is?"

"Let's just say it's an exporting opportunity in a new market, a contribution to the war effort.  I'll let you all know if it comes through."  He picked up the phone and began to dial, signaling the discussion was over.

She went back to her desk but had trouble concentrating. She knew her father was hiding something. He had never been one to make shady deals, not unusual in this business during war time. She would keep a closer watch on him.

Her uncle came back a few minutes later. He was complaining about the Customs officers, as always. "I sat for half an hour waiting. I just had to pay a few fees. It's always a chore. These Frenchman make everything a discussion. Every time they pretend to check that I have translated my English form to the proper duplicate French forms. They know my French is better than their English. 'Dis, dat, dese, dose.' Anyway, I got everything done. I need to go to the bank before it closes. Can you file these please? I'll get your father and we'll all go to lunch. My treat." He came out of her father's office a few minutes later. "The big shot is on the phone. Come, we'll go. You pick."

She picked the place they always went to as if there was any place else her uncle would go. It was right around the corner from the bank that was used by almost all the businesses near the port.

The restaurant was small. The menu never changed, but the food was good. Everyone there knew them. The waitress didn't even ask Uncle Morty what he wanted. She brought him his usual chicken sandwich with poutine. Dionne ordered fish.

She wanted to ask her uncle about her father's activities but thought about what her father had said. He would get worked up. Instead, she asked if he had heard from Harry.

"Got a letter a few days ago. It was almost three weeks old. He's fine. Can't say much about the war with the censors and all. He sends his love to everyone. Do you ever hear from him?"

Harry had written her a couple of times. The Eighth Army was on the move, and she figured he didn't have much spare time. She missed him.

"So, what's with Sammy?"

"Nothing much. We have fun together. Why don't you like him? He's very bright."

"He's a nice boy, but don't confuse wealth with brains. His family has money going back generations. They give to all the right politicians. They get favors."

"He's more of a scholar, I think."

"He can afford to be. I've heard him talk about the war at synagogue. I think he feels embarrassed about not serving."

"Everyone isn't like Harry," she smiled. "I'm sure Sammy has his reasons."

"Probably none of them good. Let me ask you something. Does he make you laugh? I mean really laugh."

"Of course!" she said a little too quickly. She couldn't remember the last time that Sammy made her do anything more than giggle. They didn't talk about much the rest of the meal.

Dionne was brought back to the present in Aix when the waiter brought her food. She loved croissants. The best were in Paris at a bakery near Sacre Coeur that was actually known more for its baguettes. She ate quickly, left a few extra coins for the waiter, and headed for the train station.

# 19

Kleet and Monroe parted at the airbase where they had started in England. "My driver will see you get back to your hospital. You are expected to report for your usual shift tomorrow morning. Good luck, Captain. And, remember, you were at a conference. Nothing more."

"Yes, sir. You know my boss is kind of curious. What do I tell him when he asks about what was discussed?"

"I'm sure you'll think of something. Just make it mundane."

The ride back to base was uneventful. Kleet's driver did not converse beyond one word answers. Monroe was dropped near the Officer Quarters. Before he could even thank the driver, he was gone. "He and Kleet must have a barrel of fun together," he thought.

Monroe reported for duty the next morning. His boss asked him how things went. Monroe mumbled something about the meeting being mostly policy and procedure oriented. His boss, who had over 20 years in and wanted his remaining time to be quiet, nodded his head and dismissed Monroe, who headed for the hospital for his shift.

Things were very quiet over the next couple of days, giving Monroe time to mull over his recent experience. He still wasn't sure what to make of the whole thing. He couldn't dismiss the questions he had had. His thoughts also kept returning to the waiter and the waitress. He remembered Kleet's warning, but still was unable to put his thoughts to rest.

He was finishing his charting when Kemp sat down across from him. "So, Doc, what's the low down on this conference deal?"

"Nothing much. Just boring medical stuff, procedures, policies."

"Don't bullshit a bullshitter, Doc. I've known you too long. The past couple of days, you've been all business, even with me. There's something else up."

Kemp had always had Monroe's back. He was smart and loyal. Against Kleet's "advice," he decided to trust him.

"Sergeant, I'm going to give you the skinny, as you would say. If any of it gets out both of our asses will be in a sling. You saw the officer who came to get me for this mission. He is as scary as he looks."

Kemp nodded his head. "Got it, Doc. Lips are sealed."

Monroe summarized his mission, leaving out the personal details of the other doctors. He also did not mention the waiter and waitress.

When Monroe finished, Kemp thought for a minute then asked, "So who's this Nazi? Sounds like he's more important than they're letting on or it could just be army BS. You really want to find out?"

" I think I do, but I wouldn't know where to start. If I try to find out through channels, I'll hit a dead end or worse."

" Doc, if you want my help, I know a guy. Met him when I was recovering from my wounds. I was at the NCO Club having a few. He goes to the bar and orders a beer. German accent. Some yahoo from supply starts giving him a hard time. They were disturbing my evening so I politely ask the guy to lay off." Monroe imagined that politely asking involved some shoving and maybe a punch or two. Anyhow I persuaded the asshole to leave the club. The other fellow then insists on buying me a beer, and we start talking. Turned out he was a Jew boy. Sorry, no offense."

"None taken."

"Anyway he got out of Germany in the 30's when things started to go bad. Enlisted so he could get citizenship and kill a few Nazis. So, they made him a translator. He translated for the army when they interviewed captured Nazis. Said he even met Fatso Goering. I think he's with SHAEF somewhere now. I might be able to find him. I know a guy at headquarters. Owes me a favor. What do you say?"

"See what you can find out - quietly."

"You don't have to tell me twice. Gimme a day or so. Oh, we may need a few items from supply for my buddy."

It turned out that Kemp's friend was working out of a manor house not far from the air base. Monroe and Kemp arranged to meet him in a pub in a village halfway between the two locations. Kemp requisitioned a jeep while Monroe got passes for the two of them to go off base for the evening.

"Listen, doc. I told this guy that you are with intelligence on a special assignment to help hunt down Nazis, that even his own boss wouldn't know anything about it. I played the Jew card pretty heavy. Thought it would grease the skids. Just trying to help."

"Not to worry.  You are stereotyping for a good cause Sergeant.  I know your heart is in the right place." Kemp appeared relieved.

They didn't talk much the rest of the way.  When they arrived at the pub, Kemp turned to Monroe.  "I'll let you out here, Doc.  I'll be close by.  The guy has a SHAEF insignia.  He's a sergeant.  Short, glasses, curly hair.  I told him you'd be the tall guy."

Monroe entered the pub.  It was dark with a fireplace at one end.  It could have been anywhere in England.  The few patrons looked like locals.  There were a few military, both British and American.  Monroe had no trouble finding Kemp's friend.  He was by himself in a corner, facing the entrance but away from the customers.  Monroe bought a pint of ale and sat down.

"You are Monroe?" the man asked.

Monroe nodded.  "And you are?"

"I am Hans.  Hans Stone.  Kemp told me you are with intelligence and that you are a Jew as well.  What kind of name is Monroe for a Jew?"

"The same kind as Stone, or was it Stein? We probably had the same immigration officer," said Monroe smiling.

Stone laughed then spoke quietly, "What information can I help you with Captain?  And, I assume no one will know the source? There are already people in my office who do not trust me, you understand?"

"I understand. I appreciate anything you can tell me. I gather information from many sources. I will keep your name out of any reports. I need to know anything you can tell me about a guy named Bormann. Maybe some of the Nazis you interviewed spoke of him."

"As you can imagine the Nazis were not the elite geniuses that they were portrayed to be in their propaganda. A few like Goebbels were still loyal to the cause and kept up an air of superiority. Others, like Himmler and Speer, would turn on their former comrades in the blink of an eye if they thought it would help their own cause. When asked about his comrades, Goebbels had very little good to say. He hated Goering and Himmler as they were his rivals for Hitler's attention. Goering didn't like the Army or the Navy because he thought they prevented his Luftwaffe from winning the war, though I think our air corps might have had a little to do with it. He only spoke of this Bormann once that I recall. Called him 'Hitler's office clerk.' Himmler felt the same way."

"Sounds like what I've heard, too."

Stone went on. "Foreign Minister Ribbentrop had more to say. He said Bormann would sit in on meetings on Hitler's behalf that he had with foreigners. Made Ribbentrop nervous, like Bormann was a spy. Said he would interrupt and even speak to some of them after Ribbentrop left. Apparently Bormann spent a lot of time with the Grand Mufti of Jerusalem. He was cut off by the interrogator when that came up."

"Anything else?"

"Not really. Bormann seemed a bit of a mystery to me, but I think someone who aroused so much dislike from Hitler's inner circle had more power than it appears. I don't know much else."

"Thank you. It helps. Let me ask you, did the G2 guys or prosecutors ever talk about finding Bormann?"

"Most of the people I worked for were after bigger fish, more high profile Nazis. You know, better headlines. I'll let Kemp know if I hear anything new."

Stone got up and looked around like he was expecting someone, then left the pub. No one seemed to notice him. Monroe waited a bit then left himself. Kemp called to him as he came out, nearly making him jump. "Jeep's over here."

As they rode back to the base, Kemp asked, "Was my guy any help, Doc?"

"Just created more questions about this whole thing, too many unknowns, and not just Bormann. Maybe I'll let it rest."

"Yeah, and I'm the King of England."

# PART II

## 20

Dionne could not stop wondering about her father's activities. She was quite sure that he was content that the matter was closed as far as she was concerned. She also knew that were the situation reversed, he would not be satisfied. When she was focused on a task, he would say, "You're like a dog with a rag in its mouth." She didn't say anything for a week or so as her father was just going about his usual routine. She and Sammy were going to meet for the Wednesday night discount movie when her father announced during supper he was meeting some business friends and would be gone a couple of hours.

As he was getting ready upstairs and her mother was cleaning up after supper, she went into the hall and called Sammy on the phone. "I can't go to the movies tonight. My throat has been sore, and I'm losing my voice," she rasped, hoping it sounded convincing.

"Can I see you on Saturday night, after Shabbas? The movie will still be on. I mean if you're feeling better." He was clearly disappointed but sounded like he believed her.

"I'll call you Friday afternoon if I think I can make it. I don't want your father getting mad at me for calling on the Sabbath."

Hope returned to his voice. "I'll be waiting."

She knew she could not have told Sammy the truth, that she was going to follow her father. He certainly would have disapproved but worse, might have wanted to go with her. For all his good qualities, Sammy could not keep a secret. The entire shule , including her father and uncle, would have known by Saturday night. She heard her father say something to her mother and go out the door. She grabbed her coat, told her mother she was meeting Sammy and left. She could still see her father about a block away as she reached the street.

Her father set a brisk pace that she managed to match. She felt a bit like the private eye, Sam Spade, from the movies. She was curious but also a little worried about where they were headed. After a few blocks, it became obvious he was heading toward the pub where she had seen him before. She was able to slow her pace when she was sure of the destination. Now the question was, what would she do when she got there? Go in? Look through the window from across the street? She decided more distant observation was the better part of valor to start. If she saw something she didn't like, she would risk her father's wrath and go in.

Her father stepped in and was greeted by two men. One looked to be in his 30's, average height with dark hair. He was clean shaven and dressed like a dock worker in a dark pea coat. The other man was at least 20 years older, short and fat. He had on a suit with no tie and an overcoat much like her own father. The older man looked Jewish so she assumed the younger one was as well. A waiter brought them beer, and they began talking. She was obviously too far away to hear them speaking, but their faces were all serious. The younger one appeared agitated at times, only to have the older one pat his arm to calm him down. Her father mostly listened and nodded in agreement. After about thirty minutes her father got up and left. The two men remained.

She couldn't follow her father home. Her parents thought she was at the movies with Sammy. She decided to watch the two men a little bit longer then go get coffee to kill time before going home. Just then the two men got up from their table and left the restaurant in opposite directions. She made a decision to follow one of them, but which one? She decided on the heavy one. If he spotted her, she was pretty sure he wouldn't try to chase her down and certainly couldn't catch her. "OK, Fat Man, let's see if you lead me to the Maltese Falcon."

The older man walked deceptively fast. Dionne was able to keep up but found her breathing getting heavier in the cold air. They were headed toward an area with many hotels and restaurants. The street became more crowded so the "Fat Man" had to slow his pace. Dionne felt more confident that she could blend in with the crowd. The Fat Man did not stop until he came to a hotel where some of her out of town relatives had stayed once. It was very popular with Jewish visitors, comfortable but not particularly elegant like the CP hotel downtown. Should she follow him in? After all, she really wasn't Sam Spade. By the time she made up her mind and entered the lobby, he was nowhere to be seen.

When she got home, her mother, as usual, was still up. "So, how was the movie?"

"I liked it. Sammy loved it. He wants to go again Saturday."

"I think it's more about the company that than the movie," she smiled.

"You know, Mom, I'm not a baby. You don't need to wait up for me. Did Dad get home yet?"

"Over an hour ago. He went to bed a while ago."

She tried not to seem too curious. "I hope he had a good time."

"It was business. Some kind of new deal. He wants to keep it quiet for now. He doesn't want Uncle Morty to know yet. He's afraid he'll get too excited, which he would. He'll tell us when he is good and ready."

At least her father kept his story consistent. She kissed her mother and went up to bed, none of her questions answered.

# 21

When Dionne returned from lunch on Friday, her father called her to his office. From his tone of voice, it was more of a summons.

"Sammy called. I told him you were at lunch. He asked that you call him back before shabbas. He said he hoped you felt better and would be able to make the movie Saturday night. Rather than completely embarrass you, I told him you would call him back when you returned from lunch. Not that I want to intrude into your personal life, but it is not like you to lie. If there is someone else, I think you need to be honest with Sammy."

"It's now or never," she thought. "There's no one else. I followed you to your business meeting. You have never done any business out side of here, so I didn't buy your story. You wouldn't have bought it either. I saw you meeting with those two men." She didn't think it would be wise to reveal that she had followed the "Fat Man" back to his hotel. She looked at her father, waiting for the explosion.

His face reddened, but he said nothing at first. He looked like he was struggling with what he would say. After a long exhale, he spoke. "To say that you shouldn't have followed me is an understatement. I think I should have earned your trust by now. But, you have always been too curious for your own good, like that summer when you and Harry got lost at the Rideau cottage looking for a bear. Do you remember that?"

She did remember that adventure. It was one of the many she and Harry had growing up at the family cottage on the Rideau River, halfway to Ottawa.

"Don't change the subject, Father."

"I was just making a point. I suspect you will not give up unless I tell you about my meeting. You are old enough. But, you must trust me and not tell your Uncle Morty or your mother. I will tell them when the time is right. Deal?"

"Deal, but why all the secrecy. Is it illegal? Are you in trouble?"

"Let's just say it is more irregular than illegal. Those men were from Palestine. The older one emigrated from Russia before the war. The younger one grew up in a kibbutz in the Galilee. He was educated in England. They are both Zionists. They are part of the movement to create a Jewish

94

state in our ancestral home after the war. There are terrible stories coming from Europe. Jews are being systematically exterminated by the Nazis and their ilk in the occupied countries. Those men want me to help them to establish a new Jewish State in the one place we have always lived."

"Do they want money? Why not go to the community? Most Jews would contribute something," she said, but was thinking that there had to be more.

"They do want money, but not from me. They need me to use my connections at the port and with some of the boat captains to get items from here to ports where they can then be transported to Jews already living in Palestine, avoiding any paperwork on both ends, shall we say."

"In other words, they want you to help them smuggle contraband. Weapons, I would guess."

"Weapons, medicine, gold and even people who the British want to keep out. The British court the Arabs and limit Jewish immigration to Palestine."

"Your friends sound dangerous."

"They are not above violence. Is that good enough? Are you satisfied now?"

"Why not tell Uncle Morty? He knows every official at the port."

"Uncle Morty is an Anglophile, at least while Harry is in the British army.  Conflict between these men and the British may be inevitable.  I'm not sure how Uncle Morty would deal with all this.  As for your mother, I know she would support me.  I just don't want her involved if things go bad, you either.  That's why I kept it a secret."

"Well it's too late for me.  So, when do I get to meet them?"

"I don't want you involved.  If something happens I need you to pick up the pieces and help your mother.  I can't allow it."

"Papa, Harry  has been doing his part in this war.  I always thought there wasn't much I could do to help.  Maybe now there is.  Even if it's just as a messenger or something."

" I know you Dionne.  You'll find a way to get  in on this no matter what I say.  I guess better with me than without.  I will see, but you must be patient.  And again, nothing leaves this room.  Now, go call Sammy.  You better sound a little sick."

# 22

The next few days were routine.  Dionne went to the show with Sammy.  They had their usual routine date.  Dionne couldn't help but dwell on the confrontation she had had with her father.  She was beginning to doubt he would let her be part of his new world.  A couple of times Sammy asked her if she was OK.  She said she was still feeling tired from her illness.  He was sympathetic.  Sammy was always nice, but her uncle's concerns kept coming back.  "So what if he doesn't make me laugh.  He's a good guy."

A few more days passed.  Then, one morning, her father stood at her desk.  His voice was near a whisper.  "I'm meeting some friends for lunch.  Wait thirty minutes and come to where you saw us before."

It had snowed the night before.  Mount Royal was covered in a white blanket of snow.  Dionne took the underground to within a couple of blocks of the pub.  She could not see her father in the window this time.  She decided to go in.  If he wasn't there, she would have a bite and confront him at work.  As she entered, she saw him in the back with the two men from before.  His back was to her.  The  Fat Man rose as if he knew her.

"So, this is the young woman who followed me last week. I didn't know you had an agent of your own, Bernie.  Don't be embarrassed my dear.  When  you come from  Russia like me, you learn to be very careful."  He had a wide grin and clapped her father on the back.  "I am Avrum, and this is Simon.  It is a pleasure to meet you, Dionne.  Here, sit, sit."

She was chagrined that she had been spotted by Avrum but couldn't help smiling herself.  "I'll be more careful next time."

"You will need to be in order to be useful to us. Simon will help you. But I am ahead of myself. Bernie said you wanted to meet us. So, here we are. What do you want to know? I will tell you what I can." The smile was still partly there but his expression was more guarded.

"My father has told me of your plans to help Jewish refugees and settlers in Palestine."

Simon spoke for the first time. "We prefer Israel. That is what we have called it as long as we have lived there."

"Okay, Israel. The plans are admirable if not ambitious."

"We look upon ourselves as a combination of the Red Cross and the Maccabees."

"So angels and rebels."

"We intend to help our people, whatever is necessary," said Simon. "To whomever stands in our way, we are avenging angels."

Avrum looked at her father. "These young people so dramatic, Bernie. Enough symbolism."

He sipped his coffee. The joviality was completely gone. Time to be serious.

"History has taught us that we can trust no one.   This has only been magnified in this war.   Germany was one of the most advanced countries in Europe and a country where Jews were more assimilated than any country in Western Europe.   Yet, they slaughtered us.   The British pledge to help us, have even promised a Jewish state since 1917.   Churchill has Jewish advisors and is for us.   Yet, the British Colonial Office deals with the thugs who answer to Hitler's war time guest the Mufti of Jerusalem.   We can barely defend our own settlements.   The United States never filled their immigration quotas from Germany.   Canada said they only wanted farmers, and we weren't that type, even though our settlements have turned the desert green.   Don't get me wrong, the Americans and your countrymen have no ill will against us.   Their bureaucrats, the professionals with their Ivy League degrees, however, are a very different story.   We are what is left. We are men and women, former soldiers, camp survivors. Some are professionals. Others are adapting to new lives with new roles. Many just do some small task to help.   We must do whatever we can for what's left of us, for ourselves.   If you choose to help us, we welcome you.   If not, we only ask for your silence about our work."

Dionne spoke quietly.   "Well, Mr. Avrum, you're not so bad at drama yourself.   I want to help and will.   One more question?"

"You are your father's daughter.   Nu, what else?"

"Who is the Mufti of Jerusalem?"

The Mufti is the religious leader of the Muslim Arabs in Palestine.  He is a fanatic Muslim and has his own army of followers who spend most of their time attacking our settlements.  The British who are spread thin make only minimal responses.  They spend more time trying to keep Jews out and taking away our guns than they do trying to deal with the Arabs.  In reality, there are simply more Arabs. We are much easier to control, for now.  The Mufti hates both the British and the Jews.  In that respect, he and Hitler have much in common.  He  has spent most of the war as Hitler's guest, directing his followers from Berlin.

# 23

*Berlin, 1944 -*

Bormann had spent the morning dealing with local party bosses who were trying to gain access to Hitler.  While he had denied all of them a personal meeting with Hitler, he reassured them that he would pass their concerns on.  Hitler, of course, was quite busy directing the war, so Bormann could not tell them when they would hear anything.  They were then all invited to one of the Fuhrer's business lunches. It was the usual two hour monologue with an occasional interruption of  agreement or praise from Goebbels, sitting on Hitler's right.  Today on Hitler's left was Field Marshall Jodl, who ate quietly if somewhat impatiently,  probably hoping an aide would save him with an urgent war development. Bormann sat next to Jodl.  When lunch was over and Hitler made his exit to prolonged applause, Bormann shook a few more hands and headed toward his office.  He was stopped by one of Hitler's security who asked that he join the Fuhrer in the leader's private office.

Hitler's private office was not particularly large or ornate. There were a few pictures of Hitler speaking to large throngs. Each celebrated some triumph, Austria, Munich, Poland and finally France.  Some were taken by Eva Braun, Hitler's mistress.  There were none after 1940.  Hitler was going through some papers, most of which Bormann had already read.  Bormann saluted and waited for Hitler to acknowledge him.  Hitler removed his glasses and bade him sit.

"Bormann, we will have a special guest at supper tonight, our friend the Mufti."

Hitler's suppers were more intimate than the large lunches.  Suppers could last for hours and could be repetitive and boring, with Hitler expounding on multiple topics. Nevertheless, invitees perceived themselves to be close to Hitler, one of the inner circle, especially earlier in the war. Most of those who attended were the usual intimates like Goering, Goebbels or Himmler.   There might be a general. Sometimes, like tonight, there would be a special guest that Hitler wanted to impress or manipulate.   Usually one of Hitler's secretaries would be present.   Bormann was always there, mostly listening, rarely speaking.

Hitler continued, "I have told the Mufti that you would escort him to supper since he is such an important ally, at least in his own mind.  I would like you to speak with him for a few minutes privately and give me your impression of his continued use to us. We need his people in Palestine to be more aggressive in raiding Jewish settlements and British installations. I, personally, see no place for him once we are victorious, but he may be of some help now."

"Yes, Mein Führer." Hitler went back to his reading. Bormann stood and left, not waiting for Hitler to dismiss him.

Bormann did not think there would be a victory. The Germans were on the defensive everywhere. He knew there were many in the military who wished Hitler dead so that they could make a deal with Western Allies to the exclusion of the Soviet Union. He knew Stalin would never allow that scenario. He doubted the Mufti's men could be more than a thorn in the side of the British at best. "Maybe, the Mufti could be of some use to me."

The Mufti arrived at the Reich Chancellory a few minutes before he was to meet with Hitler. Bormann had sent one of the Mercedes sedans that were used to chauffeur foreign dignitaries around Berlin. A pair of SS guards accompanied the Mufti. The Mufti exited the vehicle and was greeted by Bormann with a slight bow of the head. Bormann led the way with the guards in tow.

"I hope your excellency continues to enjoy our hospitality. If there is anything I can do for a guest of the Fuhrer, you need only ask."

"Perhaps, you might do something about the British air raids at night. They are most disturbing," the Mufti answered in a most condescending tone.

"We are assured by the Fuhrer that Marshall Goering will remedy the situation."

" You are a faithful servant of your leader as I am of Allah. We must determine our fates, not Marshall Goering."

The Mufti was seated next to Hitler. There were only five others in attendance. In addition to Hitler, the Mufti and Bormann were Goebbels, Speer, head of war production, and one of Hitler's secretaries. The meal was vegetarian. Hitler did not smoke, drink alcohol or eat meat. This menu suited the Mufti. The others, well aware of Hitler's tastes, usually consumed alcohol before arriving.

The meal proceeded as usual. Hitler began a monologue that might last over an hour. Goebbels would interrupt with enthusiastic endorsements of Hitler's thoughts in a practiced routine that Bormann was well used to. Speer would nod his head, but rarely spoke. He always looked preoccupied, but was likely bored as well . Bormann nodded in agreement when expected and answered Hitler's questions in one or two words. He much preferred dealing with Hitter one-on-one with none of the inner circle around sniping at each other and at him.

Finally, Hitler asked the Mufti how the Reich could aid him in combating the British and the Jews in the Middle East.

"You have been most gracious to the Arab people in our war against the Jews and their British allies. We know that there are huge battles underway in the East and the West that are consuming your resources. We ask only for small arms, explosives and financial help to pay our brave warriors," he said.

Bormann guessed that the Mufti knew he would get little in the way of heavy armament's so did not bother asking. He also knew that the Mufti had an account in Zürich where the money for his brave warriors would likely end up.

Hitler looked irritated but responded calmly. "As you know, the Reich is on a campaign to be Jew free. I can also assure you that we will destroy the Bolshevik armies and their English and American allies with new weapons that are being developed by Herr Speer. Our victory will be final as long as I control the destiny of the German people. We can honor your request. I will leave the details to Herr Bormann."

"Yes, Mein Fuhrer," said Bormann.

"You are most generous. My people and I thank you," added the Mufti.

Hitler rose, signaling the end of supper. He left the room with Goebbels in tow. Speer said he had urgent production matters to attend to and left as well. As it was late, Bormann escorted the Mufti back to his car. He asked the Mufti if they could meet the next day to discuss Hitler's offer. The Mufti agreed. Bormann said he would send a car in the morning. He stood watching as the Mufti was driven away. A few minutes later, the air raid sirens began. It was the seventh British raid in ten days. "We await the super weapons, Herr Speer," he whispered to himself dejectedly. He would help the Mufti as ordered, but for his own benefit as well.

The Mufti arrived over thirty minutes late for their scheduled appointment the next day, clearly showing Bormann who was boss. Bormann acted as if he took no offense, but made sure his adjutant interrupted several times with routine papers for him to sign. After some small talk, the bargaining began.

The Mufti gave Bormann a list of arms his fighters would need. Most were small arms with ammunition, grenades and other explosives.

"Frankly, your request is somewhat excessive," he said after browsing the list.

"I was under the impression that your armaments industry could easily meet these minimal requirements, Herr Bormann. Certainly your Jewish labor force can be motivated to meet the need." The Mufti's remark was clearly a challenge mixed with sarcasm.

"The issue is not production, but rather transportation. We can move sometimes through Turkey by paying off certain officials, but this has become more difficult and more expensive due to Allied pressure to have the Turks join the Allied powers. Most of it must be delivered by U-boat, as surface ships in the Mediterranean are easy prey for British ships and airplanes." Bormann paused for a moment. "I noticed that there is no request for financial assistance."

The Mufti looked Bormann directly in the eye. "I thought that is something that you and I would discuss privately. After all, we need not bother with book keepers and accountants. I am sure we can agree on the proper amount necessary. We, of course, would provide you with a commission or, as we say, baksheesh for your efforts on behalf of Arab freedom fighters."

Bormann had expected as much. He would pretend to be shocked at such an offer, then he and the Mufti would finally haggle out a price. Before he answered, the Mufti interjected. "I can have your commission placed in a secure account in the neutral county of your choice. Some of your colleagues seem to like Argentina. I, myself, would prefer the Swiss with whom I can facilitate a confidential transfer, saving us both any official inconveniences."

There was the hook. Each could benefit from the deal and each would have something on the other if the agreement was broken. They both had leverage on the other. Bormann thanked the Mufti. "I appreciate your kindness. It will certainly facilitate our effort to crush the Allies."

"I am happy to be of service. You are most kind, Herr Bormann."

They left the details of the arms transactions to their aides then privately arranged the "financial aid." The Mufti bowed to Bormann this time before he got into his car. Bormann returned to his office quite satisfied with their arrangement. His future contact with the Mufti would be brief and private. There were too many suspicious eyes and ears in Berlin.

# 24

*Montreal 1945-*

Time passed slowly at first. Everything was a new experience. Dionne's duties for her father and Avrum did not replace her regular work. While most of what she did occurred after work hours, there were some things that had to be done at the port during the day. In addition, she had to be trained to avoid being followed on some of her errands as well as how to lie convincingly to suspicious officials, friends and relatives. On her first day, she met Simon at the café where they had first met. They had coffee, then Simon said, " I want you to get up now and leave. I will give you a five minute head start. This is your city. Lose me."

Dionne left the café and tried to put some distance between her and Simon. She knew the neighborhood well and was able to duck down some narrow alleys that connected to some more crowded streets. She tried not to look back to see if Simon was there, running across intersections against the lights when she could. She then jumped on a bus that took her to Chinatown. After browsing in some shop windows, she went to one of her favorite restaurants and ordered a victory lunch of chow mein. Just as she took her first bite, Simon sat down with a big grin on his face. "Not bad for a first try. You actually lost me for a while."

"Then how did you find me?"

"I knew that you and your boyfriend what's his name come to Chinatown, so I took a taxi here and waited for you to come."

"You've been following me?"

"Yes. Even though your father vouched for you, we had to make sure that you were not indiscreet in your daily activities or did not associate with risky characters."

"So you cheated."

"Dionne, we deal with very dangerous people. They are smart and careful. Cheating, as you say, is a way of life for them — and for us. The better cheater wins. You have to be a better cheater. The loser rarely gets a repeat match."

For the next few weeks, Dionne and Simon played the "game" as she called it. Simon was a good teacher. She learned when to stop and look in a store window to see if anybody was following, when to speed up and slow down her gait, even what to wear to blend in. She got better, but he always caught her. One day, she was walking with Simon not too far behind. He was wearing a pea coat and a toque, but by now she knew his gait. She walked by the hospital where her grandmother had been before she died. Dionne had been there often as a child and knew the layout. She walked in the main entrance and left via the loading dock. She and her cousin Harry had gotten into trouble with her Uncle Morty for disappearing and exploring the hospital. As she entered the alley, she saw Simon by the ambulance entrance looking for her. It made sense that someone might leave that way.

She walked up behind him and tapped him on the shoulder. "Looking for someone?" Simon whirled around, trying not to look surprised.

"Very good. How did you do that?"

"I cheated."

"I guess it's time for you to go to work"

# 25

*England -*

Monroe spent the next couple of weeks on his usual duties at the hospital. He also had to clear patients for transfer home on troop transports or hospital ships. He was assigned to escort some of the sicker patients to one of the hospital ships leaving from London for Antwerp then on to the States.

He would go as far as London. Kemp was assigned to go with him. As usual, Kemp talked to somebody in headquarters and managed a layover for the two of them for three days in London.

On the troop train to London, Monroe had time to think some more about the autopsy. He still had nagging doubts about the witnesses and the evidence. Kemp noticed his distraction.

"Okay, Doc. What's up?"

"Just thinking about my little trip to Germany. Can't seem to put it to rest."

"Well, if you ask me, you're getting a little too worried about some dead Nazi asshole. The Army is happy with you, so let it rest. 'Making waves' as my sailor buddies say will not win you any medals and may get you, nor should I say us, stuck on a troopship taking the slow way home."

"I think I'm going to go see the British doctor, Smythe. He lives in London. Maybe he can give me some of his private thoughts with nobody official around. Couldn't hurt."

"I'm glad you were listening to me, Doc. You know where to find me in London if you need anything."

"I was listening to you. If anything goes screwy, I'll keep you out of it."

"Hopefully you and the Brit will just end up at his club for tea and crumpets."

# 26

Monroe checked in at the Officer's Quarters in London and then hailed a black cab. He decided to start at Guy's Hospital where Smythe did most of his surgeries. He wasn't sure that Smythe would even talk to him about the case, but maybe would at least listen. Most doctors have a need to know at some level. Monroe hoped that Smythe had a greater curiosity than he had shown in Germany.

The trip to Guy's took awhile. Though London did not look nearly as bad as Berlin, it hardly looked like the city of a victor. There were boarded up or partially destroyed buildings all along his route. It didn't help that it was a grey, drizzly day, not too different than St. Louis in March. The driver pulled up to the main entrance to Guy's Hospital. He thanked Monroe with a big smile for the fare. "Probably over tipped, but what the hell. These people have been through a lot."

He was directed to the surgical ward and asked the nurse in charge if Dr. Smythe was making rounds or operating.

"He was in early, did surgery, made rounds and left about two hours ago to go his surgery on Harley Street."

Smythe had just finished with his last patient. He had decided that he would go to his club for the evening. A couple of school chums had returned from a Mediterranean assignment with the Navy and wanted to get together. He looked out his window at the darkening sky. "Raining, and dark. Nobody on the street. Probably never get a cab."

He walked out to the street and saw a cab approaching. He stepped off the curb to flag it down. It slowed down and headed toward him. As it neared, it accelerated, struck a terrified Smythe head on, and sped away.

Monroe was lucky to find the cab that had dropped him off at the stand near the hospital. As they neared the Harley street address the nurse had given, he saw a crowd with police and an ambulance. He instructed the driver to pull over, gave the driver too much money again, and ran over to see if he could help. A bobby tried to keep him back. "I'm a doctor. I might be of some help."

"Sorry, doctor. It's too late. Poor fellow was run down. Looks like he walked out into the street and got hit. Driver ran off. Probably had too much to drink."

Monroe looked down at the body. It was Smythe.

"Who's in charge here? I know this man," he said to no one in particular.

Another policeman approached. "May I help you, Captain?"

"I know this man. His name is Dr. Smythe. We are colleagues."

"Yes, sir we are aware of who he is. Office right over there. Looks like he was struck by a car at high speed. Probably a drunk."

"Did anybody see it? Are there any skid marks?"

"Not that it's your business, but in the spirit of us being allies and all, there are no skid marks or witnesses. If that's all, I'll need for you to move along."

Monroe knew that there wasn't going to be anything more for him to do here, so he hailed a cab and headed to the Bachelor Officers Quarters. He thought the whole thing was all a little bit surreal but just chalked it up to an unfortunate coincidence.

As the cab sped away, an onlooker in the crowd turned up his collar and headed toward the Tube. He was satisfied that Smythe was dead, but was curious as to who the American officer was. He would tell his superiors, collect his pay and wait for any further instructions. There could be another opportunity in the near future.

# 27

Monroe spent a restless night at the Army BOQ in London. The facts of Smythe's demise were straightforward on their face. He had been run down by a reckless, possibly drunk driver. There was no reason to come to any other conclusion. He nevertheless found himself coming up with all kinds of secret plots and conspiracies. In the end, at 4 am, he resigned himself to what he had learned in med school. "If it looks like a duck, walks like a duck, and quacks like a duck, it's not a zebra." He had slept for about four hours when the sergeant who manned the front desk knocked at the door. "Sir, there's a British police detective to see you. Says it's about an accident that you witnessed."

"Be right down." Monroe splashed some water on his face, dressed quickly and went to the lobby. "Can't keep Scotland Yard waiting," he thought.

A medium built man approached him, hat in hand and a badge visible inside his overcoat. He looked every bit the police detective. "Captain Monroe is it? I am Detective Inspector Le Strade. Can we go  and talk about last night's events? I have a car waiting." They got into a waiting cab and drove only a few blocks to a nondescript office building with no official markings. Once they sat down in a small office, as Le Strade was about to speak, Monroe interrupted. "Detective, who the hell are you? I mean 'Le Strade.' Should I call myself Dr. Watson? I'd think you'd come up with a better fake."

"Sorry, that was more for the sergeant's benefit. Always liked Sherlock Holmes. I knew you'd figure it out. I wanted to peak your curiosity enough that you'd come willingly without any questions in public."

"So, I take it you're not with Scotland Yard."

"MI-5 actually. My name is Watson, really."

"OK, I'll play, Watson. What's this all about? MI-5 doesn't do traffic accidents."

"We do when there could be a national security issue. You see, your colleague Dr. Smythe was assigned to your mission in Germany by MI-6. They asked us to look into this because it concerns the death of an operative, though not a professional, an operative nevertheless. I might also add that he was a cousin of the MI-6 director, Menzies. They don't operate domestically so we were brought in. Don't think there's a whole lot here myself."

This was starting to look more like a zebra. "What do you want to know?"

"What was your business with Smythe?"

Monroe decided to lie with the truth until he had a better idea where this was going. "As you know, we met in Germany. Smythe was kind enough to invite me to visit if I was ever in London. I was here for a couple of days with not a whole lot to do so I decided to drop in to see him." He figured that MI-5 would have already gone to the hospital. "I went to the hospital to get the address for his surgery and got there right after the accident."

"So you did not contact him before hand? What if he hadn't been in London?"

"It was a spur of the moment thing, that's all."

"Then it wasn't about your business in Germany?"

Monroe tried to not look surprised at the question. This looked like something more than routine. He decided to reveal a little more to see what he could learn.

"I did have a few questions about the way things went, so hush hush and all. Smythe seemed so relaxed through the whole thing that I thought he might know a lot more than he let on. I guess I was trying to be a bit of a Sherlock Holmes to perpetuate your metaphor. But, I guess that's over now. Do you know any more about what happened? The police were not too forthcoming."

"It is no longer their problem. We are doing the investigation now. We do, however, agree with the police. We also have the resources to find the offender, and I assure you, we will. For my own information, did you question anything that happened in Germany as being irregular?"

" I signed the official report."

"That wasn't my question."

"Well, you'll have to take my answer. Otherwise I have to get my superior on the mission, Colonel Kleet, involved as we have our own procedures to follow." Was that a hint of recognition when he mentioned Kleet?

"Thank you Captain. That will not be necessary. I have everything I need. My driver will take you back to your quarters. I should remind you that since MI-5 is involved our interview, it falls under the Official Secrets Act and that you are under its jurisdiction while you are in England."

Monroe was dropped off in front of the BOQ. He was about to walk in when he heard a familiar voice. "Doctor, a moment?"

Kleet.

# 28

Kleet pointed Monroe to an army sedan driven by the linebacker who had escorted them to Germany. Kleet did not give the driver any destination, simply telling him to go.

"I'll be brief, Captain. I know our British allies were just speaking with you about the events involving Dr. Smythe. I'd like you to brief me on what went on with those events and your visit with our MI-5 friends."

Monroe noticed that when Kleet referred to him as Captain rather than Doctor, he was clearly pulling rank. This was to be no less an interrogation than the one that he had just been through with Watson. He suspected that Kleet knew a good deal of the story so he made sure his answers were consistent with what he had told the British.

"Smythe had invited me to visit should I ever be in London."

"Which your boy Kemp arranged."

Monroe ignored the remark but was a little surprised that Kleet knew that detail. "I went to his surgery, and he was dead. Had been struck by a car. Hit and run. Next thing I know there is a British intelligence officer at my door who drags me in for questioning. Says Smythe was considered an operative, and they were tying up loose ends. I told him what I am telling you, which I assume you could have asked him about directly. By the way, am I considered an operative? I guess I must be since you are awfully interested in the hit and run of a British citizen."

"Captain (there was the rank again), I am not interested in verbal jousting with you, though you may find it amusing. I will start by saying our British allies, especially their intelligence establishment, are not always totally forthcoming with their US allies, though sometimes we are not any different. I wanted to hear it directly from the horse's mouth. Oh, and by the way, that guy's name is not Watson.

Now, I want you to tell me if you left anything out when you spoke to him. For instance, did you go to see Smythe out of any concerns from your trip to Germany?"

"My concerns are the same ones I told you about in Germany. I didn't expect Smythe to be of any real help in that regard."

"Doctor," (Back to the professional title. He's personally curious about something.), I know you're an inquisitive guy, too much for your own good if you ask me. Off the record, did anything seem strange to you about this accident?"

Nothing was off the record with Kleet, but Monroe decided to play the game, maybe get an answer. "It seemed odd to me that there were no track marks or evidence of the driver trying to avoid Smythe. Granted, it was dark, but why run away unless you were drunk like the police thought, or some kind of criminal? In any case, I doubt we will, or at least I will never know."

"You're right, you probably never will know exactly what happened. I doubt MI-5 will be forthcoming with me either. You are not an operative and don't have the need to know any of the details. You are, however, someone we have to keep tabs on since you were involved in a confidential operation and seem to have a friend in Washington."

" I remind you I did not volunteer for the operation or use my so called connections in any way."

"True, but this is the hand the Army has dealt you. So, let me be clear, and this comes from people above us. Forget about this whole thing. Go back to your base, take care of your airmen. I do not expect to see you again, unless I run into you on the street in a few years, and even then, I will pretend I don't know you. Am I completely clear, Captain?"

"Yes, sir, Colonel." The car was just pulling up to the BOQ. Monroe wondered if Kleet and the linebacker had some secret code to time it so perfectly. He got out and had barely closed the door before Kleet was gone. Monroe knew that Kleet was deadly serious in his last remarks, but Kleet also knew that Monroe was a curious guy. He had said so himself. Kleet easily could have accepted Monroe's explanation and left it at that. Was he goading Monroe at the end? Did he want Monroe to continue poking around and then be the fall guy if things got sticky with the Brits? In the end, it didn't make any difference. Monroe was now even more fixated on finding answers. He would need Kemp.

Monroe waited until he got back to his base to speak with Kemp. He was pretty sure that Kleet had someone keeping an eye on him, and maybe Kemp, in London. He went about business as usual until he and Kemp had their weekly meeting to see what supplies needed to be requisitioned for the ward. It was a routine meeting in which only the two of them took part.

"Sergeant, I need your help with a delicate matter."

"What's her name, Doc? I'll see what I can do."

"OK, smart ass. I'm serious."

"So am I," Kemp deadpanned, but the amusement was there.

Monroe then told Kemp about the events in London with Smythe's death, MI-5, and most importantly Kleet's warning and his feeling he was being used.

Kemp was quiet for a moment, looked around, then spoke in a low voice. "Doc, whether you're being used or not, I'd take Kleet at face value. If you keep your nose clean, you go home and live your life. If you keep this up, you find out something that you don't want to know and can't tell anybody about anyway or you screw up and the Army lets you be the fall guy. And they *will* let you be the fall guy, Senator friend or not. That's my advice, which I'm pretty sure you're not going to take, so what do you need?"

"I need to go to Paris. I need to talk to the French doctor. I should have started there anyway. I could tell that he was as suspicious as me about everything. He may be in danger, if Smythe's death was not an accident. The problem is, I can't just go there on leave. I am sure that Kleet is keeping tabs on me, and I don't want him following me around Paris. I'm also not sure if someone else is keeping track of me. I need to go officially, but unofficially, if you get my drift."

"Doc, I might point out that if the Frog is in danger so are you, so going off to gay Paree might not be the best idea. I can have your back, but it may not be enough."

Monroe thought for a minute. "That could be a problem. Kleet knew you arranged our London visit, so he has his eye on you as well as me. We have to arrange this trip outside of channels, and you have to stay here. If we both leave, we'll attract the watchdogs."

"Let me see what I can do."

A few days went by. During one of Monroe's night shifts, Kemp pulled him aside. "I think I can get you to Paris. You gotta get the boss to give you a pass for some reason. Once you do that I know a guy who knows a guy. You get it. He'll get you to Paris without it coming back to me or you as long as you're not spotted there. There's one catch. It ain't free. I can take care of him with some supplies that will go missing, but he will need to take care of his guys. Like a c-note. Times two."

Monroe thought for a moment. He was now doing more than bending the rules. His mother always used to say, "Rules are for fools and a guide for the wise." He'd find out in Paris which one he was. "OK. I'll take it out of my post war Cadillac fund."

"Ok, Doc. You're going to Paris."

# PART III

## 29

*Montreal, Summer, 1945*

Dionne quickly adapted to her new role, running errands for Simon and Avrum. She knew Montreal far better than they did so she rarely had to repeat a route to the same destination. Since she was well known in the port areas, she could go nearly anywhere without being noticed. Simon would take messages and packages to the seedier areas. Though she insisted she could handle herself, her father and Avrum would not hear of her taking what they thought were undue risks. Her father gave her jobs to do that her Uncle Morty had done previously using the excuse that she had to know all aspects of the business. Her Uncle would kiddingly ask, "What's Harry going to do when he comes home?" She would tell him that she would let Harry be her assistant. Her uncle would laugh, but often got a far away, almost melancholy look on his face.

Harry was on occupation duty in Germany but was due to be rotated back to Britain soon, and then home to Canada. His letters came more often. Most were optimistic and forward looking, but some were very contemplative. They were usually about friends he had lost or who had been seriously wounded. The worst were the ones about the concentration camps that his unit had liberated. Even though his descriptions of the victims were very graphic, the only word that came to mind was "unimaginable." After reading one of the worst, her father looked up at her. "Now, you see, we are doing the right thing." She was certain he was right.

Simon continued to add new twists to her training. He taught her about signaling and dead drops for messages. He even helped her with disguises. She wasn't really sure how all that was relevant to a courier in Montreal, but she trusted Simon and went along with the lessons. Besides, she liked beating him at his own game. They spent a lot of time together, but he never showed any interest in her other than professional. Even though she was still seeing Sammy, her ego was a little deflated as she was used to men giving her more attention. One day, they were rehearsing passing a message in a downtown department store. As they walked by the perfume department, Simon stopped for a second and said, "I smell my wife's perfume," and smiled. Dionne played her role until the exercise was over. As they were walking back she asked him why he had never said anything about his wife.

"After all, Simon, you seem to know everything about me."

"That was necessary for our mission. My personal life is not."

"I thought we were friends."

He could see she was upset. "We are partners, for now at least, and I do know much about you, so I will tell you about Miriam. She is from Lebanon, part Jewish, part Christian. We met before the war in Beirut. We married about a year later. We have a son, Judah. He is two. The war has been hard on them. I was away a good deal of the time. She also had relatives who were trapped in Paris during the war. Luckily they are on the Christian side of the family or they surely would have been gone. They survived and still live in Paris. She corresponds with them. That has certainly helped. So, now you know; but I caution you, the more personal details we know about each other, the more our enemies could use those details against us."

"Simon, we are in Montreal. There may be some unsavory characters here, but I really don't see us being captured and interrogated."

"We are in Montreal - for now."

She was incredulous."What does that mean?"

"Training is over for today. We will talk. Get back to work. Your uncle is probably already asking where you are." He turned and disappeared into the crowd.

Dionne was taken aback. She had never imagined that her role would take her beyond Montreal. Maybe she would be going to the United States, perhaps New York or Boston. Since Simon had dropped the hint, she expected she would know more very soon. When she returned to work, her father was waiting with his coat in his hand. "Dionne I'm glad you're back. Come with me. We have a meeting to get to."

"I have some things that Uncle Morty asked me to do."

"Uncle Morty can wait. I'll tell him I needed you to help me."

They went to the pub where they had frequently met with Avrum and Simon. Avrum was waiting at his usual back table. He quickly got to the point. "Simon tells me that you have completed your training and have done very well. We now need the two of you to go on a more important mission. We will need you to go to Europe."

Dionne looked at her father, who simply nodded his head in agreement. "Now that the war is over, Europe is in shambles. We have a two fold duty to our people there. First, we must help the victims of Nazi atrocities to find a new life. That may be in Canada or the United States, or even Israel. The second mission is to help find those responsible for causing this horror. They need to be identified and taken to the proper authorities. The allies will undoubtedly single out the big shots who gave the orders, however, there were plenty of others who participated willingly in this Holocaust, who need to be brought to justice. You and Simon will go to Europe under a plausible cover and use that cover to assist our people openly but also to search out our enemies covertly. You will go under the guise of being a member of a Canadian Jewish relief organization.

Simon already has an identity as an international merchant. I will not lie to you. There is some danger involved. Our enemies will likely not submit willingly. We have no reservations about using any force necessary to bring them to justice. Simon is well trained in the use of force, sometimes lethal, to accomplish this goal. You will also be trained, primarily to be able to defend yourself."

Dionne looked at her father. "I assume you agree with this proposal?"

"The decision is yours. I will back whatever decision you make and everyone here will accept it as well."

"But if I do this, what am I to tell mother? Sammy?"

"I think you and I can deal with your mother. She will understand that you want to make a sacrifice for this relief effort. Of course, we will only tell her about the Jewish relief organization part. Fortunately or unfortunately, Sammy is your problem. Also, Harry will be home soon. He understands the importance of service. I'm sure he will support your decision if you decide to go ahead. That will help with both Uncle Morty and your mother."

Dionne was intrigued with the idea of foreign travel, and of the excitement of doing covert work. She also felt an obligation to help her people. She felt a sense of purpose. It had been growing since she began working with Simon and Avrum. This next phase seemed a logical extension of that purpose, and one that was necessary. "When will this happen?"

"Within the next few weeks," answered Avrum.

"I'll do it." She looked at her father. "You knew I was going to say yes, didn't you? "

Her father smiled, not from enthusiasm, more from resignation. "Yes, I suppose I did know. Let's go home, and lie to your mother."

# 30

Dionne's mother took the idea surprisingly well. It helped that her father gave his enthusiastic support, talking about the Jewish tradition of making the world better and how it would allow Dionne to see the world before she settled down. Her mother gave him a somewhat skeptical look, realizing that he was laying it on pretty thick. Dionne, on the other hand, talked about the service that Harry had done in the war and how she had felt left out. This would be her opportunity to help serve. Her mother had paused, then looked at Dionne. "You've made your bed Dionne. You'll have to lie in it."

Dionne hugged her mother. She had certainly expected at least some pushback. Her mother then asked, "What about Sammy?" Dionne had not really thought very much about

Sammy when making her decision. On reflection, she found that somewhat disconcerting. She had been dating Sammy well over a year, and they got along well. Now he appeared to be somewhat of an afterthought. Maybe it was just the excitement of going on the mission. She would talk to Sammy. She knew he would stand behind her.

Dionne asked Sammy to meet her at their favorite Chinese restaurant a couple of days later. He arrived about fifteen minutes late. "I'm sorry to be a few minutes late. We're very busy at the business. I don't have time for a long lunch. So what's so important?" He was clearly distracted.

"I've been offered a tremendous opportunity."

Before she could even get started, Sammy interrupted. "So is Uncle Morty retiring? Are you now the second in command?" He was clearly somewhat amused with himself.

"Very funny Mr. Big Shot. No, actually, I have a chance to go to Europe, to serve with a volunteer group that is helping refugees, mostly Jewish, get settled in North America. I'll be part of the Canadian group. I'm excited at the opportunity."

Sammy was clearly taken aback. "So how long will you be gone? Where in Europe will you be? Do your parents agree with this?"

"I'll probably be gone about a year. I'm not sure where in Europe I'm going to be. I guess wherever they send me. I had to talk my parents into it, but they finally agreed. I might even get to see Harry before he comes home. Of course I'll miss everybody, but I think it will be a great adventure, and I'll be helping people."

"Were you ever going to talk this over with me? I mean, I thought we were sort of in this together. We've been dating over a year; that usually means that we would be engaged someday. I don't know how I feel about this. I'm not sure I can let you go."

"I wasn't really asking your permission. This is something I've decided to do. I am looking for your support. I was hoping you'd be very excited for me."

Sammy said nothing. Dionne tried to lessen the blow. "It's a lot of new information Sammy. I'm sure you need some time to think about it, but I am going to go ahead and do it."

"So you've made up your mind."

"Yes, I have."

"I guess you're looking for something and it's clearly not here. Anyway I've got to go back to work. I'm sure I'll see you before you leave." He got up, kissed her on the cheek, and left the restaurant.

She started to get up to follow him, but then sat down. Her mother had been right. She had made her bed.

Dionne told her parents about her talk with Sammy. They were both supportive. She did not dwell on it because she didn't feel at her age that she should be burdening her parents with relationship issues.

The next day when Dionne arrived at work, her Uncle Morty took her aside. "Your father told me what went on with Sammy."

"Well, news certainly gets around quickly in this family."

"Are you alright?"

"I guess so. I expected Sammy to be a little bit more understanding. After all, we've been together for a while. I'll be fine."

Her Uncle Morty smiled. "I know you'll be fine. You and your cousin Harry are alike in that way. You see what you want to do and move ahead. As for Sammy, he's a putz."

# 31

*France,*

The train from Aix was only about an hour away from Paris. The train ride was one of the few times Dionne had been able to reflect on her life since she had come to Europe. Initially, she had spent most of her time doing exactly what she had told everyone at home she would be doing. She worked with the Red Cross helping displaced persons find a place to go. Some were able to emigrate to Canada. The local Canadian Jewish community sponsored many. The camp survivors were the hardest on her. Many were children, their parents having been gassed in the concentration camps. She was deeply moved by the experience. It only reaffirmed to her how important her mission was. She and Simon were successful in helping many of the refugees get to British controlled Palestine – legally or illegally.

They also followed leads on former Nazis or Nazi collaborators. They were tasked with looking for camp guards and lower ranking officers with a few bureaucrats mixed in. When they found them, Simon would get word to the proper authorities. Some of their targets were arrested, others disappeared. She wasn't always sure if they escaped or were dealt with by some of Simon's other colleagues. When she asked about some of them, Simon told her it was better she didn't know.

Her most recent mission had been the most important. It was the first time that she and Simon had to deal with one of the higher ranking Nazis. It was also the first time that she and Simon assumed false identities. They had been somewhat successful in finding out about the events in Wannsee. She was able to eavesdrop on some of the doctors when she served them. Simon was able to come and go in their group sessions. He had told her that the only doctor who had been truly curious was the American. Simon attributed that to him being a Jew. She had seen him arguing with the American colonel in the restaurant. She managed to only overhear a bit of their conversation but heard the determination in his voice. He also made her a little uncomfortable when he looked at her for what seemed was a little bit longer than he had to. The train pulled into Gare Lyon. After she and Simon made their reports, she was going to England to see Harry.

# 32

*London-*

Dionne met Harry in the lobby of her hotel. There were big hugs, smiles and a few tears. "So it's Captain Harry, I see."

""It's actually more like 'Hungry Harry.' Let's get something to eat and catch up."

They went across the street to a small pub. Harry stopped and ordered two pints of ale with a pub lunch. Dionne found herself directing Harry to a table in the back so she could see the entrance. When he asked why they didn't sit by the window, she realized how ingrained Simon's training had become. The operative on-off switch was always on now. They grinned at each other like a couple of kids for a few seconds. Harry looked trim and fit, maybe a little too trim. His mother would see to that when he got home. He had lost the tan she had seen from the photos he had sent from North Africa. The light in his eyes was not as bright. After her experience helping the refugees, she could only imagine what he had been through. She thought of his letters during the war where he would talk about a friend or comrade for several letters, and then there would be no more mention of them. They were gone.

"So, what can you tell me about home? My folks' letters are pretty much the same every time, mostly asking me how I am. You look great. What's your job over here? How's your folks? Sammy?"

"Everyone's healthy. Our fathers are having a competition over who can be a bigger grump. I know your dad worries a lot about you. Mine does too. Neither of our mothers are too vocal, but I see my mother shake her head whenever your name comes up. I know she's thinking, 'poor Harry.'"

"And Sammy?"

"I think Sammy and I are done. He wasn't very happy about me coming here. Got all bossy and possessive."

"Putz."

"You sound exactly like your father."

"The apple doesn't fall far from the tree. I just had too many friends get wounded or die protecting the Sammys.

The Sammys in Germany never fought back, trying to get along and go along until it was too late for them to act, and they were on a train to a camp. Anyway, you'll find somebody. I've heard you're quite the businesswoman. You know my dad wants me to come into the business as well. Somehow I knew I'd be working for you someday," he laughed then turned serious. "But you know after what I've seen here, I don't think I could do what my dad does. Don't laugh, but I'm thinking of going back to school - to be a doctor, maybe a pediatrician. I already wrote to McGill. So, I guess you'll be the big boss one day."

"You'll be a great kid doctor. Don't worry about your dad. He'll make a little stink, but I know he'll be very proud of you. Your mother will be calling all of her friends with eligible daughters."

"So what made you do this thing you're doing?"

"You in part. I saw how you felt a duty to volunteer and risk your life for us. So, this came up and I jumped at it. Mom and Dad were supportive, though with some reluctance. It's been an adventure for sure."

"So who got you into this? Anyone I know?"

Dionne decided to lie with the truth. "I went to a meeting with dad and some of his friends. They talked about the refugees and the help they needed. Most of the businessmen offered money and sponsorships with jobs. When I asked what I could do, a fellow said they needed people on the ground.  So here I am."

" I'm not surprised.  You always made your mind up pretty quickly."

Dionne was looking out at the street.   There had been a man standing outside the hotel when they had sat down.  Now he came out of the hotel and looked around like he was being careful.  "Now I'm really getting paranoid," she thought.

"See somebody you know?" asked Harry.

"No, no," she said a little too quickly.  "Just a kid chasing a dog across the street."

"I have to get back to base.   I'm heading home in a few days so there's lots to do.  Are you here for a while?  Maybe we can have dinner or something.  "

"Only a couple more days."

"I'll call you at your hotel or leave a message."

They walked out together and went opposite directions.  She waited until he was out of sight walked to the end of the next block and turned back to her hotel.

# 33

She entered the hotel and went to get her key. The desk clerk said, "A gentleman left a message for you, Miss."

She thanked him and decided to go to her room to read it. She recognized Simon's handwriting. "Go to the British Museum South Entrance at 4. Buy a copy of today's Times. There is a coffee shop across the street. Go in and order. If I am not there in 10 minutes, get up and go back to your hotel. We will contact you."

"That's Simon, cryptic to a fault." Nevertheless, she was worried He would not have come to London unless things had changed, and probably not in a good way.

She left her hotel an hour early and walked around to make sure she was not being followed. She went down into the tube and jumped on a train at the last minute, getting off a few blocks from the museum. She bought a copy of the Times from a newsstand next to the coffee shop. The proprietor handed her the paper and her change. "You might want to look at page four, Miss."

She went into the coffee shop, got coffee and a bun and sat down. As she was opening the paper, Simon came in, gave her a peck on the cheek like friends do, and sat down. The waitress delivered hot tea for him. "Page 4, about halfway down," he said with a casual smile. Just two friends talking.

It was a story about a hit and run accident involving a prominent Harley Street physician, Dr. Menzies-Smythe.

"He was the British doctor in Germany. How terrible. I hope they catch the fellow. Is this why you're here, Simon?"

Simon just looked at her, nodding slowly.

"Are you saying this was not an accident? That he was killed on purpose?"

"We have our suspicions. The American doctor had been asking about him and was questioned by MI-5 about his attempt to contact Smythe. We also spotted him with that American colonel"

"You don't think he had anything to do with this?"

"No, we don't. But you remember how upset he was at the meeting. We think he wanted to see Smythe about it, but someone prevented it. We went looking for him to pass him an anonymous warning, but he was gone."

"Probably back to his base. I don't think that colonel would want him running around London."

"We think he is going to Paris looking for the French doctor. We have people on the American bases who let us know about certain movements of people and things. If he finds him, they could both be in danger."

Dionne had not even thought about the Frenchman, just the American.

"Then we must go to Paris."

"Exactly. We leave tonight."

"I'm supposed to meet Harry," she remembered.

"We will get word to Harry. You were called away on orders. He will understand." Somehow, she didn't think he would.

# 34

*Moscow —*

Georgi Dugasvili was sitting in his office, finishing paperwork. A man dressed in an overcoat that clearly marked him as a member of the NKVD entered the room without knocking. "Comrade Doctor, you are to come with me immediately. Comrade Stalin would like to speak to you at the Kremlin."

Dugasvili got his hat and coat and followed the officer. A summons to the Kremlin was not something that was welcomed in most cases. It either ended in a very good way or, more often, in a very bad way. He could not think of anything that might have brought him to the attention of Stalin, but then Stalin generally did not require a reason for any of his actions.

The Moscow streets were dark. There were still shortages of fuel. The blackout was explained as a necessary prevention against saboteurs. Whenever someone brought up a shortage of anything, most Muscovites would smile, shrug their shoulders, and say "saboteurs."

The driver did not speak on the ride to the Kremlin. Dugasvili was escorted up to the "Little Corner," which was the area that Stalin kept as his private office. It was where most of the real business of the Soviet Union was conducted. Stalin was waiting when he arrived. He bade him to a couple of leather chairs. Tea was brought in. Stalin said nothing for a few moments, quietly, sipping his tea. He then turned to Dugasvili's file. "Georgi, you are one of my cousins. As you know, I have always trusted family first, and gave them every opportunity unless they were not honest with me. A family member who lies to you is worse than the capitalist wreckers who would destroy us. I read your report from your mission to Germany. You performed your mission as ordered. However, there has been a development. The British doctor was killed in London. We have sources there that alerted us that MI-5 and the Americans are looking into the matter. They are obviously suspicious of an assassination, as am I. It is important that we bury these Nazis and that any hope that they may be alive be silenced forever. If those who are hunting these war criminals are assassinated, it will only give hope to the Nazis that are left. We cannot have our efforts in Eastern Europe sabotaged. I want to ask you, do you think any of the other doctors or anyone who is involved with this Bormann matter are agents or potentially assassins?"

"I don't think any of the doctors were agents. They all had handlers from their government who probably were agents. We had little contact with anyone else except the staff of the hotel. There were only two or three employees who were assigned to us. Oh, the American groused about the lack of access to all the evidence, but I think it was his medical curiosity rather than any attempt at espionage. The Frenchman seemed to go along with whatever the rest of the group agreed upon."

"That is interesting. Your American friend was spotted in London and was interrogated by MI-5. He was not detained and is back at his hospital. It is important that I know if he ever spoke to you about his doubts."

Georgi realized he had to answer his cousin's question very carefully. "He only spoke to me in the presence of the rest of the group. He never approached me privately. I never gave any of his concerns any encouragement."

Stalin looked Georgi in the eye and smiled broadly. "Thank you cousin, I knew I could trust you. Now you must excuse me. I have matters to attend to. If you would, please ask the gentleman waiting outside to come in. Oh, and tell your family I think of them often."

Georgi got up and shook Stalin's hand when he offered it. He thought that Stalin thinking about your family was not necessarily a good thing, but was quite relieved that the interview was over. As he entered the anteroom, a nondescript man dressed in an ill fitting dark suit stood up. Georgi told him that Stalin would see him now. The man who had brought Georgi to the Kremlin appeared and drove him back to his office.

The man entered Stalin's office and stood at attention. He was about a foot taller than Stalin, and felt like he should try to look shorter. Stalin sat at his desk and looked up at him. He did not ask him to sit. "Dimitri, how good is your French?"

"It is excellent Comrade Stalin. As you may know, I spent two years in Paris with our comrades before the war."

"Very good. We have a mission in Paris, that we need your assistance with. It is of critical importance to the State. I trust you will not fail. Comrade Beria will give you all the details. Oh, by the way, ask him to give you a new suit. Anyone who sees you in Paris will immediately think you're a Russian spy. Dismissed."

Dimitri was in Beria's office promptly at eight in the morning. Beria handed him a manila folder. In it were

French identity papers, currency, and a name with an address to a French clinic.

"Your cover will be a cultural attaché to our embassy in Paris. Only the ambassador knows that you are working for me. He knows to be discreet. You will follow the French doctor, whose name you see printed in the folder. You are to keep your distance from him, but stay close enough to intervene and only if there is an attempt on his life. You are to terminate the assassin and return to our embassy. We will have you back home before the French can get anywhere with their investigation."

"How long will I be in Paris?"

"Long enough to see the sights and enjoy French pastry, but not long enough to get used to it. Once we determine if there is a threat and what that threat is, we will send others to deal with it. They have very effective ways of leaving very clear messages. You leave tonight for Berlin then on to Paris. The young lady in the outer office will give you your travel documents. Oh, and a new suit. A gift from Comrade Stalin."

# 35

Monroe was granted a two week furlough to travel to Frankfurt for R & R. As it was in the American occupation sector, transportation was easily arranged through official channels. It was a popular place for Americans on leave to go. He thought it better to go there than Paris. If Kleet were keeping tabs on him, and he went to Paris, Kleet would certainly follow. Once he arrived, he checked into a hotel that was frequented by American officers. The contact that Kemp had arranged would not be available until the next day. Monroe went to a café, where he could easily be observed, hoping that if Kleet had anyone following him, they would be satisfied that he was enjoying himself in Frankfurt.

The next day he packed his overnight bag, making sure he left his duffel bag in the hotel room. He left in uniform and walked to some of the popular tourist attractions, looking around to make sure he was not being followed. He had never been a spy, but felt he had seen enough private eye movies that he was at least doing a credible job. He went to a kiosk in the Frankfurt train station, where American soldiers could get free coffee and cigarettes while they waited for trains. He sat down and waited as instructed by Kemp. A few minutes later, an army corporal sat down next to him. To Monroe, he looked like every other enlisted man he had taken care of during the war. The corporal pulled out a cigarette and asked for a light. Monroe said he did not smoke. The corporal pulled an envelope out of his pocket and handed it to Monroe. "You got the password right Doc. Kemp says have a good trip."

"A lot of cloak and dagger for a train trip to Paris."

"I'm just the messenger Doc. I'm off to have me some fun, courtesy of you and Kemp."

Monroe waited for a few minutes after the corporal left, then headed over to the platform where the train for Paris was scheduled to depart.  Kemp had given him a first class ticket.  The train was crowded, but left on time.  Kemp had included the address of a hotel in Paris on the Left Bank.  It was a place where it would not be unusual for an American to stay.  Kemp noted that the staff was discreet.

Monroe had brought along a novel featuring one of his favorite characters, Inspector Magrait.  It was just about the right size for him to finish reading on the trip to Paris.  After what happened in London, he thought it would be best to meet Dr. Saint-Germaine away from his clinic or office.  He would let him pick the place.

Trying to concentrate on the book was difficult.  Monroe was becoming unsure of his goal.  He was certainly concerned about the whole  handling of the Bormann autopsy.  He was also worried about what happened to Smythe.  His new concern was, what was he going to do after he spoke to Saint-Germaine?  He doubted that the Frenchman would push for re-opening the autopsy, or for even reviewing the report.  He might not even be concerned that Smythe had been killed, attributing it to an accident as everybody else had.  He might even think Monroe was being paranoid and dismiss him entirely.  Even if he were as curious about events as Monroe was, what could they do?  Monroe had already talked with Kleet about it, and he suspected that any official inquiry that he made on his own would lead right up to Kleet.  He also doubted very much if the French would be interested in the death of an English doctor. Well, in any case, it would be worth a short trip to Paris to share his concerns with his French colleague.

The train stopped several times on the way to Paris. The French police boarded two or three times to check identity cards. Monroe's uniform saved him the trouble. On one long stretch between stops he dosed off. He dreamt that he was back in Germany, and the waitress with the striking eyes was serving him in the hotel. She smiled at him, and then was gone. He began frantically searching for her to no avail. He woke up with a start. He hadn't thought of her since Germany. He laughed to himself that she had certainly left an impression on his subconscious. He opened his book and read the rest of the way to Paris.

Monroe arrived at Gare de l'Est. It was only a mile to his hotel, so he decided to walk. He had been to Paris twice before. The first time he had been there, he realized why so many people fell in love with the city. Between the boulevards, the cafés and the food there was no place like it, especially on a day like today when the sun was shining and the streets were filled with people.

As he made his way along the Seine, he thought of his next steps. He would make contact with Saint-Germaine and arrange their meeting place. He decided he would go in civilian clothes, and while he didn't look like the average Frenchman, he would attract much less attention than if he were in his uniform. He found his hotel on a side street, not much wider than an alley, off the Rue Mazarine. A stylishly dressed woman sat behind the desk in the small front lobby.

He told her his name, and that he had a reservation.  She did not ask him for any identification.  He was glad that Kemp had been his travel agent for this trip.  His room was on the third floor with a view of the street.  The bed was comfortable and there was a small bathroom in the room.

He found a telephone in the lobby and called the hospital where Saint-Germaine worked.  The nurse said that Saint-Germaine had not returned from lunch.  She said that he usually took a leisurely lunch and would be back around 3 o'clock.  Monroe said he would call back.  He had an uneasy feeling, as the situation was similar to what had occurred in London.  He dismissed his concerns as being overly cautious.  The French did take long lunches, and Saint-Germaine was the epitome of a Frenchman.  He decided that he would have some lunch himself, and then call the hospital again.  If Saint-Germaine still was not there, he would go to his home.

He took the Metro to the hospital, where he found a small café nearby.  He sat outside, ordered a plate of cold cheeses and meats with a glass of rosé and tried to relax and enjoy the Parisian ambience.

# 36

Saint-Germaine lived in an exclusive area of Paris, not very far from the Georges Cinq Hotel.  Simon was watching his apartment from a cafe across the street.  He had seen no movement the entire morning.  He wondered if Saint-

Germaine had gone in early for some kind of an emergency. Dionne was watching the hospital, but he had heard nothing from her. They had a prearranged telephone call in a few minutes. He hadn't noticed anyone else observing the apartment or any activity other than routine deliveries.

Dionne was watching the staff entrance to the hospital from the window of a restaurant nearby. She had not seen Saint-Germaine enter or leave in the few hours she had been there. She was worried she might have missed him but was somewhat reassured that Simon was watching his apartment. She went to the telephone at the back of the restaurant and called Simon at the prearranged time.

Simon answered after four rings. "I have not seen him leave his apartment."

"I haven't seen him around the hospital either. We need to come up with a plan if he doesn't appear soon."

"I think we should both stay put for now. Paris is a big city, and he could be anywhere. He could be with a mistress somewhere for all we know, and we would waste time and energy looking for him. I think we should have another call in two hours."

Dionne was scanning the immediate area as she was speaking to Simon. She was startled to see the American doctor across the street at a café with a glass of wine observing the hospital as she had been.

"Dionne, Dionne are you there?"

"Simon, it's the American doctor. He is sitting in a café across the street from the hospital. He must be looking for the Frenchman as well. What do we do?"

"If the people we think are following the Frenchman see the American, they will both be in danger. You need to get the American away from there."

"What about the Frenchman?"

"Right now we have no idea of his whereabouts. We have the American in sight so he should take priority."

"What do I tell him? He saw me in Germany. He will wonder who I am or who I am working for. He may be reluctant to come with me."

"Tell him you will take him to Saint-Germaine. He will likely be suspicious, but if we haven't seen Saint-Germaine, then he hasn't either. From the way he behaved in Germany, he wants answers. You will be the best opportunity for him to get them."

"What do I do if he still won't come?"

"Tell him that you have armed associates nearby, and it would be best if he came quietly."

"So now I am a kidnapper?"

"The situation is fluid. We have to recognize and react. Be persuasive."

"Where shall I take him?"

"Take him to the emergency address I made you memorize before we came to Paris."

"I'll do my best."

"Get it done Dionne. I know you can." He hung up. Dionne looked around the area. Nothing looked suspicious. She crossed the street and moved toward the café.

As Dionne approached the café, a waiter came to show her to a table. Fortunately, Monroe was already sitting at a table for two. She looked at the waiter, winked and pointed toward Monroe with a big smile. The waiter smiled back, assuming he was now part of a surprise.

Dionne sat down next to Monroe. He was indeed surprised when he saw her. She smiled at him and said "pretend you're glad to see me," and gave him a peck on the cheek.

Monroe couldn't believe his suspicion about the girl had been right. He needed to follow this through. He smiled back and kissed her on both cheeks. "This is certainly a surprise."

"You need to come with me.  You may be in danger."

"And I should trust you because?"

Dionne had known this was not going to be easy.  "We know you are here looking for the Frenchman.  We are too. He is nowhere to be found.  We are concerned for his safety. We don't want him to suffer the fate that the Englishman did. Now you are here and could be a target as well."

"How do I know I'm not your target?"

"If we had wanted to harm you, we could've done it at any number of places between Germany and here.  I am asking you to trust me.  Besides, I have armed compatriots nearby."

Monroe had always been pretty good at reading people. He thought she was being at least partially honest.  "You're a terrible liar.  I've been sitting here for over an hour.  You have no compatriots nearby."  He saw her try to hide the frown that her ploy had not worked.  He almost had to laugh at her frustration.  "OK,  I'll come.  What about Saint-Germaine?"

"We have someone else watching for him."

"The waiter from Germany?"

"Yes, if you must know."

Now maybe he was getting somewhere.  "OK, I've always wanted to see Paris with a beautiful woman."

Dionne rolled her eyes but was inwardly flattered. "Very original. Let's go."

Monroe left some money for the waiter. Just as he stood up, there was a clamor from people yelling down the street. There was a man helping another man up from the pavement. It looked like a flower cart had rolled down the street, nearly striking him. Monroe could see that it was Saint-Germaine who was on the ground. There was a man in a dark suit helping him up. The cart man was nowhere to be seen. Monroe started across the street but was held back by Dionne. "We should go help him," he said.

"That may have been an attempt on his life. He appears to be fine. You don't want to be seen or you could be the next target. Do you want whoever it is to know you're in Paris?"

Monroe's instincts told him that she was right. He certainly didn't want to run into Kleet in these circumstances. They turned around and headed in the opposite direction.

# 37

Dimitri sat in a small public square across the street from the hospital entrance. He had set a briefcase next to him, and was reading a newspaper, a businessman taking a break, someone no one would remember on a normal day in Paris. He was very good at surveillance. He had never tried disguises, or looked for hiding places to watch his targets.

His talent was that he could blend into the surroundings. No one noticed him. He could be a peasant, a laborer or a waiter, never a soldier or a policeman. He never dressed well or shabbily. He would be a little more evasive if he thought he was trailing a trained agent, but most of his targets were ordinary people that had been identified by the state as potential threats. His usual role was to observe the suspect and report to his superiors, while there were others that the state used to send its message publicly by arrest or more privately by disappearance. The end was the same. His instructions from Comrade Beria had been to observe the French doctor to see if he was meeting with anyone from foreign intelligence services. He was to monitor the doctor's activity for a few days and report his findings to Beria directly via a secure line from the Russian Embassy. In addition to him, there were operatives watching the doctor's home and the apartment of his mistress. They reported to Dimitri daily. So far the mission had been very routine, even boring. He expected he would be back on his way to Moscow in a few days.

If the doctor followed his usual routine, he would be arriving at the hospital in the next few minutes after a visit to his mistress. Dimitri soon observed him coming around the corner and crossing the street to the hospital entrance. Out of the corner of his eye, he saw a flower cart, heading directly toward the doctor. No one was running after it or yelling a warning. A swarthy, bearded man was running in the opposite direction and turned down a narrow street. Dimitri was the only one close enough to act, so he had no choice but to try to save his target. He ran across the street and tackled the doctor just as the cart went by. It crashed into a telephone booth about fifty meters away. "Are you all right?" he asked the doctor.

Saint-Germaine was visibly shaken, but appeared not to be hurt. "Merci, monsieur. I must've been thinking about something else, not paying attention. I believe I am all right."

"Do you want me to take you inside to the hospital?"

"No, that will be quite unnecessary. I am a physician. I work in the hospital."

"Then I will be on my way." Dimitri wanted to leave the area as soon as possible to maintain his anonymity and see if he could find the man that had run away from the cart. He headed in the direction that the flower cart had come from. There were people beginning to gather, but no one seemed to be the one who owned the cart. This was not an accident.

As he was hurrying up the street he happened to notice a tall man with a dark-haired woman leaving a café. He recognized the man from the file that Beria had given him. It was the American doctor. He had no idea who the woman was. He decided that whoever had pushed the cart was long gone and guessed that the American was just as important to Moscow as the Frenchman. The woman was unknown and might be a threat to his mission. She might even be working with whomever had tried to kill the Frenchman. He would have his underlings keep an eye on the French doctor. He would follow the American and deal with the woman if she became a problem. In the near chaotic environment of post-war Paris, he could make her disappear.

# 38

Dionne and Monroe boarded a bus a block or so from the café. She and Simon had a plan if one of them did not check in at the designated time. Simon had given her an address of one of his contacts in the Marais. She had never been there before, but Simon had assured her it was a safe place, and the woman who lived there was very discreet. He had warned her to make sure she was never followed there as it would compromise the woman and her family. They got off the bus on an avenue that bordered the Seine and was crowded with book stalls and souvenir stands. She took Monroe's hand. "We are going for a stroll along the Seine. I have to make sure we are not being followed. Hold my hand and talk to me as we walk." They kept a leisurely pace, stopping at the book stalls or watching street artists sketching tourists. Monroe knew she was looking for a potential tail. He could tell she had done it before.

She led him down some steps, and they walked directly along the riverbank. Although Monroe was enjoying holding her hand, it was time for some answers. "Can you give me some idea of where we're going and what it has to do with what went on back there?"

"We are going to a safe place to meet my compatriots. We can then try and figure out what is going on. Right now, we are two young people walking down the Seine in Paris. We need to keep up that appearance."

Monroe decided not to ask any more questions until they reached their destination. He had decided to trust her back at the café. He was a good judge of people, though not always women in romantic situations. But, this wasn't romantic. He noticed that she didn't appear to be armed. He was bigger, stronger, and faster and could get away from her if he needed to. In the meantime he would enjoy walking along the Seine in Paris with a pretty girl.

They walked up from the river and were walking across a pedestrian bridge not far from the Pont Neuf. Street vendors selling everything from maps and flags to pastry were pushing their wares to anyone who did not aggressively send them away.

"Watch your wallet. Some of these street merchants are pickpockets," warned Dionne.

Just as she finished her warning, an old man came up to them. He was carrying a large canvas bag. He spoke directly to Monroe. "Voulez-vous acheter une serrure pour la belle jeune femme?" He opened his bag, which was full of padlocks.

Dionne whispered in his ear, keeping a big smile on her face, "He wants you to buy a lock for me. We don't want to cause attention. Buy it. I'll explain later."

"How much?" asked Monroe.

"Cinq francs," replied the lock man.

Monroe reached for his wallet and was about to open it when Dionne interjected, "Deux francs."

"Quatre."

"Trois."

"Bon Mademoiselle."

"Give him three francs. You have to bargain with these guys."

"I got the idea," said Monroe and paid the man. The lock man gave him a small brass lock. "Merci, monsieur." He walked away toward his next target.

Dionne led Monroe toward the bridge railing. "Fasten the lock onto the bridge and throw the key into the river." Monroe wasn't sure why he was doing any of this but did as instructed. "Now, kiss me." Before Monroe could respond, Dionne kissed him, looked at him for a moment, and led him across the bridge. Monroe tried not to look surprised, but he was - pleasantly.

They moved away from the Seine through a maze of streets and alleys. Monroe finally asked, "What was that all about on the bridge?"

"It's a custom. Lovers buy a lock and lock it to the bridge. They throw the key into the Seine, which means their love is locked forever," Dionne answered with a mischievous grin. "We had to keep up appearances."

Monroe wondered if she was kidding or flirting or both. "I'll hold you to that," he quipped.

Her grin diminished but did not go away. "We are nearing our meeting place. We need to be on guard."

Simon came up the street toward Monroe and Dionne and spoke directly to her. "I heard about the Frenchman and was afraid something happened to you after the attempt on his life. Are you all right? Were you followed?"

"We're fine. I don't think anybody saw us at the café. No one followed us."

Monroe interrupted, " Attempt? Are you sure? And by the way, who the hell are *you*?"

" I will explain. First, we must get off the street." They walked only a few paces to a door flush to the sidewalk.

Simon took a key from his pocket and opened the door. He led them to a flat on the third floor. He knocked four times. A woman opened the door and quickly ushered them in.

The woman introduced herself as Cosette. It was pretty clear to Monroe that she was related to the fellow called Simon. The physical resemblance was obvious, and she addressed him as only a sibling would.

She led them into a sitting room and asked if they were thirsty or hungry. She was thin, not unattractive, with long black hair, polite, but not friendly. She kept looking at her brother out of the corner of her eye. It was clear by her manner that her guests were unexpected and probably unwanted.

Addressing no one in particular, she said, "My husband Michel will be home soon. He will be able to get you all on your way."

"You must forgive my sister's caution. She and her husband spent the war in Paris, pretending to be Lebanese Christians. Their caution saved their lives," said Simon. "They have helped us from time to time in some of our operations."

"And just who are 'us'? And what are the operations?" asked Monroe.

"All in good time, doctor. We will talk more when Michel arrives."

"Please be patient. We know what we're doing," interjected Dionne. Monroe was impatient. He wanted answers and was not about to wait for this Michel to arrive.

"If you had to disguise yourselves as Lebanese Christians, then I must conclude that you're Lebanese Jews." He looked at Dionne and smiled, "You, however, are not Lebanese. You do have a bit of a French accent, though. Maybe from New Orleans, or no, better yet, Quebec."

The looks on their faces told Monroe that his deductions were correct. Just as he was about to ask more questions, a very large man, at least six and half feet tall and every bit of 250 pounds, came in through the back door of the flat. He too had black hair but also a cold black beard and mustache. He wore a beret that looked tiny on his large round head and a red scarf. Before he could speak, Monroe greeted him. "So you are the famous Michel. Maybe now we can get down to business."

Michel turned to Simon. "Simon, I will forgive this man's poor manners since you and Dionne brought him here." He then turned to Monroe, all business. "Yes, I am Michel and you are a guest in my home. First, we will all have a glass of wine, and then we can discuss our business." The look on his face told Monroe that the best policy would be to back off.

"Sorry. It's been a bit of a hectic day."

Michel got a broad grin on his face and clapped Monroe on both shoulders. "All is forgiven mon ami." The tension evaporated. Monroe had to laugh.

# 39

There was barely enough room for the five of them in the kitchen. Cosette had prepared a plate of cheese and bread. Michel poured them each a glass of wine. Michel raised his glass and after a quick "L chiam" downed his wine. They ate in silence. Monroe did not realize how hungry he was. After Cosette filled their glasses again, Simon turned to Michel, "I've put two men on the doctor's apartment and one on the hospital. The doctor is still at work as far as we know. Have you turned up anything?"

"I spoke to a policeman that I've done business with in the past. I helped him to acquire certain commodities during the occupation. I still help him out from time to time. A young lady friend of his has expensive taste. He told me that a couple of witnesses reported someone who looked like an Arab ran away after the cart was let loose."

"What about the fellow who helped the doctor?"

"Disappeared."

They both appeared to be thinking about what to do next. Monroe now spoke up. "I think I've been more than patient. What is your interest in Dr. Saint-Germaine? And if I'm not being too impertinent, who are you?"

Monroe reminded Dionne of her cousin Harry. She smiled to herself, not realizing that Monroe was looking at her. She quickly turned to Simon. "I think we need to tell him."

Simon looked directly at Monroe. "I think, doctor, that we share a similar interest in your French colleague. Like you, we have some doubts about the autopsy that was done in Germany. We were going to try to find a way to speak with Dr. Saint-Germaine, but our questions became even more critical because of what happened to Dr. Smythe in London. We don't think that his death was an accident, nor do we think that the cart that almost killed Dr. Saint-Germaine was either. We wanted to speak to you as well, but it is difficult for civilians like ourselves to get on an American military base. It was very convenient of you to appear in London. We couldn't get to you there because you were otherwise occupied by MI-5 and your American watchdog. Then we spotted you here. I should tell you that you are in as much danger as Dr. Saint-Germaine."

"You've explained part of the why. Now let's get to the who."

"We are Jews helping our people, the victims of this war," answered Dionne.

"That's very noble and I'm sure at least partially true. But, you and your friends do not look like a bunch of Red Cross volunteers. Also, refugee agency workers tend not to skulk around Paris doing their jobs."

Simon spoke up. "Dionne is correct. We are trying to help our people. We work for a Jewish group that is part of the larger movement to bring about a Jewish state. Let us just say that we are a small part of that group that is tasked with righting some of the wrongs that the Nazis inflicted upon us."

"So what are you, spies, assassins, vigilantes?"

Michel answered almost in a whisper, "We do what we have to do. The rest of the world is not concerned enough about justice for those who butchered us. We cannot ever let them feel secure. They must believe that they will all be hunted down eventually." Cosette put her hand on her husband's trying to calm him.

Simon turned to Monroe again. "So, Doctor, let me ask you a couple of questions. Did you think that the autopsy done in Germany was completed in a satisfactory manner? You certainly voiced your concerns to the others. Yet you signed the document, I suspect under pressure, and then you went on an expedition of your own to try to get your questions answered. Am I correct?"

"I did have questions. I thought the autopsy was rushed, and that simple medical questions and procedures were glossed over. It bothered me enough that I wanted to speak to the other doctors about it. Frankly, I wasn't sure what I would have done if they'd agreed with me. Our superiors seemed to have wanted the matter closed quickly."

"Let me be blunt doctor," said Simon. "Do you think that the corpse that you and your colleagues said was Martin Bormann was indeed Martin Bormann?"

"When you put it that way, no. I have my concerns."

"Doctor, we don't believe that the body was Martin Bormann. We believe he is alive. We also believe that there are those who are trying to help and protect him. They want him to be dead. Your superiors just don't want to deal with the problem of ex-Nazis. There are others who want Bormann and those like him to be able to vanish. They used a staged autopsy to confirm Bormann's death allowing him to disappear. They also want anyone who could potentially raise questions about the autopsy to disappear as well. That is why they killed the English doctor and why they tried to kill the French doctor today. That is also why you are in grave danger."

Monroe had had similar suspicions. Simon's explanation of events brought clarity to Monroe's own thoughts of the past few weeks. "I understand your theory, and tend to agree with it, but why all the concern about some Nazi that nobody's ever heard of?"

Simon hesitated for a moment. He looked like he was trying to organize his thoughts. "Bormann was Hitler's Private Secretary. He knew everything that went on in Hitler's headquarters. No one could see or talk to Hitler without going through Bormann. He was present at most meetings of the Nazi Party hierarchy and those with the army. If Hitler was there, Bormann was never far away. He knows personal and financial information about most of the big Nazis. We think he may know where some of them went, and how they are financed. More importantly, he was yet another participant in the Holocaust. It is said that he used his own influence to get Hitler's ideas implemented, but without Hitler's name on them. Everyone knew Bormann spoke for Hitler. He has as much blood on his hands as any of the Nazis that the allies have already hung. We intend to find Bormann, interrogate him and see to his final disposition, whether in a court room or by other measures."

"You all certainly don't occupy your time with frivolous tasks, do you? So what now? When can I speak with Saint-Germaine?"

Simon looked annoyed. "Dr. Monroe, I do not think you comprehend. You are a target. Contacting Dr. Saint-Germaine or even staying in Paris is out of the question. We will see to your colleague in the near future. Michel will get you to a safe place for tonight then back to your base tomorrow. You will be more secure there until you go back home. We trust you to keep our mission a secret."

"Not a hope. I'm involved now. I am going to find a way to see this through, with or without you. If what you say is true, I may not be safe even if I'm back in the States. I've treated enough soldiers for social diseases who have snuck on and off the base to know that it's not secure. At least you guys know the threat."

Dionne spoke up. "Simon, part of our mission is to protect those involved. If we find Bormann, alive or dead, Jack can testify as to his identity. If Jack dies, we will have failed."

Simon thought for a moment. "Well, *Jack*, it seems you have an advocate. We will get you to the safe house tonight. I will speak to my superiors. I make no promises. If they do agree, you will have to find a way to keep your MP's from looking for you. We have too many players in this game already. At any rate, I have other business to attend to now." Simon nodded to Michel, kissed his sister goodbye and left by the back door.

Michel watched Simon leave from the window then turned toward Monroe. "We will wait a few minutes then leave ourselves. I will take you and Dionne to the place Simon spoke about. He will find you in the morning and give you his decision. You two will walk with Cosette and me, just friends out for a stroll. When we get there, we will stop and say goodbye. Open the door to the building directly behind you and go to the flat on the right. Wait there until Simon returns."

The two couples left Michel's flat and strolled through the Marais, stopping to look in shop windows and chatting with friends they happened to meet. If Monroe had not known that Michel was making sure they were not followed, he never would have guessed. Dionne seemed more relaxed, glad to let Michel do most of the work. She and Cosette acted like two girlfriends out for the evening, speaking in French most of the time. Monroe was left to mostly nodding his head or giving one or two word answers to Michel.

They arrived at a small apartment building after about an hour. It seemed they had been walking for quite a distance but were actually not very far from where they had started. Michel hugged Monroe, slipping a key into his pocket. "The flat is on the ground floor to the right. There is a back door. Simon has a key. We will be watching. If anyone knocks at the front, get out the back as quickly as you can. Good luck. A bientôt, mon ami." He kissed Dionne on both cheeks. Monroe did the same with Cosette, and the two walked away without looking back. Monroe opened the door to the building and led Dionne into the flat.

# 40

Dimitri had been following the couple since they had left the café. One or both of them had been taught how to evade surveillance, probably the woman. He didn't know of too many doctors who were spies. He almost slipped up on the bridge while they were negotiating with a street hawker. He had to buy a map and a pastry to keep an eye on them. He walked past them as the American put the lock on the bridge, threw the key into the river, and kissed the girl. The American's file had not indicated any romantic attachments. A new twist. This assignment was becoming more interesting. He continued to follow them but had to be careful of his distance as they twisted and turned down narrow streets that were largely deserted, but he was good at what he did. He was sure they didn't know he was there. Another man approached them. They spoke for a moment and headed into a building that could only be entered with a key. Dimitri would have to contact some of his agents. They would watch the building in shifts until the American emerged. In the meantime, he needed to find out who lived there and how they were connected to all of this.

One of Dimitri's agents was about to relieve him in front of Michel and Cosette's apartment when the two couples had emerged. He left his man to watch the flat while he followed them. The big Frenchman was cautious, and almost lost Dimitri a couple of times. But his size was to his disadvantage and Dimitri was just able to keep his targets in view.

As the couples parted, Dimitri had decisions to make. His people were getting spread thin. One was watching the French doctor's home and the other was watching the big Frenchman's apartment. These men would have to be relieved at some point. Now the American was in this new location. Fortunately, it appeared that everyone was settled in for the night. Dimitri felt confident that the French couple was heading home and saw no reason to follow them. However, in the morning, he could have as many as four different players on the move. He would need at least a pair of agents to trail each of them. He decided he would leave the French doctor to just one agent. Whoever had tried to assassinate him had likely been scared away. The French couple were probably temporary helpers for the man who had brought the girl and the American to their home. He decided he would follow the American and the woman along with their handler. Hopefully the three of them would move together, and his task would become much easier. He decided to gamble that the American and the girl would be in the flat for the night. If they were going to be moving tonight, the Frenchman would not have brought them here. He would go back to his room, get a few hours sleep and return before dawn.

# 41

The apartment was decent size, but minimally furnished. There was one bedroom, a bathroom, kitchen and the living room. Monroe looked at the couch in the living room and tried to estimate if his 6'4" frame would fit on it. He figured that Dionne would want the bedroom. She was rummaging around the kitchen to find something for them to drink. "We have bottled water, tea and wine. I am having tea. Do you want some?"

Monroe would've loved to have had a glass of wine with her, but decided that he better keep his wits about him. He was not a tea drinker so water was the only choice. There was a small refrigerator but no ice. What was it about Europeans? He thought. There is never any ice.

She sat at the table while she prepared her tea. "So, what did you do in Montreal? And how did you get into this business?" he asked.

I have worked for my father and my uncle since finishing university. We are in the shipping business at the Port of Montreal. My father got involved with helping Jews and Jewish refugees during the war. I have a cousin, Harry, who served with the British. I wanted to do something, too. It took some persuading, but my parents finally agreed. I am not sure that they would like it if they knew that I would be sneaking around Germany and Paris. What about you? I know you're a doctor."

"Well, my folks immigrated to the US from Russia. I grew up in the Bronx. I got a scholarship to Washington University in St. Louis, where I stayed through medical school and my post-graduate training. I decided to get my service obligation out of the way and enlisted in early 1941. Then came Pearl Harbor, and here I am."

"So how did you end up in Germany with the other doctors? Are you some kind of a specialist?"

Monroe didn't know how much he should tell her about how he was picked to go to Germany or about Kleet or the whole mission. He liked talking to her. For some reason, he felt she could be trusted but thought it would be best to give her only a basic explanation. "It's kind of a long story."

"Well, it doesn't appear we're going anywhere."

"Well, you see, I was engaged to a woman whose father is very powerful. He knew that I was over here and suggested that I be picked for the mission. Believe me, I didn't volunteer."

"So what happened to the woman?"

Monroe wasn't sure where this conversation was going, but decided he would tell her the story. "Well, I was finishing my training and was deciding where I would go next. My then-fiancé had already planned out the rest of our lives, without asking me how I felt or what I wanted to do. When I told her that that was not how I saw us going, we broke up. You think you know someone. She did find a guy who fit her version of how things should be. I'm sure she's happy. I really have nothing against her anymore. And you? Are you and that Simon guy a couple?"

"Oh no, Simon and I are colleagues - and friends. He was the one who taught me, but he is married. His wife is in Israel."

"So is there anybody back home?"

Dionne paused. He could see that she was trying to decide how much to tell him. "That's OK if you don't wanna talk about it. It's really none of my business."

Dionne wasn't sure how much she should tell Jack. He was easy to talk to. When they had walked along the Seine it felt very natural, but this was a mission. He had trusted her with his personal life so maybe she would tell him something about Sammy. "I had a boyfriend. We went together for a couple of years after McGill. We had fun together. Our families knew each other and all that. When I told him that I was going to do this - something really important to me - he didn't even try to get it. He told me that he would not allow it. It's not like we were engaged or anything. I saw then that he maybe wasn't the right person for me. I don't like being told what to do."

"What a putz," thought Monroe. "I can see that," his tone lighthearted. She looked a bit sheepish and smiled.

He found himself looking into those eyes of hers and feeling sheepish himself. Neither spoke for a minute. Monroe decided to move things in another direction. "Well, I guess we better turn in. Your friend Simon could come back at any time. I'll stand guard here out on the couch."

Dionne looked relieved that he had given her an out. "I'll see you in the morning. If Simon comes, he will knock only twice. Wake me up. We should both open the door just in case." Monroe nodded. He was unnerved. He realized he didn't want her to leave.

# 42

Monroe had not realized how much the day's events had exhausted him. In spite of being crammed on the short couch, he slept surprisingly well. When two knocks came at the door, he bolted upright, startled. He saw Dionne out of the corner of his eye, obviously amused at his reaction. "My guardian, let's answer the door."

Simon came in quickly, a bag of pastry in his hand.

"Let's eat. We have much to discuss."

"And good morning to you, my friend," said Monroe, a bit annoyed.

"You will forgive me doctor, but I do not have time for niceties. We think we may have an idea who tried to kill your French friend. He appears to be an Arab. He could be someone hired by the Germans or maybe one of the mufti's gangsters. At any rate, there are now new players in the game."

"What about the guy who saved Saint-Germaine?"

We know nothing of him. He seems to have disappeared. For all we know he could be a British or American agent.

The involvement of the Arabs and possibly the mufti changes things quite a bit. We may now be confronting Arabs and Germans. We need to proceed very carefully. An incident with the Arabs could affect matters more important than your safety."

"Easy for you to say. But, I get it."

"Doctor, you are going to have to find a way to extend your leave another few days without arousing any suspicion. Michel is checking you out of your hotel as we speak. He will bring your things. You and Dionne are going on a trip. I will be with you, but we will not acknowledge each other."

"Would it be too much to ask where we're going?"

"You are going to meet a chemist and a painter."

Monroe still had another 48 hours leave. He thought it best not to ask for an extension this early. Anyway, he had to think of something that his boss would buy. He was due to start night coverage when he returned. Whoever covered for him would be pissed off. Monroe would owe big favors to someone. His thoughts were interrupted by another knock at the door. It was Michel with his suitcase. Monroe changed into a plain pair of pants with a dark shirt. Michel gave him a beret and a scarf to put around his neck. The big Frenchman smiled. "Now you look like a Parisian." Dionne wore a similar outfit, all black with a short, fuchsia jacket.

"Striking. If this is camouflage on her part, I don't think it will be successful," thought Monroe.

They took the underground to the Gare d'Lyon. Simon had purchased a compartment for Monroe and Dionne. He would be sitting in the car behind them. He handed Monroe a newspaper and gave Dionne a cheap paper back to read. "Try to look as routine as possible," he said."The train will be crowded at this hour which will allow you to blend in better. It will also allow anyone following you to blend in as well. If we need to switch trains because we are being followed, I will walk by your compartment as the train pulls into the station. Otherwise, I will see you in Aix-en-Provence."

Monroe and Dionne went to their compartment. They sat across from each other. Monroe's newspaper was in French. He could only understand a few words, but decided he would just look at the photographs and pretend to be reading. After a while, he looked up to see Dionne smiling at him. "What's so funny?"

"You look about as French as a priest at a Bar Mitzvah."

"I guess I missed the disguise class in medical school." Now they were both laughing. He hadn't laughed this hard with a girl in a long time.

Dimitri had jumped on the train right before the conductor. He had been right to wait outside the flat where the American and the girl spent the night. When he saw the big Frenchman come in the morning, he knew they would be on the move. His operatives had the French doctor under observation, so once again he decided to follow the couple. He knew he was to protect the French doctor, not follow the American, and was technically violating his mission parameters. He would certainly pay the ultimate price if he failed. That eventuality had been made clear by Beria. If he could deal with both the American and the Frenchman, however, then Comrade Stalin would reward him. He walked through the train at a leisurely pace, just a passenger looking for a seat. The train was crowded, but he found a seat on the aisle next to an old man who was fast asleep. Hopefully he wouldn't wake up and want to talk.

Simon had noticed the tall man in the rumpled suit walk by him. Something in the back of his mind was nagging at him. He had been on guard since the French doctor was almost killed. He was pretty sure none of them had been followed. Then he remembered that Dionne had noticed a man in a suit who had saved the French doctor then disappeared. Was this passenger that man? Maybe he was being overly cautious, but that was his job. If they got off the train before Aix and he followed, it would confirm his suspicions. If not they would just be late. He needed to find the conductor. He would be the key to his plan. It would be expensive.

The conductor knocked at the compartment door. Monroe got their tickets and opened it.

"Bonjour, monsieur. Votre billets s'il vous plait." Monroe handed him the tickets. He seemed to study them for quite

awhile before returning them. "Merci, monsieur, madame."
He left and moved to the next compartment. As Monroe put
the tickets back into his wallet, he noticed a note in French.
He looked at it and handed it to Dionne.

"It's from Simon," she said as she read.

"I figured."

"He wants us to follow the conductor off the train at the
next stop. We are to stay right behind him. I am to act ill.
Simon will find us at the station. He thinks we are being
followed."

"Thinks or knows?"

"Does it really make a difference? Better to be late than
end up like your English friend."

"I guess not." He noticed the train begin to slow. People
were lining up to get off. The conductor was at the door.
Monroe looked at Dionne. He ruffled her hair. He put his
arm around her. "Look sick." They moved down the aisle
with Dionne leaning heavily on Monroe. The conductor was
hurrying passengers to get off. As Dionne and Monroe
stepped off the train the conductor stood behind them
blocking any further exit. They headed for the station.

Dimitri saw the commotion in front of him. It looked like
his targets were leaving. The woman looked ill. He got up
quickly to follow. Just as he got to the door the train began

to move. The conductor blocked his way. Then they were gone. They must have suspected they were being followed. He had no choice but to go on to Aix and wait for them there.

Simon had watched the tall man get up and head for the door. The conductor played his part well. He had earned his pay. As the train started to move he jumped off at the rear door to meet Monroe and Dionne.

"Well, that was thrilling," said Monroe.

"It was timed well. Simon must have been very generous with the conductor. Jack?"

"Yeah?"

"You can take your arm off me now."

"Um, sorry, all the excitement." He felt like a stupid teenager. Just then Simon stepped up.

"There was someone following us. It might be the fellow who saved the French doctor. We will have to find another way to our destination. He will be watching the trains. Michel has a cousin nearby. He can take us or find someone who will get us there. Wait here." Simon headed for a phone booth outside the station entrance.

Monroe looked after him somewhat incredulously. "So let me get this straight. Here we are in the middle of nowhere being followed by someone we don't know and Michel has a cousin who just happens to live nearby?"

" Simon told me that Michel was part of an underground network during the war. Most of his so-called 'cousins' were operatives in that network. Even though the war is over, they continue to help each other with various enterprises. Some legal, some not so much," explained Dionne. "I only hope Simon is able to reach him soon. Otherwise, we will be on our own."

"I see a bunch of cabs out front. I bet some American dollars would get us where we need to go."

"If some of those guys see you flashing around American dollars, they would probably want to get more from you, and they won't ask nicely. We also don't want someone coming around looking for us and buying information from them."

"I was lucky to get in touch with Michel," said Simon as he walked up to them. "He has to make some calls. He has a friend he trusts with a car in the next village. We can pay him to take us near where we need to go. Someone else will take us the rest of the way. I have his phone number. I am to call him in thirty minutes. So, let's pretend we're exactly what we are, travelers on our way to southern France. There is a small café right outside the station. You two go there and get something to eat. I will stay here. Dionne, be on guard."

Dionne and Monroe went to the café and picked a table a bit back from the street but looking out. The waiter came to take their order. Dionne, who spoke much better French, quickly ordered for the two of them. "Did I understand that you ordered bread, cheese and ham?" asked Monroe.

"I think bagels and lox might have drawn suspicion," said Dionne somewhat sarcastically. "I also ordered two glasses of rosé. We are in Provence. As they say, 'Rosé all day.'"

"It's OK. Pork is one of my favorite dishes, but there's nothing like a corn beef on rye with a little kraut."

"In Montreal we call it smoked meat. My father, my uncle, and their cronies often go to a particular delicatessen in Montreal for lunch. It has become a weekly event."

"You miss them don't you?"

"I guess I do. I wanted to be on my own, to have a new adventure. I have loved every minute of it, but sometimes you think about home and you do miss it. Both my dad and my uncle can be hard on me, but I know they love me."

Monroe could see why they did. The food arrived. Again, Monroe didn't realize how hungry he was. This spy stuff took a lot of energy. He noticed Dionne was eating heartily as well. The wine was light and fresh, perfect for lunch.

"Jack, what happened on the train may be a preview of events to come. Things could become very dangerous.

Simon and I are trained for these situations. I need for you to trust me and follow my lead as we go on. We can't have anything happening to you." She paused, "or the mission." Monroe thought he heard genuine concern in her voice. He rather liked it.

They continued to talk about more mundane things for half an hour. Dionne saw Simon across the street. He signaled to her that they were to follow him. Monroe paid the bill with some francs he had gotten in Paris. They followed Simon at a distance away from the center of the village. Dionne put her arm inside Monroe's, tugging at him to stop or to turn and look in the window of a shop, making sure they were not being followed. Monroe was starting to get the hang of it but still was uncomfortable with not knowing completely what was going on. He was more trusting of her but still wasn't sure if they wanted the same ends out of the mission. He wanted to solve a mystery. He wasn't sure that everyone had the same goals once the mystery was solved. They followed Simon down a small side street. At the end an old sedan was waiting with the motor running. Simon spoke to the driver, gave him some bills and got in next to him. He motioned for Dionne and Monroe to get in the backseat.

"This is Laurent. He will be taking us to our next stop," said Simon.

"Bonjour, mes amis. I will take you on a brief tour of Provence. It is a most beautiful part of France. Let us enjoy our journey." His easy manner was contagious. Monroe relaxed and enjoyed the scenery. As they drove, Simon and Dionne spoke quietly in French. Monroe looked out at the striking scenery. They drove through hilltop villages and down into valleys dotted with farms and vineyards. Dionne fell asleep, her head on Monroe's shoulder. Soon, Monroe noticed the smell of lavender. As they came around the bend, lavender fields came into view. Laurent said, "It is beautiful is it not? In the next village we can stop and you can buy some perfume for the lady."

Before Monroe could answer, Simon interrupted. "A very romantic notion, Laurent, but we have business. Let's keep moving."

"Ça va, Simon."

# 43

*Paris -*

Michel's man had been watching Saint-Germaine for the past several hours. He had relieved one of his compatriots just before sunrise. He would follow Saint-Germaine to the hospital, then sit across the street in the café until Saint-Germaine left for his usual lunch. The danger for the doctor would be on his way to work and when he left for lunch. There was really no one on the street when he took up his post near Saint-Germaine's house. As he was looking around, he saw another man, obviously European, also scouting the area. He wondered if it were possible this newcomer was watching the doctor as well. He did not want to leave the area to notify Michel, so he decided he would continue to focus on the doctor and also try to keep track of the other man, at least until the doctor got to work.

Saint-Germaine took the same route to work every day. This practice made him much easier to follow for both friend and enemy. Michel's man saw him kiss his wife at the door and start off towards the hospital. He followed, keeping his usual distance. It quickly became apparent that the other man was indeed also following Saint-Germaine.

Saint-Germaine stopped at a newsstand and purchased a newspaper as he always did on his way to work. Both of his watchers had to pause and conceal themselves so that he would not see them. After a brief chat with the newsboy, he went on to work.

Saint-Germaine admitted to himself that he had been somewhat shaken by almost being killed by the runaway cart. He presumed it was basically a random act of negligence. The police had asked him if he had seen anything strange, but he had not. He told them of the stranger that tried to help him but could not really give a detailed description of the fellow. They left with a perfunctory admonishment of "be careful." He had been less nonchalant about his walk to work this morning, making sure he checked the streets before crossing and looking behind him periodically. He approached the main entrance to the hospital. As he was walking in, a man appearing to be Arab bumped into him. Then he felt the blade. He could not even utter a scream. He was dead within seconds. The Arab man kept walking at a relaxed pace out of the hospital.

Michel's man saw the collision at the hospital entrance. He did not think it was random. He saw Saint-Germaine crumple to the ground and ran to his assistance. By the time he got to the doctor, it was clear he was dead. He ran out of the hospital to look for the assassin, but he'd already disappeared. He needed to get away from the area that was now crowding with hospital personnel and onlookers and contact Michel with the gruesome news.

Meanwhile, the man that Dimitri had assigned to watch Saint-Germaine had picked up Michel's man very soon after the doctor started off. He could not be sure whether he was protecting the doctor or planning to do him harm. Once the doctor was inside the hospital, he'd deal with this unknown Frenchman.

Dimitri's man saw the assassination and the Frenchman running to the doctor's aid. There was no point in him continuing to watch the two of them. He saw the Arab moving away from the hospital and decided to follow him. The Arab went down into the Paris Metro and went to the platform with trains headed for the 19th and 20th arrondissements. He jumped on the train a few steps behind his quarry. He followed him through a maze of street markets and cafés. He was trying to decide whether to follow him to his potential associates or to deal with him immediately. He knew Dimitri would be very angry with him for not protecting the doctor. He was no strategist. He thought that the best result would be to stop the Arab, find out what he knew and then dispose of him.

The Arab stopped in a fruit stand very close to an alley. Dimitri's man came up behind him and shoved his pistol into the man's back. "We are going for a little walk. Do not cry out or try to get away, or you will die."

They entered the alley, where Dimitri's man stripped the Arab of his knife and pushed him up against the wall, the gun under his chin. "Now, you will tell me who you are working for and why you killed the French doctor."

"If I tell you, you will kill me anyway. So go ahead." Dimitri's man plunged the Arab's knife under his ribs into his heart. He lowered him to the ground covered him with some of the refuse in the alley, then ran out the  way opposite way that he had come in. He would be able to tell Dimitri that the assassin was an Arab. It wasn't much but he hoped it would save him from the same fate as he had dealt the Arab.

# 44

Dionne awoke just as Laurent was pulling the car over in the village square of Gordes. "We will be leaving you now, Laurent. We have made other arrangements from here," said Simon. "We trust you will remain silent about today." He then handed Laurent a few more bills.

Simon turned to Monroe and Dionne. "Michel thinks Laurent is a good man. I find him a little too chatty. We had arranged for someone to pick us up at the train station. Obviously that was not possible. I will call the Chemist who has arranged for another man to come and get us. There is a hotel across the street where I can call. You two continue your tourist act. Be vigilant, Dionne. There is still no guarantee that we are safe."

Monroe took Dionne's hand. "Have to keep up appearances." Dionne barely acknowledged him. Her thoughts were obviously concentrated on their security. They walked about the market stands purchasing souvenirs and some pieces of fruit. He bought Dionne some lavender. Just as she was about to thank Monroe, Simon came up to them. The look on his face told Monroe that something was very wrong.

"I just spoke to the Chemist. There has been a development. Your friend Saint-Germaine was killed today by an assailant with a knife. Michel's man tried to help him but he died instantly. The assassin disappeared. Doctor, they will obviously be coming for you next. We don't know anything about the Russian doctor. He may be dead as well. Our driver will be coming soon. He will take us to the Chemist and the Painter. We can then decide how best to protect you."

Monroe just nodded his head. He had liked Saint-Germaine. He realized now more than before that he was a target. While he trusted his bodyguards, their track record thus far didn't inspire a lot of confidence.

The three of them headed away from the market area. They were met near a hotel by a late model American car, typically used by military brass or politicians. The driver was British. They didn't say much during the hour long drive, all of them trying to make sense out of the latest developments. The car smelled faintly of the lavender that Monroe had purchased in town. They pulled off the road and went up a long, tree lined drive to a villa perched on a hill overlooking the Mediterranean. It was guarded by British soldiers. Dionne was surprised when Avrum came down the steps to greet them. She had not seen him since Montreal. He was not smiling.

Avrum greeted the three of them as they got out of the car. "Thank God, you are all right. I was quite worried about you. Oh, forgive my manners doctor. I am Avrum. I am, as you Americans would say, the boss of these two. I know you all have had quite an experience. We have much to discuss as there have been developments of which none of you are aware. One of the valets will show you to a room where you can get changed. We have taken the liberty of obtaining some suitable clothing for you. I hope we have gotten the right sizes for you, doctor. There are not many your height in this part of France. We are going to meet on the terrace where it is a bit cooler in about an hour. Our hosts are anxious to meet you."

As Monroe shook hands with Avrum he thought that the man looked like everybody's Jewish grandfather. He was short, overweight, and balding. What hair he had was in disarray. He wore a white shirt open at the neck. He was perspiring in the dry heat of Provence. His Russian accent reminded Monroe of his mother. "Nice to meet you Mr..."

"Call me Avrum. No need for formalities."

"And no need for anyone knowing who this guy is," thought Monroe. While intrigued, he was also getting weary of all the cloak and dagger. "If I may ask, who might our hosts be?"

"One is Dr. Chaim Weizmann, a chemist by profession. He has been one of the great advocates for a Jewish homeland as well as for justice for the victims of the Nazi genocide. You may have heard of him. He has traveled to your country and spoken to Jewish groups and to government officials."

Monroe vaguely remembered some of the Jewish doctors in St. Louis going to a fundraiser where a Jewish scientist was raising money for Jews in Palestine.

"So, he's the chemist."

"Very good, doctor."

"And the painter?"

Now Avrum had a twinkle in his eye. "While his art is actually quite good, in my opinion, he is known more for his political career. His name is Winston Churchill."

Monroe had no reply. He looked at Simon and Dionne. Simon did not seem at all phased. Dionne looked as surprised as he was.

"Now doctor, if you'll excuse us, I must speak to my two colleagues. We will be able to tell you more when we meet later. Someone will show you to your room." It was clear to Monroe that he was being dismissed. He decided not to ask any questions now. He would later.

After Monroe left, Avrum took Dionne and Simon into a small room off the entrance of the villa. He looked at Dionne. "I saw your father a month or so ago before I returned to Europe. He sends his love. I can tell he is worried about you. Your uncle, too. I told them you were doing a good job for us and that you were contributing to our cause. He is quite proud of you."

"I miss them all very much. I will be glad to go home when this is all over."

"Yes, when it is all over. I am not sure it will ever be finished. As you know, the French doctor is dead, leaving our American friend as the only one left from the Bormann autopsy besides the Russian. Right now, the American is safe in our hands, but I am sure he is the next target. I need to know a couple of things. First, do you think that he has the courage and the wherewithal to continue? We can get him safely back to a base where it will be the Americans' problem to take care of him."

Before he could go on Dionne interrupted, "I have no doubt that he can continue. He can be abrupt but he is smart and wants answers. I don't think he will go back to his base unless he is forced to."

"Well, it appears he has an admirer," quipped Simon.

Avrum let Simon's remark go. He looked at the two of them, "This is becoming more dangerous. I need to know if the two of you are willing to kill Bormann if we cannot capture him."

Simon answered without any emotion, "absolutely." Dionne looked a little more thoughtful. After a pause she looked at the two of them, "I will do what is necessary."

"Very well then. We will not go into further detail right now. Mr. Churchill takes great delight in being part of adventures like this. He appears to have some information that has not been made available to us as yet. Be prepared for an interesting dinner. Now go and get ready."

# 45

Monroe was led to a spacious bedroom with a view of the Provence countryside. As with many villages and homes in

Provence, this villa was perched on a hill with the valley on display out the large window. It was a wide expanse of vineyards and lavender fields. On the bed there was a pair of pants with a blazer and a shirt. Monroe held them up and noted that they appeared to be the correct size. He shook his head. "How do they always do this?" He decided he would lay down for a few minutes rest before getting ready for dinner. He was awakened over an hour later by the man who had shown him to his room.

"Sir, dinner will be in 45 minutes in the garden where you met before. May I be of any assistance?"

Monroe's voice was sleepy. He had not realized how tired he had been after the events of the last several days. "No... no I'm good. Thank you." Monroe freshened up and dressed quickly. As he had thought, the suit did fit well. Even the shoes fit. He made his way to the garden. The only persons there were Weizmann and Avrum. Weizmann greeted Monroe, "Well doctor, you look refreshed. Simon and Dionne will join us in a few minutes. It took us some time to complete our business."

Monroe smiled back. "I don't suppose now would be a good time to ask you what that business is, assuming that it may involve me."

Avrum replied, "Your assumption is correct, but your timing is off. All will be revealed soon."

At that moment, Simon and Dionne entered the garden. Simon was dressed in a similar outfit to Monroe's. Dionne was in a floral dress with canvas shoes. Monroe had never seen her dressed this way and found himself staring. She was striking. He quickly averted his gaze elsewhere but wasn't sure that she hadn't noticed him staring at her. He was about to make some kind of innocuous remark to fill the conversational gap when the servant called to them from the entrance to the house. "Madame et messieurs, please follow me. Mr. Churchill has asked that you join him for drinks before dinner."

They were escorted into a large drawing room with three walls of glass windows overlooking the countryside. Churchill stood by a table with several bottles of liquor and seltzer. He was dressed in a one-piece linen "siren suit" with a floppy hat like he had been painting. He was shorter and rounder than Monroe had imagined him. Like most of the free world, Monroe had listened to Churchill's broadcasts when England was alone and then later during the war. Listening to him, you imagined him to be well over six feet tall like Monroe himself. He had seen pictures of Stalin, who was also short in stature. Roosevelt had been the tallest, but of course was confined to his wheelchair a good deal of the time. "It just shows that anyone is capable of changing the world given the right set of circumstances," he thought.

There was another man with Churchill. He was more formally dressed, and looked "official." Weizmann made the introductions of Monroe, Dionne, and Simon. Churchill then introduced his colleague, Desmond Morton, as his unofficial source of information. "Yet another spy," thought Monroe.

Churchill shook hands with all of the men, looking each one in the eye. When he got to Monroe, he said "I am glad to meet you, doctor. My own doctor certainly helped me keep going during the war, though I do have my own medical opinions." There was a twinkle in his eye. "General Bedell-Smith sends his regards." Again, a twinkle.

"Thank you, sir. I, for one, am grateful to your doctor as well."

"I shall tell him. I think he feels neglected at times as I am his only patient."

He then kissed Dionne's hand. "Avrum tells me you are from Montreal, a lovely city. As you know, I have spent time in Quebec City and Ottawa as well. Canada has always been our friend and ally." He then got a distant look in his eyes and muttered, "Flanders in the last war and Dieppe in this one. Canadians...brave, brave men." Churchill came out of his revery. "Let us all have something to drink. I am having whiskey and soda, but we have rosé and champagne as well. Please, get something and sit." Monroe took gin with tonic. He noticed Dionne took the rosé. Avrum and Weizmann joined Churchill with a whisky each. Everyone sat. Churchill remained standing.

"My friend, Dr. Weizmann, has brought me up-to-date on the autopsy in Germany and the recent affair in England. I understand also that the life of a French doctor has been taken. We cannot have this type of villainy occurring. Though I am currently and, hopefully, only temporarily out of power, I am not without my sources of information. My friend, Mr. Morton, has been invaluable to me in this regard since before the war started. I am going to ask him to tell us all whatever information he has, then we will decide what action we will take."

Morton took the floor. He was very businesslike and was obviously a confidant of both Churchill and Weizmann. "Thank you, Winston. We have been trying to piece together the events of the past few days. It seems there is an organized effort to eliminate the key participants in the Bormann autopsy. The reasons are not clear, but it appears that there are suspicions about the conduct of the autopsy and its results. The most obvious, though not proven explanation is that the person that was autopsied was not Martin Bormann. While Bormann was not very well known to the Germans or public at large, we are more concerned that there are other Nazi sympathizers and war criminals who are leaving Germany and establishing themselves elsewhere. If they are willing to go to such lengths to eliminate inquiries into a minor bureaucrat then we are facing a well organized group, likely funded from wartime loot."

Churchill got up. "Thank you, Desmond." Morton did not appear to be finished but took a seat. "It is my opinion that we must find the perpetrators of these crimes and eliminate them one way or another. Even though I am out of power, I am not without influence. I have contacts in the intelligence communities of both Britain and France and have them looking into the matter. Unfortunately, they will likely plod their way through. We need to act more quickly. Dr. Weizmann has promised his assistance. We are asking you here to help."

Weizmann replied, "I think I can speak for my colleagues. They will cooperate in any way that they can. Fugitive war criminals must be brought to justice." He looked directly at Monroe. "Of course, it would be presumptive of me to speak for Dr. Monroe."

Churchill addressed Monroe. "Well, doctor, what do you say?"

It was clear to Monroe that he had only one choice. As with Eisenhower earlier, he was being asked by a leader of the free world for help. "Mr. Churchill, I have had questions about this whole affair since the beginning. At every turn my inquiries were resisted by members of my own government as well as yours. I would like to see justice done as well. More importantly, I am obviously a target of whoever is doing this, so my self preservation is clearly at stake. So, yes, I will help. The problem is it will be very difficult for me to help with any kind of investigation as I am on active duty. I am expected back at my base in a day or so. It will certainly arouse some suspicion if I don't return."

Churchill's irritation was visible. "Doctor, I can only apologize for the misguided efforts of the government of

Great Britain in this matter. The current leadership is more interested in moving on with their programs rather than finishing the tasks left undone during the war. In their minds, now, making the war go away as quickly as possible will help them politically. Obviously I disagree. " He looked at Morton. "Desmond, come up with something so that we can keep the doctor with us for a while. I am sure you have some sympathetic friends in the American military. Now, let us make our plans over dinner."

In Monroe's wildest dreams, he did not ever think he would be eating dinner and drinking Pol Roger champagne with Winston Churchill. Unfortunately, he didn't think he would ever be able to tell anyone about it. Morton and Weizmann sat on either side of Churchill. Monroe was seated next to Morton and Avrum with Donne and Simon seated next to Weizmann across the table.

Churchill and Weizmann went back and forth discussing the potential consequences of Nazis on the loose. They discussed different strategies to find the Nazis and the assassins, intertwined with some of Churchill's war reminiscences and barbs at the Labour government currently in power. While Monroe was fascinated by much of the conversation, he wasn't sure it was leading to anything concrete. His expression must have been obvious to Churchill.

"Doctor, we have not heard from you but I sense some impatience on your part." The table became quiet.

"Well sir, in my business running through the possibilities and the options are important, but at some point you have to act or the patient dies. I think we need to pick a direction to move and go. I would say it comes down to what we know and what we should do based on that."

Churchill stared at Monroe, then broke into a smile. Weizmann and Morton looked relieved. They had both experienced an unhappy Churchill.

"Pray doctor, what direction would you have us go?"

Monroe had not really developed a plan. Now he had to think on his feet with people far more experienced at this stuff than him waiting for an answer. "I suppose I would look at what we know about Nazis getting out of Germany. Who's helping? Where are they going? How are they financed? On a more narrow scale I'd look back at the autopsy itself. It seemed to me at the time that the results were already a forgone conclusion. Dr. Monod dismissed any questions or disagreement. I'd like to know a little bit more about Dr. Monod and how he is connected to all of this. He may turn out to be a target, too."

Morton looked at Churchill as if asking permission to speak freely. Churchill nodded assent.

"We know that there is an underground of Nazis and their sympathizers trying to get both former leaders and war criminals out of Germany. It looks like many are going to South America via Italy. They have help there from sympathetic Catholic church officials who believe that the Nazis are bulwarks against the atheism of communism. They have friends in the Italian bureaucracy who are more than happy to help them for financial compensation. The funds appear to be coming from accounts in Switzerland. Of course the Swiss will not reveal anything about what is in their banks and who it belongs to. We know that high ranking Nazis sent money to Switzerland, much of it taken from German Jews and later from conquered peoples. In fact there is a banking family called Monod. I wonder if your doctor is connected to them."

Monroe responded, "In my line of work we usually say 'if it looks like a duck, walks like a duck and quacks, it's not a zebra.'"

Churchill laughed. "In this case doctor we may be insulting the poor duck."

"It seems to me that it will be difficult to get anything out of the Swiss via the usual channels, but I'll see what we can find out," offered Morton.

Churchill looked at Weizmann. "Chaim, I think our three young people here should proceed on more unofficial lines. Perhaps Dr. Monroe could persuade his Swiss colleague to help us."

Avrum spoke for the first time. "We have people in Switzerland. Simon can be very persuasive if Dr. Monod is hesitant."

Churchill slapped the table with his open palm. "Then it is settled. Desmond and I have other matters to discuss if you all will excuse us." He turned to Monroe, "I like your spirit doctor. Keep buggering on." Before Monroe could reply, Churchill and Morton had turned and left the room.

Weizmann smiled at Monroe. "You appear to have made a new friend, who will be a loyal one. We should not disappoint him. Avrum, we have plans to make. The rest of you should get some rest. The next days will be busy."

# 46

Monroe didn't feel like sleeping. He decided to walk around the grounds of the château. The meeting with Churchill had been nothing short of incredible. What the hell was he involved in? Not only was he dealing with international leaders but dealing in espionage at their behest. A few weeks ago he had been a doctor and a soldier just waiting to go home. He wondered if he was doing the right thing by joining in this escapade. He felt pretty sure that he could be excused and allowed to go on with his life if he told them he couldn't continue and would keep his mouth shut. He certainly was not excited by the cloak and dagger stuff. Maybe he should just go home. But there was something about what Weizmann had said when they parted. Winston

199

Churchill had been impressed with him, and was now his "loyal friend," at least according to Weizmann. He actually felt that he would be letting Winston Churchill down if he did not continue. On its face that seemed ridiculous, but he now understood at some level how someone like Churchill could inspire people to "keep buggering on."

His thoughts turned to Dionne. Weizmann, Avrum and Simon seemed totally committed and unquestioning about their mission. He wondered about Dionne. Did she feel the same way he did? After all she was no professional spy, though he could see that she had dedication and no shortage of determination, maybe even some stubbornness. It made him smile to himself.

It had always been in his nature to want to get to the answer to a question. This was certainly the biggest question he had ever been faced with. He didn't think he could resume his usual life without knowing the answer. He would continue. He walked over to a stonewall overlooking the valley below, just thinking about random things and enjoying the view.

"I couldn't go to sleep, either, Jack." He was so surprised that as he turned around he nearly fell.

"You scared the hell out of me. After what's been going on the past couple of days, I really don't think it's a good idea to sneak up on someone."

Dionne was laughing. Her smile took his breath away. "Simon taught me how to do that during our training. I'm probably actually better at it than he is now. So what's keeping you up?"

"A lot has happened since we first ran into each other. I am now involved in international war crimes and on an espionage mission. It's just a little bit jarring. I wanted to think it through, sort of clear my head."

She stood next to him and took his hand. "I'm a little bit scared too, but I've made up my mind to follow through. I know my dad would tell me that I was crazy. Simon and Avrum have been doing this for years. They are professionals, like soldiers. I'm just a beginner and well, you're an amateur."

"Thanks for the vote of confidence."

"I didn't mean it the way it sounded. You never asked for any of this. You were following orders and doing your job, not thinking your life would ever be at risk. I would understand if you didn't want to go through with it."

"Well, my dear, I am going to go through with it, but I need someone as stubborn as me to go through it with me. "

She squeezed his hand and kissed him. "We'll see it through together." She turned away and headed toward the château.

Monroe was stuck for a reply. He didn't say anything, just watched her walk away. He realized then that the real reason he was continuing this mission and going on to Zürich was Dionne.

Dionne lay in her bed trying to fall asleep. She was glad that Jack was continuing on the mission and that they would continue to be partners. Funny, Simon was her partner as well, but she never thought of him the way she was thinking about Jack. She actually felt excited that he was staying on the mission and selfishly hoped she was the reason. That night she had a dream about home. She was at the Montreal Forum with her cousin Harry watching the Canadiens play. They were sitting in the first row on the glass. One of the Canadiens skated by, pounded the glass and winked at her. It was Jack.

# 47

*Southern England*

Sergeant Kemp, can I see you a minute please?" It was the C.O. When the C.O. asked to see a lowly sergeant, the news was not usually good. Kemp walked over quickly and saluted. "I am reassigning you to Dr. Keilly for the next little while."

Kemp was not fond of Keilly. Keilly was a snob. "Sir, if I might ask, uh, Dr. Monroe and I have been together awhile. Did I do something wrong? Is he OK?"

"Though I don't need to explain my orders, I know you two are as thick as thieves. I received a call from command saying that Dr. Monroe would be detained there on some kind of official business indefinitely. No further explanation was given. I don't suppose you would know anything about all this?"

"Uh, no sir. I don't know anything … about this that is."

"I thought as much. Well, you are dismissed. Oh, and Sergeant, being assigned to Dr. Keilly is not a punishment."

"He didn't sound like he believed that," thought Kemp.

Kemp was worried about Monroe. That British doc was dead. Monroe was running around France and, now, it appeared big shots were involved. He knew some guys at HQ. Maybe they heard some scuttlebutt.

On the way back to his barracks he saw Kleet approaching. "The day just keeps on getting better and better," he thought.

"Sergeant, a word."

"Yes, sir."

"I came here to speak with your boss about some worrisome events in France. I find out that he is not only not here, but the Colonel has no idea about where he is or what

he is doing. Says he was informed by headquarters that
Captain Monroe was on assignment. Well Sergeant, I am
headquarters and no one told me anything, so I think there is
mischief or worse going on. I think you know about some of
it. So why don't you tell me the real story."

Kemp knew this guy had the clout to get what he wanted.
Time to fess up. He was worried about Monroe. Kleet had
the pull to help Monroe if he were in trouble. "He is in
France sir. At least, last I knew. Wanted to talk to a French
doctor."

"I won't ask how he got to France though I think you did
what you do to get him there. Well, that French doctor is
now dead. So if your boss gets in touch with you, tell him
he'd better get his tail back here and contact me at the
number on this card. He is in danger. Am I clear Sergeant?"

"Crystal, sir."

# 48

Dimitri was stuck in Provence and frustrated after losing
the American and the girl. He was waiting impatiently for
his train back to Paris. He had heard nothing from his agents
about the American or the girl. He thought it best to go back
to Paris and start over, maybe put some pressure on their
French helpers. He had better people and greater resources
there as well. His superiors would be unhappy, but he was
confident that they knew no one was better at this than him.

He happened to look up from his newspaper and was shocked to see the American and the girl with another man who looked either British or American. The two purchased tickets and walked over to the first class gate for the train to Zürich. A porter took their luggage. The man shook hands and left them both there.

Dimitri looked at the schedule. The train to Switzerland would be leaving in 15 minutes. He gabbed his valise, ran to the ticket office, and bought a ticket to the last stop on the train to Zürich. He would contact Paris when he could. He got on the train a few cars behind his targets and found a seat alone. He wondered if even the ex-divinity student Stalin would admit that the gods had been kind to him.

The conductor led Monroe and Dionne to their compartment. The trip to Zürich was over 12 hours, and they were both grateful that someone, probably Morton, had arranged for a compartment, allowing them to be able to get some sleep. It was also more anonymous and secure. Monroe suspected that Simon was lurking around the train somewhere as well. The compartment was large by European standards and equipped with a water closet with upper and lower berths. "Less awkward for sleeping," thought Monroe.

They decided to go to the dining car for dinner before retiring. They each had soupe au pistou. Dionne then ordered ratatouille while Jack opted for a salade niçoise. They shared a bottle of rosé. While they were waiting for their main course, Dionne reached over and took Jack's hand. "Have to keep up appearances," she said, then started to laugh.

"What's so funny about holding my hand?" said Jack.

"It's the look."

"What do you mean 'the look'?"

"Every time you are uncomfortable or annoyed, you get this look. I saw it when you were annoyed with Weizmann and when Churchill asked your opinion. So you are annoyed or uncomfortable?"

"This mission was getting better by the minute, " thought Monroe. Here he was holding hands with a beautiful woman. He was flattered that she was paying so much attention to him and couldn't help but like it.

"Let's just say I'm comfortably uncomfortable."

"Very diplomatic answer." She took a sip of wine and they both laughed, but she still held his hand.

After a dessert of traditional Aix-en-Provence calissons - diamond shaped sweets with almonds and candied melons, covered with icing - followed by coffee, they made their way back to their compartment.

They sat across from each other, Dionne on the bed and Jack in a chair by a small writing desk. "We arrive in Zürich tomorrow morning. What then?" he asked.

"The papers that Mr. Morton gave us should get us through Swiss customs. Someone from the British embassy, probably one of his operatives, will meet us and take us to the bank where Monod's brother works. It's up to us to find out what he knows."

"Sounds like a better job for Simon. I suspect he can be very convincing."

"Maybe they think your professional gravitas and my good looks and personality will be more convincing. Anyway, Simon can always help if things become difficult."

"So Simon will be in Zürich?"

"Knowing Avrum and Simon, he's probably on this train to watch over us."

"Scary but reassuring. I think we should get some sleep."

"I'll go change and take the top. You'll be more comfortable on the bottom. It looks like it will fit you better."

Monroe  stripped down to his skivvies and got in to bed. Dionne came out in a pair of pajamas and climbed up to the top berth. "Do those pajamas have feet?" he said with not a little bit of sarcasm.

"We're going into the mountains. It'll get cold. Where I come from these are standard issue. Good night."

Jack turned off the light and turned toward the wall. With the motion of the train he was asleep in no time. Awhile later, he felt Dionne get in bed with him. She snuggled up into his back and wrapped her arms around his waist.

"Where'd the feet go?"

"I don't expect I'll need them to keep warm for a while."

# 49

The train would be arriving in Zürich in about 20 minutes. Dionne had awakened before Monroe and was in the water closet getting ready. Last night's events were a jumble in Monroe's head. His first thought was that he was in love with this girl. He had to admit that he had been attracted to her from the time they met. He had thought she might have felt the same way. That was now confirmed. "This is good," he thought. Much to his consternation his rational side tried to take hold. Was this some kind of a war time thing, two people under pressure and thrown together by events? They had known each other a couple of weeks. There were guys at the base who jumped into relationships with British girls.

Only a few ended well. He could imagine what Simon and Avrum would think. They might even pull the plug on the whole thing if they knew. Even though he didn't want to, he knew they would have to talk. "When I was kid, having to talk usually meant someone was getting dumped," he almost said out-loud.

He looked up from the berth as Dionne came in. There were those eyes and that smile. "Let me guess," she said. "You're wondering if this is some kind of wartime pressure cooked romance thing and trying to decide in your logical, doctor mind how you are going to manage it. Well, Jack Monroe, I do not make romantic decisions lightly nor can I predict the future, but I think there is something kind of special here as I think you do. So let's put the doubts to rest."

Monroe walked over to her. He hadn't really realized he was almost a foot taller than her. He kissed her for a long time then laughed. "Just wanted to confirm that I agreed with you."

A few minutes later the train pulled into the station. The porter took their luggage. Monroe hung back a minute. "So what do we tell your buddy Simon? I don't really think that he or Avrum are my biggest fans."

"We'll tell them when it's necessary. I know Simon pretty well, and I think he suspects that we are attracted to each other. He is actually quite passionate. Avrum is like my father. I can handle him."

"So we're going to dodge telling them anything."

"Exactly. We have to complete this mission then I'll handle them. Of course, it will go a lot better if we're successful."

"I guess I'm comfortable with that."

# 50

Dimitri jumped off the train before it had quite stopped. He wanted to be able to spot the American as soon as he and the girl got off the train. He would also be able to spot anyone jumping off to follow him. He saw the couple being led by a porter off of the train. They went to the office and had their luggage put in a cab and sent off then strode away together arm in arm. He noticed how close they were to each other. "Hmm. Maybe they are more than colleagues. All the better. It will make them sloppy." The station was crowded but he was able to blend into the crowd and keep them in sight. They did not appear to be trying to hide their presence.

Simon had seen the man from Paris jump off the train. "A pro move," he thought. The move had forced Simon to try to catch up without being noticed. When Monroe and Dionne stopped to tend to their luggage, he had time to spot their tail again.

Dionne and Monroe were led by the porter to an office near the  platform.  A grey haired man sat behind the counter.  He was clearly all business.

"How can I be of service?" he asked, directing his question to Monroe.  Dionne answered.

"We were told by Herr Mises that you could  have our baggage sent to our hotel."

A look of recognition came over his face with a bit of a smile. "Yes. Yes.  Herr Mises is a good customer.  I imagine he told you the fee.  We take dollars, pounds and Swiss francs."

Dionne handed him some bills.  He directed the porter to take the bags to a waiting car. "The driver will see to your things. They will be waiting at your hotel. Here is your receipt."

After they left the office, Dionne opened the envelope labeled "Receipt." On a single sheet of paper were two names and addresses. The first was Dr. Monod's clinic, the second his brother's home. "Where shall we go first?"

"Maybe we should split up," suggested Jack.

"Too dangerous. We might be followed, and I don't think you would be able detect a tail, much less evade one."

"Thanks for the vote of confidence, but I guess you're right."

"Hey, I don't do medical stuff," she said and poked him in the ribs.

"I say we see the doctor first. I've interacted with him, and we speak the same language. He can't BS me with medical babble as he would you. If he tells us anything, it might help leverage his brother to tell us about his business with the Nazis."

She took his arm. "Let's go."

It was a short taxi ride to Monod's clinic. The sun was sparkling. Zürich was the picturesque city that Monroe had imagined it would be. The prosperity was evident, if reserved. Stately buildings, expensive sedans and well dressed people everywhere. "You can tell there was no war here," he said to Dionne.

"Only the profits from it," she said quietly.

They had the taxi stop a few blocks away from the clinic. It was set on a small square with a fountain in the center. Dionne was headed to the door when Monroe squeezed her arm and steered her away. "This might be nuts but I think I saw the guy from Paris who helped Saint-Germaine a ways behind us."

She  pointed at a café like any tourist and said,  "Go over there and sit.  We'll make sure then figure out what we should do.  We can still see if Monod enters or leaves the clinic."

They made a point of looking around for a table, allowing Dionne to see where Monroe thought the man was.  They sat. Dionne leaned over and kissed Monroe then whispered.  "It is him.  He's looking at a guide book pretending to be searching for something.  We can't go into the clinic.  He or an accomplice would be waiting for us when we leave."

Just as she finished, Monroe saw Simon talking to a policeman who was standing on the opposite end of the square.  Dionne's back was to him.  "Don't turn around, but your friend Simon is here and talking to a cop."  Simon walked away from the policeman, who smiled at him and nodded.  The policeman walked over to the man who had been following them.  There was some shouting and then the policeman was taking him away.

Simon came and sat at the next table, not acknowledging them.

"What was that all about?" asked Monroe.

"The Swiss are very proud of  the cleanliness of their country.  Do you know that you can drink from any fountain here the water is so clean?  I merely informed the officer that the gentleman who has been following you emptied the remainder of his drink into the fountain.  Here, that's a minor crime, what you call a misdemeanor. He will be taken to the police station, given a stern lecture and likely have to pay a small fine. It should give us an hour or so. We need to move quickly."

Dionne looked at Simon and said, "Since Simon is here, I think we can split up. Jack and I will see the doctor. You can see the banker."

"Good idea. You two can try and get information from the doctor. I will find out what his brother knows."

"Good luck," offered Monroe.

"Thank you, but I can be very persuasive, if necessary." Simon walked off. Monroe and Dionne waited a few minutes and went across the square to the clinic. A couple of workers had arrived and were starting to "clean up" the fountain.

# 51

The clinic waiting room was empty when they walked in . Monroe walked up to the receptionist.

"Do you have an appointment, sir?

"Dr. Monroe to see Dr. Monod. It's professional. I need his opinion on a clinical matter involving an important patient."

As she reached for the intercom, Monod opened the door to see a patient out. He noticed Monroe and made a move to shut the door. Monroe crossed the room quickly, Dionne behind him. He grabbed Monod's hand and shook it but did not let go. "My friend, so good to see you," he said with a big smile.

"And you as well," Monod said with much less enthusiasm. "Come in." He turned to his assistant. "You may go for today."

They walked through a spotless exam room, all white and stainless steel. Monroe observed that all the equipment was top of the line and fitting for Monod's elite clientele. His private office was much more traditional looking. Diplomas and certificates from top schools in Switzerland were displayed prominently along side certificates and awards from medical and charitable organizations. There were no pictures of friends or family. Bookcases were on three walls. Monod sat behind a large wooden desk that looked like it took a crane to move. His desk accessories were all leather as was his high back chair. The desk was uncluttered, with a telephone and intercom along with three Mont Blanc fountain pens. Monroe and Dionne sat in plush leather chairs as well. There was one small window in the room.

Monod wore a traditional white coat over a dark blue vested suit that appeared to be tailor made. He had glasses on a gold chain around his neck. He addressed Monroe in the same officious manner as he had at the autopsy. "I assume your unannounced presence here has something to do with the events in Germany. I have rendered my findings so I am not sure what the issues are."

Monroe ignored the man's tone. "Well Dr. Monod, I came here with some concerns about the manner and thoroughness of the autopsy, but after walking in here and seeing your operation, I am more than convinced that my concerns are valid. You see, we were told that a Swiss pathologist endorsed by the Red Cross was going to perform the autopsy to assure that there would be no hint of cover up or politics. In looking at your walls here, I don't see any evidence that you are a pathologist at all, no certificates or diplomas. What that tells me is that your presence was to make sure there was a cover up. You and I both know that whoever was on that table was not Martin Bormann. I am most interested in your answers."

It was clear by the expression on his face that Monod wished he had not let them in. "I have performed autopsies in the past. I was advised that there was no one available on such short notice and that my expenses would be covered."

"I bet you have performed as many autopsies as I have delivered babies. Probably helped out or were supervised on a couple in medical school. By the way, who contacted you about doing this service?"

"I resent your implications. You are not a pathologist either, and besides, your colleagues raised no objections."

"You are correct. I was ordered to participate. I don't know about the others, which brings me to the second part of my visit. I am also here to do you a service. You see, Drs. Smythe and Saint-Germaine have both been killed. I have been followed. I suspect that loose ends are being cleaned up by someone and that either you will be a target or are part of the murders."

Monod was visibly shaken. He began sputtering. "I know nothing about these murders. I was contacted by someone in government who knew from my brother that I was a doctor. I was just doing as I was asked."

"Just following orders? Like all the Nazis."

Monod stood. "I am no Nazi. I would ask that you and your Jewish waitress - yes I know who you are young lady. I remember you from Germany - leave my office, now."

Monroe had had enough. He was in Monod's face. "You are a naive fool with an over-inflated opinion of himself. I would be very careful doctor. The people behind this have no more use for you." He was about to push Monod into his chair when the window shattered. Monod collapsed into Monroe's arms as Dionne pulled them both to the floor. Monroe had heard no shot, but Monod had obviously been killed by a bullet to the head.

"Jack, are you alright?" asked Dionne, her voice cracking.

"I'm fine. The blood is his. He's dead."

"We need to get out of here before there are more shots or the police come." They crawled on their bellies to the exam room. Monroe closed the door and they stood up. He went to the sink and washed the blood from his hands. Fortunately there was none on his clothing. Dionne peaked into the outer office. It was empty. Before they walked out, Monroe grabbed a scalpel from a tray by the exam table. Dionne looked at him. "What exactly are you going to do with that?"

Monroe really didn't know what he would do but felt better having some kind of weapon. "I'm going to defend your honor," he answered sheepishly.

"I'm touched, but you are ridiculous. Let's go."

"Where?"

Dionne was now all business. "First, away from here. Then we contact Simon."

As it was by now approaching the end of the day, the square was more crowded with people leaving work. Most were older men and women who did not appear threatening. Dionne and Monroe joined the crowd and got on a street car headed toward the center of Zürich. After a couple of stops they got off in an area with several taverns and restaurants. They went into a bar that was full of people socializing after work. Monroe got a beer for himself and red wine for Dionne, who had found a table in the back. She took the beer from Monroe and took a generous drink. She looked at him staring. "What? I'm Canadian. We start drinking beer in grade school." Monroe laughed. "Nothing like a stereotype."

Monroe sipped the wine, which wasn't what he preferred, but wasn't bad either. "What now?"

"We need to find Simon. He was going to the brother's home. He probably hasn't made contact. The brother's been at work and wouldn't be there yet."

They finished their drinks and took a taxi, again getting off a few blocks before their destination. Both were hyper aware of potential pursuers.

"I'll find Simon," said Dionne.

"How? He doesn't know we're coming."

"True, but we have the address and I know how he observes targets. I think I can find him."

The neighborhood where Monod's brother lived was clearly a wealthy one fitting for a successful banker. As they neared the address, Dionne began scanning the streets. She spotted Simon close to a streetcar stop, close enough to look like he was waiting for a streetcar but probably not close enough for it to stop for him. She and Monroe sat down on a bench where he could see them. He casually walked over and sat at one nearby. Dionne brought him up to date on Monod's questioning and subsequent assassination.

"This makes talking to the brother even more important.
The police will be looking for his brother's killer and will
probably come to see him. Also, the receptionist saw you, so
if he doesn't arrive soon, we'll need to get you two out of
Switzerland. We can get you to Geneva and across to
France. I will stay here and get in touch with you later."

As if on cue, Monod's brother walked up to his
townhouse.

"Let's go. Quickly," he said.

Monroe spoke up. "Let's not tell him his brother was
murdered right away. It might be useful if he's resistant."

"Good idea, doctor. But he will tell us one way or another.
I can assure you."

Conrad Monod was feeling content. He was a manager at
his bank, and while it was not a well known Zürich
establishment, its assets were some of the largest in Europe.
He was on the short list to be its next president, which would
move him into the highest echelons of Swiss business and
society. While still unmarried, his mistress was lovely and
above all discreet. Tonight he would go home and open a
bottle of wine and spend a quiet evening reviewing the latest
balance sheets, which he knew would make him look even
better to the bank's board. He turned his door key. Just as
the lock clicked he was pushed into his entry way by a man
accompanied by another and a dark haired woman. They

closed the door and walked him into his kitchen, pushing him down into a chair.

"Who are you? What do you want? I don't keep much money here but you can have what little there is," he sputtered.

"Herr Monod, we are not thieves. We are here to discuss business. We need some information about some of your clients," said Simon in an almost matter-of-fact way.

Monod regained some of his composure. He raised his voice. "That is totally improper. Our records are strictly confidential. You have no authority. Please get out."

Simon's tone became more serious. He would turn up the intensity as the situation warranted. "We do not need authority because we don't care about your rules. We know how your bank became so wealthy during the war. We want to know about some of your clients who acquired their wealth over the dead bodies of others."

"So, you are Jews."

"Who we are does not matter. What does matter is that we are not leaving until we get answers."

"I have nothing to say."

Simon was about to slap Monod when Monroe interjected. "Your brother was murdered today. He was shot in the head by a sniper. We know the two of you worked together and that you recommended him for an assignment in Germany. That is where I met him. Now my life is threatened as well. I am becoming impatient."

He pulled the scalpel that he had taken earlier out of his pocket. "I am as skilled with this as he was. My associate was trying to make this easy, which you still can, but I am more desperate than he is."

Monod turned pale and began to sweat. News of his brother's death and Monroe's threats changed his attitude.

"My brother is dead? Who? Why?"

"I think you know the answers to both of those questions. The longer you take to answer ours, the more time you give them to find you and the less time you have to get away." He turned to Simon and Dionne, who looked almost as shocked as Monod at Monroe's threat. "My friends have a few questions for you now."

"I...I will tell you what I can."

Simon sat across from Monod. "We need to know about only one client, Martin Bormann."

"Yes, I remember the name. His account was opened a couple of years after the other Nazis started making deposits. There was a large deposit followed by regular, smaller ones every few months. In fact, it wasn't really a deposit from the outside. It was transferred from another account, as were all his other deposits."

"Who owned that account?"

" An Arab, Hajj Amin Al-Husseini."

Simon was taken aback. "The Grand Mufti of Jerusalem was giving money to Martin Bormann?"

"All I know is that the money was transferred."

"Has it been withdrawn?"

"About half of it was withdrawn in the spring of 1945. The rest is still there as far as I know, but I cannot be sure."

"And the mufti?"

"He or his agent makes regular deposits and withdrawals to this day."

"So why was it so important that you arranged to have your brother declare Bormann dead?"

"Some of our other, more well known clients are trying to disappear in the wind. If they are dead, no one will hunt them, except for a few Jews." Simon bristled at the remark. Monod turned away avoiding his glare. "They reached out to my superior for help. He knew my brother was a doctor. My superior used his own influence to get my brother sent to

Germany. I know my brother suspected something irregular, but he did it for me. I think he did it to protect me, and now he is dead. That is all I know."

Dionne spoke up now. "These clients are obviously trying to get away and take their loot with them. What do you know of that?"

"Nothing. Now please go. Your presence is putting me in more danger."

Simon put his pistol on Monod's knee and looked at Monroe. "I don't think our friend is being truthful. Do you doctor?"

Monroe looked at Monod. "My friend is going to shoot you if you don't answer. If he does, you will never walk normally again."

"Alright! All I know is that they send money to a church official in Rome who must handle things for them."

"His name?"

"I don't know. They called him the Red Hat."

Simon seemed satisfied. He turned to Monod. We'll leave you now. I warn you again, which you don't deserve, these people are deadly."

They left by the back door. In the alley behind the house, they decided to split up and meet at a safe house that Simon had been given by the British.

# 52

Monroe and Dionne walked silently for a while. Finally she turned and faced him. "What was all that cowboy stuff back there? Twirling that scalpel. You were right out of a movie."

"I'm a man of many talents. I couldn't let Simon have all the fun. And besides, that guy might have taken more time to break if he thought we were just thugs. He had to decide if he was better off talking to us and getting out alive or getting killed by whoever killed his brother. Impressed?"

"More like appalled." She tried to give him a scolding look but couldn't hold back her smile. She took his arm and they headed to the safe house.

The safe house was above a real estate office in a nondescript part of Zürich that would be relatively deserted after business hours making a tail easier to spot. Nevertheless, Dionne and Monroe took a circuitous route to get there. By the time they arrived it was dark and the street was indeed deserted. A light rain was falling, causing them to run the last block. Simon buzzed them upstairs. The stairway was narrow and dark. A perfect place for an ambush if Simon has been compromised. He stood at the top of the stairs. "Welcome, cousin," he said. Apparently this was some kind of code for saying everything was good. Dionne and Monroe climbed the stairway and went into the apartment. Like the other safe houses Monroe had been in so far, it was small and utilitarian, even for Switzerland. "Who do you guys use for decorators? Love what you've done with the place," said Monroe. Dionne was only mildly amused. Simon clearly was offended.

"It's ok Simon," she said. "Jack is making a poor attempt at humor. It's an American thing."

"Hey, you gotta laugh once in a while or life will overwhelm you," said Monroe.

Simon ignored both of them "Sit, we need to figure out our next move. I will contact Avrum tomorrow. I think we can get him to talk to Weizmann about Monod's bank. Maybe Churchill can put some pressure on the bank, though I doubt it will do any good. The Swiss have made a religion out of being discreet. Many important people take advantage of that, so I don't think there will be much enthusiasm to freeze any suspicious accounts."

"It won't help us find Bormann either," replied Dionne.

"We also need to find out what the Mufti has to do with all of this. He and his thugs pose a direct threat to Israel and its people. We need to know if the Mufti and the Nazis are connected by more than money laundering."

"I think we need to go after this Red Hat guy," said Monroe. "It would be nice to know who he is."

"He may be a high church official," answered Simon. "Cardinals wear the red hat. I will see if Avrum knows anything. Maybe Mr. Morton can help. I can contact Avrum in the morning. In the meantime, we are safe here. Let's get some rest."

They got up. Simon headed toward one bedroom. Monroe volunteered to take the couch. Simon smiled and looked at Dionne. "Give me some credit Dionne. The two of you are pretty obvious. Take the other bedroom. I will be discreet, as should you. Avrum and your father are very close. I'm pretty sure I know how they will react."

"I can handle my father," said Dionne.

"I'm not worried about you," he said, looking at Monroe. He then turned and went to bed.

"Why would he be worried about me?" asked Monroe.

"My father can be rather gruff, to put it mildly, but he loves me. And besides, you're a doctor. My mother will love you."

"Now I'm chasing Nazis, being shot at and meeting her parents. I'm not sure which is scarier," thought Monroe.

"Penny for your thoughts, Jack."

"Sorry, just thinking about the mission.  Let's get some sleep."

# 53

They actually didn't go to sleep right away.  Monroe awoke early.  He decided to get dressed and eat something. Simon was already gone.  Monroe found coffee brewing along with a few pastries that looked  a couple of days old. There was some ham in the refrigerator.  "I guess if someone were to search this place, they'd never think it was a Jewish safe house," he said to himself.  He put some food on a plate with a cup of coffee and went back to the bedroom.  Dionne was sitting up in bed stretching.  She smiled at Jack.  "You're up early."

"Simon is already gone.  Besides, if we woke up together we might still be in bed when he got back.  We need to be ready to move when he returns."

"You are correct on both counts.  Jack, about last night, when I spoke about my parents that wasn't meant to pressure you or anything."

He let her squirm a few seconds before he answered.  "I didn't take it that way.  You are both right and wrong."

She looked at him quizzically, "I'm not sure what you mean."

"Well, you are wrong about your father. I actually can handle your father. And you are right in the sense that your mother will love me, not only because I am a doctor, but because I love you."

"Did I hear that correctly?" Now she was having fun with him.

Monroe thought, "That wasn't supposed to come out," but he knew that's how he felt. "OK. You got me. I'm nuts about you."

She hugged him tightly. "Took you long enough."

At that moment they heard Simon coming in. "You go keep Simon company. I'll finish dressing. Leave the pastry."

Simon was all business as usual. "We have a meeting with one of Morton's people from the British Consulate. I have the address. It will take us awhile to get there. We have to make sure we are not followed. Besides our current unknown enemies, all the diplomatic officials in Zürich are being routinely watched by someone, either from another government or their own. While many in the British government are sympathetic to the establishment of a Jewish state, there are those who are not, especially in the foreign service. So we must be wary of friend and foe. You and Dionne will go together as usual to a place we know is safe. I will meet our contact and bring him there. He may be reluctant with the change in plans so it may take some time to convince him.  If I do not arrive by 11, come back here and wait."

Dionne had walked in while Simon  was explaining things to Monroe.  She listened quietly, then asked, "What if I think we are being followed?"

"Then just be the happy tourists having a romantic trip in Switzerland and try to lose them.  Once you are clear, go to the bar at the Zürich Haus hotel.  Someone will find you."

Monroe asked, "Should we be armed?  These guys are ruthless.  You have a pistol, maybe one or both of us should too."

"Unfortunately, doctor, we cannot afford any incidents.  The Swiss authorities and your government would not take kindly to an American officer getting into a gunfight in Zürich.  If someone gets close, use that scalpel.  If they want to get you from far away, you'll just have to hope they are not a good shot."

"And Dionne?"

"You will be the target, not her.  She knows how to get away.  She is also a terrible shot."

"You are indeed a breath of sunshine.  You remind me of Colonel Kleet."

"We are both professionals, doctor, like you. We all deal with death in one way or another."

Dionne spoke up, "If you boys are finished with your debate, it's time to get going."

# 54

Dimitri's hunch to follow the couple to Zürich had paid off. He had lost them at the train station, but Zürich was not France. The Russians had a much better espionage network headquartered here in their Zürich embassy. There were Soviet agents posted around the other embassies in the city as well as undercover agents inside some of the embassies themselves. When he had approached the resident agent in Zürich, the man had been officious and uncooperative. After a conversation with Beria over a secure line, his manner had changed one hundred and eighty degrees. Dimitri only heard one side of the conversation, which was mostly a repetition of "Yes, Comrade Beria." When he had hung up the telephone, the agent was glistening with perspiration. From there the Russian intelligence apparatus had been put at Dimitri's disposal.

Early in the morning a Soviet agent placed within the British Embassy had messaged Dimitri that one of the attachés known to be MI-6 had been huddled on the phone with his superior. The attaché then notified the duty officer that he had an important errand to run. While that might have had nothing to do with Dimitri's mission, he was betting it did. Another Soviet agent picked up the attaché's trail until Dimitri could take over. While the attaché was careful, Dimitri was able to follow him to his meeting with the man he had seen on the train. The two of them walked to a restaurant. Dimitri waited outside and was rewarded when the couple appeared. Dimitri would wait and follow the couple. He would have some of his other agents deal with their associate.

# 55

Dionne and Monroe took yet another circuitous route to their rendezvous. "At least I'm getting some exercise," thought Monroe. Simon was already there with the British contact who was wearing a tweed coat and club tie. Simon had placed his beer on his left, indicating he had not been followed. Dionne wore a scarf tied with the knot on the right side, indicating the same. They sat down at the table. The British agent spoke with an Oxford accent and was clearly a product of one of its colleges. He introduced himself as Ian, not giving his last name or credentials.

"I must admit this is highly irregular. As you know, Mr. Churchill and Mr. Morton are not currently in government. I served in the Special Operations Executive under them during the war. Mr. Morton can be very persuasive. At any rate, our sources in Italy and specifically the Vatican have suspicions that certain Church officials have been helping former Nazis get out of Europe. Some clergy are motivated by their abject hatred of Communism. They believe the Germans were a bulwark against Communism and remain sympathetic to aiding them. This person referred to as the Red Hat is Cardinal Gabriel Garronini. He runs the operation but does not get his hands dirty. His assistant Father Giuseppe Lordo is the actual hands on man, arranging false papers, money transfers and passage to South America, usually to Argentina. President Perone of Argentina is sympathetic to the Nazis and profits the bribes they provide to get into his country. Lordo would be the one to give you the information if indeed there is any. He rarely leaves the Vatican during the day. Our agent believes he has a mistress outside the Vatican. I will give you a contact, an Italian, who we employ from time to time who may be able to help you. Mr. Morton also wanted me to tell you that Mr. Churchill is doing what he can to make your banker friend's career come to a rapid conclusion, but makes no promises. The Swiss will put up their usual wall of neutrality. Now, I must go. Good luck."

He handed Simon a piece of paper, presumably with the Italian agent's contact information and left the restaurant.

Simon showed Monroe and Dionne the information. "I'll meet you back at the safe house." They waited a few minutes to let Simon get away.

"This isn't how I imagined touring Europe," said Monroe.

They met later at the safe house to make plans. Simon had already contacted Avrum. "Avrum is going to see if any of our people know of this priest. The Italian contact that the British gave us may be someone who is available to the highest bidder. In that case we could be walking into a disaster. I will contact him alone so that if something is wrong, the two of you will not be compromised. The priest should be easy enough to follow, but knowing who his mistress is in advance will give us an advantage in finding them. Catching them together would be ideal for leverage, but we may have to go after them separately. I leave in an hour. You two will follow in the morning. Going separately should make it harder to be followed, but you two will need to be more careful as you will have no backup. By the time you arrive in Rome, I should have the information we need and maybe some helpers as well. Rome is still a political mess - fascists, communists, right wing religious fanatics and a few social democrats. They all hate each other and their alliances change almost daily."

"What else is new?" said Monroe.

"One other thing, I have secured these for each of you." He handed them each a German handgun. "These are the easiest to get here. If you are threatened, please do not hesitate to use them. It would be best to kill your attacker. Fewer questions." He looked at Dionne.

"Before you ask, Simon, I can kill someone if I have to. These people have already shown themselves to be murderers."

"I believe that you believe what you say, but until you are faced with killing someone, you cannot predict how you will act. Don't think it through. It will get you killed. And you, doctor, have spent your life saving lives. Can you take one?"

"Simon, you're right about what I do. I have treated friend and foe alike, but I have seen what evil has done in this war. If Hitler were brought to me for help, I would skin him alive and sleep very well. Does that answer your question?"

Simon nodded. "I hope neither of you need to use your weapons, but you are correct doctor. There is evil in this world, even in the Vatican."

# 56

*Southern England*

Kleet was reviewing some intelligence reports, or, more accurately, dissecting them when there was a knock on his office door. One of his junior officers poked his head in.

"Sir," he said.

"Come," he said curtly.

"Yes, sir. I, um , think I have information about that doctor you are looking for. I was just wondering, sir, why we are looking for him? It says he is on assignment, sir."

"Well, Lieutenant Jordan, is it? I was not aware that I had to justify to you any of my requests. The doctor may be up to his eyeballs in shit and against my better nature, I am trying to help him out of it. Any other questions?"

"Uh, no sir. Thank you, sir."

"Then get on with it man."

"Well, we haven't actually found him. What we have found is that the Russians are looking all over for someone, the British, too. When we looked where he was last seen, in Paris, we found the Russians and the Brits on high alert. The same pattern occurred in Zürich just a few days ago. I don't know if they are looking for your man, but I thought I should tell you in any case."

"Anything else?"

"Yes sir, we are now seeing Russian code traffic directed to Rome talking about following some Jewish agents. I mean, the doctor is Jewish."

"Not much to go on Lieutenant, but good work. Keep looking. Report your findings directly to our embassy in Rome."

"Not to you, sir?"

"I will be in Rome. Dismissed."

# 57

Monroe and Dionne made their way to Rome without incident. The safe house was in the Jewish ghetto in Rome, near the Tiber River and the Vatican, where it had been for hundreds of years. Its residents had been called the "Pope's Jews" in earlier times, as some had been useful to the Popes in various financial dealings. In the end, that did not spare them once the Nazis occupied Rome. This time, Dionne and Monroe had their own flat with Simon next door. Dionne wondered if Simon had arranged it that way on purpose. They were both tired and fell asleep until they heard a knock at the door.

Monroe got his gun. Dionne said, "It's probably Simon. Please don't shoot him."

"Just being cautious."

"Who is it?"

"It's Simon. I have a letter from your father."

Dionne turned toward Monroe. "It's OK. It means he wasn't followed. If the letter was from my 'uncle', we'd have a problem."

She opened the door and Simon entered. He looked at Monroe holding the gun. "Easy cowboy."

Monroe had not realized that he hadn't put the gun down. "Sorry, pardner," he replied sheepishly.

"I have news. I met with the British attaché's contact. He provided me with the information we need to get started. Our priest visits his mistress every Wednesday, which is tomorrow. We have people following him as well as watching her flat. After he leaves her, I will follow him with the doctor. Dionne, I think you should go to her flat. Use some pretense to get her to let you in and find out what she knows about all this. Hopefully he will tell us what we want to know. If not, we may have to use her as leverage."

"Do you think the contact is reliable?"

"I think the British are paying him enough, for now at least, that his information is good."

"What if the girl knows nothing?" asked Dionne.

"She's having an affair with a priest, one with a Vatican position. I doubt she is totally in the dark about some of his activities. Feel free to question her."

"I also have some more potentially disturbing news. We have people watching all of the important embassies in Rome. There has been an increase in activity at both the American and the Russian embassies. There are more agents of both countries making inquiries. Hopefully, they are more worried about each other than about us. However, we need to remain on guard. Colonel Kleet has probably been alerted by the American embassy in Rome. We do have his description that we have passed on to our people. Should we spot him, it is likely that the Russians will, too. Hopefully, your colonel will come to Rome to be your guardian angel, not hunt you down. We cannot have the politics of the United States and the Soviet Union interfering with our mission. I doubt that all of our goals are the same."

Monroe paused for a bit then answered, "I will have to deal with Kleet at some point. I do agree with you that now is probably not the time. If we find Bormann, I'll need to determine when to bring him in on our activities."

"Events may not allow you that luxury."

# 58

Father Lordo left the Vatican early Wednesday afternoon. Fortunately, their informant had provided them with a good description, as the priest was not in religious garb. He didn't appear concerned about being followed, which made their work easier. He went to a two story apartment. Soon after he entered, the blinds were drawn on the second floor.

"I imagine they'll be in there for a while," said Simon. "I will go check the alley behind the building to see if there is a rear exit. You two watch the front."

Monroe and Dionne sat on a bench with a good view of the front door of the apartment. Simon returned a few minutes later.

"Fortunately there is no rear entrance to this building. I will go across the street and keep an eye on things. We should not be seen together. When the priest leaves, I will follow him. Doctor, you follow behind me close enough that you won't lose me. Dionne you can then go and see the girl."

Almost two hours later, the priest walked out of the apartment. Simon let him get a little bit ahead and began to follow. Monroe got up to follow Simon. He bent over and whispered to Dionne, "Be careful. I'll see you soon."

"Try to keep Simon under control. He knows we're getting closer. He may be more extreme."

As Monroe followed Simon he realized that this was the first time he and Dionne had been apart since all this started. His gut churned a bit. "Must be love," he thought.

Simon followed the priest back toward the Vatican. He took a route along less traveled streets, which played into to Simon's plan. Simon slowly decreased the distance between himself and his quarry until he was nearly beside him. He brushed right by the priest then quickly turned toward him, hoping Monroe would play his part.

"Excuse me, aren't you Father Lordo?"

"You must be mistaken," said Lordo, though his expression revealed otherwise. He started to turn away and ran right into Monroe. Simon grabbed his arm.

"Please come with us, Father." It was not an invitation. "And do not cry out or try to run. We are watching your mistress."

Any thought of escape left Lordo. "I will come with you, but you have made a mistake."

They took Lordo back into the ghetto to a boarded up shop that was padlocked closed. It appeared to have been a bakery. Simon had a key and let them in. The scent of baked bread remained in the shop. They took Lordo to the back where they would not be seen. Simon sat him in a chair. Before he could start his interrogation, Lordo spoke up indignantly.

"I am a man of God. You have made a grievous mistake. I work in the Vatican for Cardinal Garoninni. If you let me go, nothing will happen. I will forgive you."

Monroe replied. "You seem to have forgotten a few commandments Father."

"I will admit my spirit has been weak."

"We are not here to discuss your pursuit of the flesh. We are here to find out about the Nazis you and your boss have been helping get out of Europe."

"I don't know what you are talking about," replied Lordo, but his indignity was rapidly fading.

"We know you have been helping Nazi fugitives get papers and transportation out of Europe. We know that others in the Vatican are involved. We also know that you are the intermediary. You are the most involved in the day to day transactions. You are the Cardinal's shield."

"The Cardinal is not involved in what you say."

" I am sure that is what he would say as well. Do you think he would protect you as you do him? You will take the fall from grace, as you might say, if these dealings are exposed. And let's not forget your own personal sins. Your time as a priest is done. Be truthful now and you may just survive. "

"The Cardinal is a good man, a holy man. He protects the Church from the communist atheists. I have nothing else to say."

Simon was thinking about what to say next when Monroe spoke. "You know the good Father may not feel it is in his interest to talk to us. Maybe his girlfriend will. She may even be in on it. We should quit wasting our time with this guy and ask her. She might be more easily persuaded."

"You may be right," said Simon. "Come, we'll tie up the Father here and go speak to her."

"No, no. She is innocent. I will tell you what I know. Please do not hurt her. She is everything to me." There was no fight left in him now.

"You are correct. I do help get documents and arrange passage for certain people. Refugees from the communists."

"Nazis, let's be clear who they are," said Simon with contempt in his voice.

"They fought the communists who threaten the Church by their very existence," argued the priest.

"And you do this with Christian charity out of the goodness of your heart?"

"There is some cost to what we do and an obligatory donation."

"Which you and your boss and God knows who else split up," said Monroe.

"I don't know what happens to the money other than the things I have to pay for."

"We are trying to find out about one particular individual, though I am sure others will have more questions when your operation is exposed."

"I don't know names. I am given a photo by a contact. I don't recognize the person. The famous Nazis have been arrested or are dead. I take the document to a forger who provides the papers. There are ship captains who are willing to take passengers with papers on their freighters, no questions asked, for a fee."

"Where do they take them?"

"To South America, usually Argentina or Uruguay. That's all I know, honestly."

"How many in the last few months?"

"Eight, maybe ten. But I don't know who they are."

Simon gave Lordo a pen and paper. "The names of the ships and your forger. We will be in the next room."

Simon and Monroe stepped into the front of the bakery where they could not be heard but could still see Lordo.

"Very good bringing the girl in, doctor. You are getting better at this game."

"I'll take that as a compliment from an expert. What now?"

"I don't think he'll be of much further help. We need to find the forger. I will get someone to watch over the Father. I don't think he will be a problem as long as we keep the girl in play. He will be anxious to disappear. He is now in disgrace."

"A modern money changer in the Temple," added Monroe.

# 59

Dionne waited several minutes after Monroe and Simon were out of sight, making sure the priest wasn't going to return. She had never done anything like this before. She felt somewhat reassured by the fact that Simon had so nonchalantly given her the assignment. Either he was very confident in her or he had no other choice, or a little bit of both.

The front door to the apartment building was unlocked. She knocked on the girl's apartment door. "I found a cat outside. I was wondering if it was yours," she yelled through the door. She knocked again. "Is anyone there?"

She heard footsteps rapidly approaching the door. A woman about her own size opened the door. She wore a plain gray dress, had mossy brown hair and wore no makeup. "Not what I would expect a mistress to look like," thought Dionne.

"I don't have a cat. Maybe you should check downstairs." Dionne charged past her into the apartment. "Please leave. You have no business barging in here," said the woman.

Dionne looked at her, pretending to be concerned. She was not intimidating like Simon. She would have to somehow win the woman's confidence. "I need to talk to you about your lover. He may be in trouble."

Color left the woman's face. "Can we sit down?"asked Dionne. They sat. Dionne introduced herself as Diana. The woman was Marie

"Has someone harmed him? Is he hurt?" Dionne sensed her concern was genuine. She suspected the romance was more than casual, which she might be able to use to her advantage.

"He is not hurt yet, but he is involved with dangerous people."

"Who are you? Are you police? Are you from the Vatican?"

"I work with a group helping victims of the war," she said, trying to sound official. "We have found information that there are some in the Church who may be helping some of their former tormenters to slip away from justice. Your lover may be helping them."

"Giuseppe is a good man. I have known him a long time, since he was in seminary. He loves the Church."

"How long have you known him like this?"

"Why should I tell you? You won't tell me who you are or how he is in danger. Her expression hardened. "I will tell you nothing more."

"I think you will. I can see you are worried about him. You know more than you say you do. I will tell you that my associates have him now and are questioning him. If you know anything about his recent activities, it will be much easier on him. I will leave if you like, but I think we both know that it would be best for the two of you if you helped me. We wish you no harm."

Marie was silent for a couple of minutes. As she spoke, she wiped away tears. "Giuseppe and I met when he was studying to be a priest and I was studying to be a nun. I realized that while I loved the Church, it was not my calling. I left and became a teacher. I didn't see him for several years. Then one day I went to Church for confession. When I heard his voice, I knew who he was. He was so kind and reassuring. I kept going back and managed to run into him on a couple of occasions outside of church. We fell in love and have been lovers for two years."

Dionne decided to take a gamble. Marie didn't strike her as devious. She hoped that this confession was an act of trust. "But something changed, didn't it?"

Marie briefly hesitated again. The words came more slowly this time. "We .. were.. discovered. I don't know how, but it must have been the Cardinal. He has people, not just in the Vatican, but all over Rome. This is hard for me.

I love the Church and so does Giuseppe. The Cardinal is not of the Church we believe in."

Dionne wanted to keep the momentum going. "I know. He is a bad actor among good people. Don't worry, go on."

"He told Giuseppe that he knew about us. That he could have him dismissed from the Vatican, from the Church, but would protect him if he would help him with certain tasks that would help the Church but were frowned upon. He even offered to pay him. Giuseppe came to me distraught. Finally, he decided to do it. He would keep the money so we could run away. He knew of places where we could go and help people. Places where no one would ask about our past."

"What does he do?"

"He gets forged passports and visas for Nazis." She started to sob. "He says we would use their bad money for good."

"Tell me. How does it all work?"

"I know very little. Sometimes when Giuseppe comes, he brings an envelope and leaves it with me. The next day, I place it by the front door behind the potted plant where someone picks it up. We have few visitors here and all the residents mind their own business, especially since the war. It all went well until a few months ago. Since then I have been very frightened."

"What changed?"

"He came to see me again with an envelope. It looked like all the others. I could see he was worried. When I asked him what was wrong, he told me that the Cardinal had warned him that he had to be careful and make sure that nothing happened, that his client was very important and very dangerous. Giuseppe told me that it had taken him much longer to make the arrangements. He had to deal with someone he had never used before to get passage."

"To where?"

"I don't know. I just know that the ship was leaving from Bari - not Rome or Venice. After Giuseppe left the next morning, I went across the street to see who picked up the envelope. There were two men. Not Italian, foreigners."

"Were they Arabs?"

Marie thought for a second. "They might have been."

"One more thing. Did you look in the envelope?"

"No, honestly. I was too scared."

Dionne didn't think there was much more she could get out of Marie. "Thank you."

"Wait what will happen to Giuseppe and me? We are in danger, aren't we?"

Dionne had some empathy for Marie. She realized she might have done the same thing if Jack were in trouble. "Marie, my associates and I are not a threat to you, but maybe some of the people Giuseppe is working for are. I would go stay with someone if you can, some place where Giuseppe would look for you. If he tells my friends the truth, they will release him. I would advise the two of you to leave Rome. I don't think the Cardinal will protect Giuseppe if he is in danger."

Dionne left Marie, who was already getting her things to leave. She walked for nearly an hour to make sure she was not being followed, then headed to the safe house.

# 60

Fortunately for Dimitri, the Russians also had sources in the British embassy in Zürich who found out about the meeting between Monroe, Dionne and Simon with Churchill's man. The Russian was able to piece together why the three of them were heading to the Vatican and that the Vatican had people helping Germans escape. This time, Dimitri was able to follow Monroe and Dionne to Rome without being detected. Dimitri had been following Simon and Monroe as they followed the priest. He left another agent to watch the apartment where Dionne was questioning Marie.

Dimitri followed Monroe and Simon with the priest to the bakery in the ghetto. He decided that he would wait until Monroe and Simon left. If the priest were left behind, he would go in and persuade him to reveal what he had told the other two. Dimitri knew he was close to finding Bormann, and that the priest would likely be the key. Now the question would be what to do about the other two. He was not concerned about collateral damage as long as he could complete his mission. If a corrupt priest and a couple of Western agents were casualties in the process, so be it.

As he was observing the bakery and contemplating his next move, he felt the barrel of a gun in the back of his neck.

"OK, my friend, let's just keep this very calm. I want you to take the revolver you have under your coat, place it on the ground next to you, then you and I are going to have a little talk."

Dimitri could not see who was behind him. He had been so fixated on following Monroe and Simon that he had not been aware that he was being followed. He silently cursed himself for his error. The accent was clearly American. He turned around slowly.

Kleet had used a series of agents to follow Monroe. He knew Monroe was traveling with two other people, probably Jewish agents. But now, there was a new twist. Kleet was informed that another agent, probably Russian, had also been spotted following Monroe and his companions. "That dumb bastard has no idea what he's getting into. It's time for me to get involved," he thought. Monroe and Simon had been spotted outside of an apartment near the Vatican. Kleet got there just as Monroe and Simon were leaving. He also saw the Russian agent trailing Monroe and his companion. He needed to find out what Monroe was up to. He was pretty sure that it was involved with Bormann. He followed them all, trying to stay far enough away from the Russian, but close enough to help Monroe should the situation go south. "This is like a goddamn caravan. You couldn't make it up if you wanted to,"he muttered. Suddenly, Monroe and Simon stopped another man and looked to be forcing him to go along with them. They took him to a bakery and went inside.

He kept his eye on the Russian waiting outside of the bakery. He was pretty sure that the Russian had not spotted him, but that could change quickly, especially if more Russian agents were on the way. He had to find out what the Russian knew and then get Monroe the hell out of Rome.

Before Kleet could speak, Dimitri attempted to take control of the situation. "Colonel, it is colonel is it not? Let me assure you that I am no threat to your doctor."

Kleet was not totally surprised by the thoroughness of Russian intelligence. They obviously had some kind of a file on him. Though he knew his adversary was with Russian intelligence, he knew little else about him. He kept his expression blank. "You have me at a slight disadvantage. I know that you are with Russian intelligence but haven't had the time to review your file."

Dimitri thought that he knew more about the situation than the American, giving him somewhat of an advantage. However, that advantage shrunk to nothing with the American pointing a gun directly at him. He decided that the best course might be to bide his time and try to cooperate with the American for now. "Colonel, I suspect that you and I are seeking complimentary goals. You are trying to protect your doctor, who is out of his depth in this operation. Two of his colleagues have already been assassinated. I am trying to hunt down a Nazi war criminal. If we work together, we may be able to accomplish both of our goals and go our separate ways."

"And how do I know that you aren't the bastard that killed the other two doctors?"

"I did see the French doctor get nearly killed by the runaway cart. In fact, I saw your doctor run away from the scene with two others, one of whom is in that bakery with him. The other is back at the apartment we were both watching. I think he saw me try to help the French doctor. I had no interest in killing him. He was far more valuable to me alive. I also saw a man who looked like an Arab running away at the same time."

Kleet was at a crossroads. He could not easily get rid of the Russian without detaining him or killing him. The former course could cause an international incident and the latter would be messy for all kinds of reasons. He also wondered why the Russians were so interested in a Nazi who appeared to be nothing more than an exalted clerk. Finding out why might be more important than getting Monroe out right now. Should he gamble that he could save Monroe and find out what made Bormann so important to the Russians? He decided to make the deal with the Devil.

"How very noble of you. Now let me tell you what I think. I don't think that you have any interest in bringing a Nazi war criminal to face justice but would rather move right to your own verdict and execution. I also think, judging by how your boss, Stalin, treats failure, that you cannot afford to fail on this mission, or you will face his justice."

"I think you also know, Colonel, that your doctor is obsessed with finding the same man, Martin Bormann, that I am looking for. I doubt that he will willingly go with you. I also don't think that you want to arrest him or court martial him. That would be very embarrassing for a certain Senator from New York. Don't look so surprised. We had dossiers on all of the participants in the Bormann autopsy just as you did. So, I think we have a bit of a stalemate here. "

"OK. Here's the deal. You and I follow the doc and his two new friends. If they lead us to Bormann, he's yours. You get to go back to your boss and be a hero, and I get my guy out of harm's way. There are two conditions. First, it's just the two of us. The fewer people involved in this the better. You tell me everything you know and I will do the same.  Second, should you deviate from this course and try to harm the doctor or his friends, I will kill you."

"Do you trust that I will not kill you?"

"Well, I figure you're in the same boat that I'm in right now.  If you kill me, there will be hell to pay for you and your government.  I think your boss would have no trouble in making you the sacrificial lamb to preserve diplomatic relations.  Also, I don't give a hoot in hell about what you do with some Nazi war criminal.  So, I think we can help each other.  I also think it's about 50-50 whether I would kill you before you could kill me, and I don't think you like those odds anymore than I do." Kleet lowered his gun but kept Dimitri's.  "Don't worry, I'll give it to you if you're gonna need it.  Now what can you tell me?"

# 61

One of Simon's men had arrived to watch Father Lordo.  He was instructed to let the priest go after Simon and Monroe were well clear of the area.  Simon spoke to Lordo before they left, "Father, I would advise you to leave Rome with your girlfriend.  You have no future in the Vatican.  Your Cardinal will soon be tending to a flock far from here.  He cannot protect you."

"Do you think he'll go back to the Vatican and report what happened?" asked Monroe.

"I think the father is basically a decent man who got caught up in events that he could not control. In a way, we have given him an out. He seems to love his girlfriend, which gives him a purpose to keep going. I don't think we need to worry about him." Simon smiled, "but just to be safe, my man will follow him to make sure he will not be of any danger to us."

"I know that we don't always agree, but I think you're doing the right thing," replied Monroe. They didn't speak again until they reached the safe house.

Monroe and Simon were eating sandwiches that they had picked up at a small shop on their way back to the safe house. Monroe had to refrain from eating the sandwich that they had gotten for Dionne. With his mouth still half full, he asked Simon, "what now?"

"Well, we know Bormann is or was in Italy. He has a new identity and papers that will get him out of the country. We need to know what his new identity is and where he is going. We need to get to the forger who made the papers, then we need to find out which ship was used to get him out of Rome. I have contacts at the port of Rome that may be able to help us. We can also reach out to the British, unofficially, of course."

"He's not leaving from Rome." It was Dionne, who had entered the safe house without making a sound to Simon's irritation and Monroe's amusement.

Dionne related what she had learned from Marie.

"If what you say is true, Dionne, most of our assumptions about Bormann leaving Italy are wrong," said Simon.

"It's true."

"Is this assumption of yours supported by any fact or is it just your intuition?"

"Marie was scared. I got there too soon after he had left for her to have time to make up false details. She also doesn't want anything to happen to him. She just wants the two of them to get out. I think we have to believe what she told us."

Monroe had kept quiet for most of the discussion. "I have to agree with Dionne. If Marie loves this priest as much as he appeared to love her, and if she is even half as scared as he was, she probably is telling the truth. It would have been very easy for her to deny everything or to give us the easy answer, which was that Bormann was like all the other Nazis they helped to go to South America. She didn't have to tell Dionne about Bari and the two Arabs. The story is different enough that it probably is true. I think the test will be if your man follows the priest back to her. Dionne said she was already packing to get out. I don't think that either of them would leave the other behind. If we can find this forger and see what he knows it may confirm everything for us."

"Then we need to hurry," said Simon, getting up and grabbing his hat.

Monroe grabbed the last sandwich and handed it to Dionne. "I saved this for you."

Dionne smiled, "I think I arrived just before you ate it, but I'll give you the benefit of the doubt for your chivalry."

# 62

Father Lordo had told Monroe and Simon that the forger worked out of a pawnshop. The shop opened onto a nearly deserted street. It would have been very easy to walk by it. There was a sign in the window instructing patrons to ring the bell. Simon did so and was greeted by a short, bald rotund man who looked both ways before he closed the door. Monroe and Dionne waited around the corner. Simon had told them to approach the shop about 10 minutes after he was let in.

"How may I help you, sir?" Asked the pawnbroker. "A loan perhaps or maybe you would like to redeem a ticket or make a purchase."

Actually I am here to make a purchase of sorts. I was told by my priest, Father Lordo, that you might be able to provide some documents for me that would allow me to travel without interference from officials."

"I have heard that such documents are very hard to come by, especially ones that will fool the authorities. They are quite expensive. But as you can see, I run a pawn shop. "

"Well, I have some jewelry and other items that I obtained during the war from some people I know will never return to get them. I'm sure we can make a trade if you can help. My associates are nearby with the items. If you can provide such a service, I will bring them to you."

The pawn broker was all business "Very well. Have them come. I will appraise the items. I can make no promises."

After a few minutes, Monroe and Dionne came to the store and rang the bell. When the shopkeeper opened the door, Monroe said, "Our friend," pointing at Simon, "told us to meet him here." The shopkeeper let them in and once again looked down the street in both directions before shutting the door. He then turned the sign in the window to indicate that the store was closed. He turned to them, and Simon grabbed him and twisted his arm near breaking and pushed him to the back of the shop.

"Now my fat friend, we need some information. Let me assure you that I will go to any lengths to obtain it. Your priest friend has been exposed. I suspect that you will not be far behind. We have no interest in harming you if we don't have to. I'm sure that you have resources, including forged documents of your own to fool the authorities. If you tell us what we need to know, you may have a chance of getting away. If not, we will wait for them to arrive or maybe we will let some of your more unsavory customers know that you have been compromised. In either case, we are your best option."

The shopkeeper was sweating profusely and looked pale. Monroe ordered Simon, "Sit him down, now." He checked the pawnbroker's pulse. "His pulse is weak and rapid, get him some water. I am a doctor. Do you have a heart condition? Are you in pain?"

"Yes I do. No pain, feel lightheaded, breathing is hard. The doctor gave me some pills. In my jacket, on the hook. Over there."

Dionne rifled through the coat and gave Monroe a small case. He opened the case and slipped a pill under the man's tongue. After a few minutes he began to look better.

"His pulse is coming down. Is your breathing easier?"

"Yes. The pill always helps. Thank you. My doctor tells me I eat too much bread. I tell him my father was a baker."

"You need to go to your doctor or a hospital. This lady will call an ambulance for you, but first you must help us," he said, pocketing the pills.

"Yes, yes. Those papers are not worth my life. Go to that cabinet. Inside is a box. Here is the key. There is a notebook with the names of everyone I made papers for. It is an insurance policy of sorts."

Dionne retrieved the box. In it was a ledger with all of the Nazis that had gotten forged papers, including dates with new names side by side with the old.

"We'll take it with us," said Simon "We need to go."

Monroe picked up the phone and told the operator to send an ambulance. He bent down and got close to the pawnbroker. He could smell tobacco on his breath. "When was the last time you saw the priest?"

"He comes once a month. He was to come tomorrow."

"How many documents did you give him last month?"

"I gave him around twenty. Like always."

Monroe handed him the nitro pills. "If you still feel bad in five minutes take another one. The ambulance will be here soon. We were never here. Listen to your doctor and cut out the cigarettes. Some people think cigarettes are bad for your heart."

# 63

When they returned to the safe house, Dionne began going through the ledger. "This is like a directory of the Nazi elite. I can see why the pawnbroker thought of it as insurance. "

"Let's see if we can find the information on Bormann. But more importantly, we have to decide what to do with this thing. What do you think Simon?"

Simon did not answer. He seemed to be lost in thought. He had not spoken at all since they left the pawnshop.

"Simon, Simon?" said Dionne.

"Hey buddy, you're quiet, even for you," said Monroe.

Simon looked at the two of them. "I didn't mean to hurt him, at least not like that. I do what I have to do, but I want you to understand I'm not a bad man."

"There was no way you could've known that he had a bad heart. Maybe I should've said something sooner. I am the doctor. Just looking at him, he was a heart attack waiting to happen. I got caught up in it too. I held back the second dose of nitroglycerin to get him to talk."

"You two realize the guy helped murderers," said Dionne.

Simon sighed, "Yes, of course. We just don't want to become like them."

"Maybe we did the wrong thing but we did it for the right reasons. The thing we need to do now is to find this bastard," said Monroe.

"I've been looking over the past few months. I don't see any Bormann," she said.

"Go back a year," said Simon.

Dionne continued to search but found nothing.

"He must've used a fake name, even with the forger, to protect himself," said Monroe.

"Then we may never find him. If we have to start looking at a big port in Italy, much less the smaller ones, he will disappear. We just don't have the people or the time," said a frustrated Simon.

"Wait," Monroe said. "Let's think about this for a second. He's using an alias. Most people pick names that they can remember. If he's as slippery as we think he is that's what he'll do. He won't want to get caught not answering to the new name. So the first name will probably start with an M."

"Unless he's using a nickname," said Dionne.

"Well, hopefully the nickname would start with M. If not, we have a problem. We can also look for last names that start with a B, though that would be less likely."

"No B here," said Dionne.

Simon joined in, "Maybe it's about what he did, how he was addressed. He was Hitler's private secretary. In German it could be sekretar or a name like that, maybe Schreiber, like a scribe."

Dionne got a big grin on her face. "There is a Schreiber. He got papers a couple of months ago."

"What's the first name?" Monroe and Simon asked in unison.

"Ludwig."

"It's his middle name. It was on the autopsy documents. It's him," said Monroe.

"So we have a name, and if we believe the priest's girlfriend, we have a place - Bari. He left from Bari. We go there next."

"What about this?" asked Dionne, holding up the book. "We can't take it with us. It's too dangerous. We need to get it to someone who can use it to find these people."

"How about Churchill?" asked Monroe. "He seems pretty interested and he has that friend Morton who's some kind of a spy."

"We can't give it to the British or the Americans," answered Simon. "It could be buried for a hundred political reasons. Remember, the allies are tired of war. We Jews do not have the luxury to forget."

"Then who?" asked Dionne.

"There is a man in Vienna that has helped Avrum and vice versa. He is a survivor himself. He hunts Nazis and is relentless."

"I don't think we have time to go to Vienna to drop this off," said Monroe.

"We don't have to go to Vienna. Avrum has a contact in Rome, married to a cousin of a cousin. He has helped us before. I will take this to him. The two of you wait here. It will be a few hours."

After Simon left, Monroe said, "That Simon is a barrel of laughs." He sat down on the small couch in the front room. "Any suggestions? I saw a restaurant a couple of blocks from here. Looked cozy, or… we could think of something to do here."

Dionne sat down next to him and kissed him on the cheek. "Jack, we need to talk."

"Oh shit," thought Jack. "It's 'the need to talk' talk." He hadn't had that talk in a couple of years since his engagement had ended. He and Kathy were at their favorite restaurant on the Hill in St. Louis. It was not a surprise. They had both seen it coming. There was almost a sense of relief that time. He was genuinely surprised this time.

"Jack, Jack. Look at me." Monroe returned to the present.

"Sorry, old memory. Not important."

"Well, this is important." He could see she was upset. God he hated "the talk."

"I think we have something special. The last few weeks have been exciting, but I worry. It's getting more dangerous. I know we have to keep on, but what if one of us gets hurt or worse?"

This certainly was not the talk that Monroe had expected Before he could try to reassure Dionne, she spoke. Her voice was near to breaking. "If I get killed, I want you to go to Montreal and find my cousin Harry. Tell him what happened. Then the two of you go to my parents. I want you to meet them. Let them know about us. It may give them some comfort. Will you do that for me?"

"Of course," he answered without hesitation. "And I would want you to do the same. My mother would take some solace that I fell in love with a nice Jewish girl," he said, trying to lighten the mood.

When he had told families about loved ones dying, most of the time it was expected and there was almost relief. When it was unexpected, it was a hard thing to witness, especially when a stranger brought the news. As many times as he had done it, it was never easy. He could only imagine how hard it would be for Dionne. He also knew she would do it. "Let's try not to get killed, ok?"

"Deal. Let's go to that restaurant. I could use a glass of wine."

"Or two."

# 64

Father Lordo had returned to his Vatican apartment after being held another hour by Simon's man. He quickly packed some clothes and a few personal mementos. He left behind the crucifix that the Cardinal had given him when he started at the Vatican. He had a suitcase with a false bottom that he had used to bring money back to the Cardinal from the clients who had purchased papers and passage. He had held back a portion for such an occasion as this. It would be, along with the false passports he had procured for himself and Marie, enough to get them out of the country to a place where they could be together. He believed that, as long as he disappeared, the Cardinal would forget about him. He felt a sense of regret that he could no longer be a priest but also a sense of relief that he and Marie could move on.

He was able to slip out of the Vatican unseen, or so he thought. He went straight to Marie's apartment, taking no precautions to avoid being followed. When he got to Marie's apartment, there was a small crowd across the street from the entrance. As he approached, he saw several police cars and an ambulance. As he was trying to get closer, he saw two men bringing out a stretcher. Somehow he knew that the body was Marie's. He was too late. He had brought her into this, and now her death was on his hands. He also knew he had to get away fast. Whoever had killed Marie knew who he was. Marie had been the easier target. Now that he had fled the Vatican, he would be much easier to find if he did not disappear quickly.

Kleet and Dimitri had split up at the bakery. Kleet had followed Lordo back to the Vatican while Dimitri had followed Monroe and Simon back to their safe house. They had agreed to meet in three hours. Each had called agents to continue surveillance in their absence. In addition, the train stations and ports were covered.

Kleet waited at the Vatican until he saw the priest leaving with his suitcase. It was no challenge following him as he headed toward his girlfriend's apartment. Kleet was as surprised as the priest when he saw the police at the apartment. It was pretty clear that whoever was behind this was tying up loose ends. The priest would likely be next and would be little challenge to the assassins.

As Lordo moved away from Marie's apartment, Kleet sidled up to him and pressed his gun into the priest's back. "Easy does it Padre. Let's take a walk."

"Why should I go with you? You killed Marie and now you are going to kill me."

"Well, first, I didn't kill your girlfriend. Second, I don't think you'll call the police. You're a priest in civilian clothes, carrying a suitcase, which I would bet has money and false passports in it. I don't think you want the police looking into that."

Kleet moved Lordo along toward where Dimitri was watching Monroe and Simon at the safe house. The priest offered no resistance. He seemed resigned to whatever awaited him. When they met Dimitri, Kleet quickly updated him on what had happened to Marie. Dimitri knew of a place where they could question the priest and find out what he had told Monroe. They waited until one of Dimitri's men came to watch the safe house.

# 65

Dimitri shoved Lordo into a chair and raised a hand to strike him. Kleet stepped in and pushed Dimitri back. "Father, my Russian friend here wants some answers from you. I am sure he will get them. Now, I consider myself to be a bit more civilized, so I'm going to offer you a deal. The people who killed your girlfriend are coming after you. Considering how easy it was for us to find you, I am pretty sure they will too. So, here's my proposition. You are going to answer all of our questions one way or another. If we can save time and can get on with our business, I am prepared to get you out of Rome to the United States, where no one will find you. If you choose the option to not cooperate, then my friend here will get the answers we need, and we will leave you to your fate."

"Why should I trust you?"

"I really don't see that you have a lot of choices." Lordo said nothing but nodded his head.

"Let's begin by you telling us what you told the men who took you to the bakery."

"They wanted to know about a man who I had helped get papers to get out of the country. I did not know who the man was but  he is important. I sent them to the forger that we use for passports."

"And where was this man trying to go?"

"That's what was unusual. He did not want to go to South America, where most of them go. He wanted to get on a ship going to the east."

"Where in the east?"

"He said Beirut or Haifa."

"Which one? "

"I told him Beirut would be easier. The British are watching Haifa, trying to keep out Jews. He didn't seem to be worried about that. Said he had friends."

"If you knew which port would be the safest for him to land, you would also know the safest route," Kleet said indicating that it was a fact not a question.

Lordo was now a the point where he actually wanted to help these men, almost like a confession of sins. He would seek absolution later from God. Maybe this was a start.

"I told him to go to Bari. Too many customs and police in Venice. There are freighters that go to the east, mostly to Greece but a few to Beirut and Haifa. The shipmasters are hungrier and ask fewer questions."

Kleet looked at Dimitri, who nodded his head. The priest had nothing more to offer. They left him and went into the other room.

Kleet said, "I will call my people. They will take him to the embassy and then get him out of Rome, but first I imagine they will want to know a little bit more information about that network. That's not my concern nor is how they get it. I'll have them get what they can about ships that go to Haifa and Beirut. Maybe we can find out something, but I doubt they keep passenger manifests. By the way, you did a pretty good job in there playing the tough guy. I think it made him talk a lot quicker. "

"I wasn't playing," said Dimitri.

Dimitri and Kleet decided to split up. Kleet waited for one of his people to pick up Father Lordo while Dimitri went to check on his man watching Monroe and Dionne from an off duty taxi near their apartment. He found him just as the American and the girl were leaving. Dimitri noticed someone he did not recognize head in the same direction as the couple. The bulge in his jacket appeared to be a weapon. The man looked to be alone. He told his man to continue following Monroe and Dionne on foot from the other side of the street while he followed the new player.

Monroe and Dionne abruptly ducked into a restaurant. Dimitri's man remained across the narrow street.The couple's quick move forced the stranger to slow his pace. When he did, Dimitri quickened his and bumped into the man causing him to stumble. As Dimitri helped him up, he shoved a knife up into the man's chest, killing him instantly, and dragged him into an alley bordering the street. He quickly searched him. There was no identification. He was carrying a revolver. Dimitri dragged him behind two garbage cans that looked like they had not been emptied for days. He crossed the street and told his man to continue to follow the couple. He would go back to the taxi and wait for Kleet.

# 66

Monroe and Dionne ate quietly. The "talk" had left both in a contemplative mood. After a glass of wine they both relaxed a bit. They ordered the house pasta dish followed by veal parmigiana. Dionne talked about life in Montreal and spending her summers as a child at a friend's lake cottage. "It's so peaceful, you forget what day it is. It never gets too hot.  The water is crystal clear and always cold because the lake is spring fed."

Monroe said, "I grew up in the city.  Hot as hell  in the summer.  We used to go to a pool in the park.  It wasn't much cooler.  I think I would have liked yours better."

Dionne smiled, "I hope you get to see it when all this is over."

"Speaking of which, I'm no spy, or maybe just a tad paranoid, but I just felt someone was following us.  I couldn't really turn around and get a good look so I don't know for sure."

"I should have been more careful.  I've been trained to spot that kind of thing.  My mind was elsewhere.  We need to be more careful on the way back.  You could have been right.  A little paranoia is necessary in this situation."

They left about an hour later.  Dionne took them across the street to avoid the alley next to the restaurant.  They stopped a couple of times to look in shop windows and once to get gelato from a street vendor but couldn't detect anyone following them.  When they arrived at the safe house, Simon was waiting for them inside after taking the ledger to Avrum's people.

"The ledger is on its way to Vienna.  I also had a copy made for Avrum in case there is any mishap.  We have people in South America who are looking for Nazis.  The world can never forget what happened to our people. Now we have to decide our next steps in finding Bormann."

"It seems to me based on what we've learned so far that he is heading east," said Monroe.

"Yes, based on what Marie said, but I am concerned that that may be a deception, allowing Bormann to disappear in Latin America. After all, he will have his compatriots there as well as sympathetic politicians to help him establish a new persona," replied Simon.

"I believe Marie," said Dionne. "She was not directly involved in all of this, so I think her information is more credible."

"Unless they fooled her, too," answered Simon.

"I don't think so. Lordo cared too much about her to lie to her."

Monroe was becoming impatient. "We can go back-and-forth about this all day. Meanwhile, Bormann gets farther away. I've been thinking about what we've learned so far. There are a few pieces of evidence that take us east. First, Bormann used the Mufti to set up his Swiss bank accounts. If he were going to South America, there were certainly people around him who could have made that possible. The Mufti has no organization in South America as far as we can tell. He does have significant resources in the Middle East. It's also not a place where the allies and even your people are looking for war criminals. Second, from what we know of Bormann, he seems to have been sort of a shadowy figure but a survivor, nevertheless. He's a planner. He opened his Swiss accounts with the Mufti when the outcome of the war was still in doubt. We really have no idea what the other high-ranking Nazis thought of him. Maybe he didn't trust them or they him, so he decided to go where they weren't. They would have wanted us to go east, while Bormann escaped elsewhere."

"You make a compelling case, doctor. Maybe you should have been a lawyer."

"It was my mother's third choice right after dentist," answered Monroe.

"Nevertheless, we cannot afford to be wrong."

"I agree with Jack," said Dionne.

"As I would expect," replied Simon.

Dionne looked at Simon with daggers. "I agree with him because the facts support his argument."

"I'm sorry. I know you are trying to help us make the right decision, but I cannot afford to put all of our energy to go east without more certainty," answered Simon.

"I have an idea," said Monroe. "Let's split up. Dionne and I can work on the 'east' angle. You can check out the people that the Nazis have used to get to South America. We should have enough information from the forger's log to help us. If we can confirm that Bormann is headed east, then we can follow and meet up in Haifa or Beirut. It sounds to me like you have plenty of people there who can help us."

"Too dangerous for the two of you," answered Simon.

"I think we've proven ourselves," replied Dionne.

"And besides, we don't have time to look in both directions together," said Monroe.

"Let's just say you are correct. How will you get to Beirut or especially Haifa? The British are watching Haifa very closely to keep out Jews and placate the Arabs. The British only care about managing their colonial empire with as little trouble as possible."

"Simon, you have family in Beirut. Perhaps they can be of help to us, maybe even smuggle us into Haifa," said Dionne.

"I also think that maybe Avrum, with the help of Mr. Morton, could help us evade British surveillance," offered Monroe.

Still somewhat reluctant, Simon agreed. "The two of you will go to Bari and see if we can get concrete information that Bormann is heading east. I will stay here and see what I can find out at the port of Rome. We will then meet wherever the information takes us. I will get a car to take you to Bari. We have an agent who helped smuggle Jews out of Italy. He knows all of the freighter captains who might smuggle someone like Bormann."

# 67

Nearby, Dimitri was updating Kleet. He told him about killing the armed Arab who was tracking Monroe and the girl. "I guess I owe you. You may have saved my guy, " said Kleet.

"It was in my interest," replied Dimitri. "I think most of the evidence that the priest gave points toward Bormann heading east. I don't know if your doctor and his friends have the same information. It may be time for us to go east on our own. My mission is to find Bormann. So far, our interests have been compatible but may not be any longer."

Kleet was at a crossroads. He could stop Monroe now and leave Bormann to Dimitri, but as before his curiosity about the Russian's interest in Bormann won out. "My people are checking out the port of Rome. If they see the doctor heading that direction, then I have to follow. I'll leave Bormann to you. If they go east, I think we can still help each other. So, until we see them move, I say we stick together," replied Kleet.

"Very well. We have assets in Beirut and Haifa. I will alert them. Oh, since I saved the doctor, can I have my weapon back?"

While Kleet was reluctant to give the Russian his weapon back, but things were getting more precarious. "Here. Just remember, I'm one of the good guys."

Dimitri took it and smiled. "For now."

# 68

The drive to Bari was uneventful. Simon had gotten word through contacts that the Chief of the Customs House at the Port was amenable to providing information for a price.

Monroe and Dionne developed a plan on the way to Bari to try to get information on Bormann without revealing their own identities. They found the customs house rather easily. They entered and asked to speak to the person in charge. After a short wait, an officious looking man greeted them, acting as if their visit was an inconvenience in his busy day. "How may I help you?"

Dionne spoke very quietly, her voice breaking. "It's my uncle. We are trying to find him. We've been looking for weeks. The last we heard he was in a displaced person's camp. Someone there told us he might be headed to Beirut or maybe Haifa. Please, can you help us? We're desperate."

"There are many people who come through this port, and since the war many are refugees. I don't think I can be of service to you. Is there anything else?"

"As you can see, my cousin is desperate to find our uncle," said Monroe. "Maybe you could direct us to someone else who might be able to help. We would be willing to pay for information on my uncle's whereabouts."

The official took a quick look around. "Maybe we should step into my office. I might be able to help you after all."

The three of them entered the small office with a desk and only one chair. Dionne set opposite the customs official continuing to dab her eyes with a handkerchief. Monroe stood.

"The information that you seek is very difficult to come by. I may have to pay ship's pursers or crewmen to find out about your uncle. Of course, I charge a modest fee for my services. The price may be higher if he is a Jew. Is he? Are you?"

"We are people looking for information and are willing to pay for it," answered Monroe.

"When do you need the information?"

"The sooner the better, within 24 hours."

"That will be very expensive, 200,000 lira."

"100,000 lira."

"You insult me. You are asking quite a lot and are unwilling to pay for it."

"125,000 lira – in US dollars. "

"Very well. I will need the money in advance."

Monroe gave him $50 from money that Simon had given them for this very purpose. "You'll get the rest when we have the information."

"Come back tomorrow. The office is closed between 12 and two for lunch. I will be here."

"We saw an open air market at the entrance to the port. There is a stall selling women's purses. We will meet you there. Come alone. If your information looks convincing, there is an extra twenty in it for you."

Monroe and Dionne gave him the information they had on Ludwig Schreiber and left the port. They found a small hotel in town and ate at a restaurant next door.

"I could get used to the pasta and the wine here. You were very convincing. I think he might've even felt the slightest bit sorry for you," said Monroe.

"I can be a very sympathetic character when I choose to be," laughed Dionne with that smile Monroe couldn't resist. "Do you trust him?"

"We really don't have much choice. Time is not on our side. Besides, I think I bribed him with more money than he makes in a month on a government salary. He'll get us the information, if he can. We just have to be careful after we get it. He could easily be playing two sides."

They met the customs official the next day at the market. He handed them a copy of Schreiber's exit papers. "Your uncle left on a freighter for Haifa. The name of the ship is there along with the captain's. You are fortunate. The ship is returning to Bari tomorrow. I know the captain. He will cooperate with you, for a slight fee, of course."

Dionne thanked the man effusively. Monroe gave him the rest of his money, and his bonus as promised.

"We need to get word to Simon to get here right away," said Dionne. "We need to talk to that captain and, while I love you dearly, I think he will make a more threatening impression."

"No argument here."

They decided to stay at a different hotel that night in case they were being followed. "Nothing to do but wait until tomorrow," said Monroe.

"I imagine you'll think of something."

"Again, no argument here."

# 69

Simon arrived the next morning. Dionne updated him on what they had found out at the port. "I think we are close," she said.

"Closer than you think," answered Simon. "While I was in Rome, I met with a colleague of Desmond Morton. The British looked into Monod's bank. Apparently, money has gone from there to anti-British Arab groups in Palestine, which supports our theory that the Mufti could be involved with ex-Nazis. They have not identified any higher ups, yet."

"Maybe this ship captain can give us another piece of the puzzle. Somebody had to pay him. I bet he charges a lot to overlook certain irregularities and keep quiet. My impression from the customs guy was that this is a regular sideline business," said Monroe.

"There is more. Doctor, when you went to the autopsy, were you shown any photos of Bormann?"

"Just a picture of Hitler and his cronies taken from a distance with Bormann in the background. Dr. Monod passed it around quickly and said it was Bormann. The body was close enough in appearance and the picture grainy enough that we took his word for it."

Simon took out a photo and showed it to Monroe and Dionne. "I got this from Morton's man. It was taken in Munich, before the war, when the Munich Agreement was signed. Of course he was younger, but it's him."

"He doesn't look like much," said Dionne.

Monroe looked at the photo. Bormann's head was looking down at his dinner plate as if he really didn't want to be photographed, but his face was clear. He was the man in Monod's picture. He had no particularly outstanding features. He could have been any faceless bureaucrat.

"Let's go see if the ship's captain recognizes him."

"He might lie to us for the money and say that's who he took, and then we end up wasting more time," said Dionne.

"I brought three other pictures, all of cousins of mine. He will have to earn his money," said Simon.

"What if he won't talk?"

"If our generous offer does not persuade, I will persuade him to tell us for nothing," said Simon in a very matter of fact tone.

The ship was not much bigger than a trawler. It was called the *Bella Regina*. It was neither beautiful nor regal, just one of hundreds of ships that sailed the Mediterranean.

A crewman unloading cargo told them that they could find the captain in a tavern not far away and gave them a description. Monroe and Dionne had been given his name by the customs official. The bar was a seedy place, just the way Monroe would have imagined, smokey, a few tables, sailors keeping mostly to themselves and a few barmaids who went about their business looking bored.

Captain Antonio Civelli was sitting in the back of the bar entertaining a woman who was clearly a "professional." He was unshaven and wore a uniform that looked like it hadn't been laundered for a while. He had a red kerchief around his neck that the sailor had told them about.

They walked back to the table. Simon spoke first. "Captain, my friends and I are looking for some information, about a relation of ours that may have gone on a voyage with you."

Civelli was irritated at being disturbed. "I take many people on many voyages. I can't help you."

"We can pay you."

"I'm listening."

"Why doesn't your friend here go have a drink with my associate?" Civelli jerked his head to the side, indicating that the girl should leave. Dionne not so gently escorted her to another table. Dionne signaled the waitress to bring them a couple of drinks.

Simon and Monroe turned back to Civelli. "How much are you willing to pay?"

"One hundred American dollars to talk. One hundred more if your information proves to be reliable," answered Simon.

"Five hundred American dollars now."

"One hundred now and another two hundred if the information is good."

"I will need at least another $50," he said, looking over at the girl. "And maybe another $50 for your friend?"

Monroe covered Civelli's hand and strategically put pressure on his wrist. Civelli cried out in pain. Monroe did not let up. "You're not very funny. I think you should agree to my friend's offer. I'm sure that he is insulted as well. Our next offer will involve how many fingers you wish not to be broken."

"All right, all right. I agree. Please let go."

Simon had said nothing and almost looked amused at Monroe's outburst. He put $100 on the table that Civelli snatched up and put in his pocket.

"You took a man to Haifa several weeks ago. I am going to show you his picture. I want you to tell me everything that you know about him." Simon laid four photographs on the table. "Is the man you took to Haifa one of the men in these pictures?" Civelli pretended to study each picture very carefully, but it was clear he recognized Bormann's photo immediately.

"It's this one," he said, pointing at Bormann's photo.

"Tell me about him. His name? What did he talk about? Did he say where he was going after he landed? Was anyone else with him? Did anyone meet him at Haifa?"

"His name was Schroeder or Schreiber or something like that. He was very quiet, spent most of the voyage in his cabin. He paid me in Swiss francs. He never talked about where he was going or where he had come from. He was clearly German. A soldier maybe. He was used to giving orders. I didn't like him, you understand, but one has to make a living."

"What about when you got to Haifa?"

"He stayed on board until after dark. Two Arabs came looking for him. He did not know them, but they handed him a note. After he read it, he went with them to a car on the dock. They drove away, and I never saw him again. "

"Our business is done. Do not tell anyone about our conversation. Mr. Schreiber's friends would be very upset if they found out about it." Simon gave the captain the rest of his money. Before they left the bar, Monroe leaned over and whispered something to the captain's girl.

Once they reached the street, Simon outlined their next move. "I think we can now be sure that Bormann is somewhere in Palestine. I suspect the two Arabs who fetched him work for the Mufti. Mr. Morton has agreed to provide a plane for the two of you to go to Palestine. If we find Bormann, the doctor will need to identify him so we can show that he is not dead. It will be much more credible coming from an American, especially one who was involved in the original case."

"I'll go, but Dionne doesn't need to be exposed to the risk." As soon as he said it, Monroe realized that his chivalry was in vain.

"I'm going. We are a team. And let's face it, I'm better at this 'spy stuff' as you call it than you are."

Monroe started to argue, but realized there was no chance in winning. Besides, he was actually glad that she was coming.

"Are you coming with us Simon?" asked Dionne.

"Mr. Morton was able to get the British to fly an American doctor and the Canadian relief worker to Palestine. He didn't think it wise that a Jewish agent be on the plane. I will meet up with you. Avrum has arranged for my passage."

Later, as Monroe and Dionne rode to the airstrip, she asked, "What did you say to that girl in the bar?"

"Well, Civelli had made certain inquiries about your availability to him. I explained to him that you weren't that kind of girl."

"That was the yelp I heard."

"That was the yelp."

"That was very gallant," she said, and gave him a peck on the cheek. "But you didn't answer my question. What did you say to the girl?"

"I told her that the captain just got $300, and she might want to charge more."

# 70

Kleet entered the restaurant in Rome. He saw that Dimitri had already arrived and was waiting for him at a table in the back of the restaurant. Dimitri had taken the chair with its back to the wall, giving a him good view of the restaurant. Kleet took the seat across from him but looked around before he sat down.

Kleet spoke first. "My people at the port couldn't find out anything about any Germans leaving by illegal means. I'm sorry to admit it, but we have also lost track of Dr. Monroe.

We last saw him and the girl heading east toward a possible port on the Adriatic."

"They are going to Palestine. The British have arranged a plane to take them," answered Dimitri.

"You seem awfully sure."

"I cannot afford to guess. We have reliable sources at the port of Bari, who spotted a man and a woman fitting their descriptions. We have also tracked them to a British airbase. The British military attaché in Rome arranged for the flight."

"I don't suppose that you're going to tell me how you know what the British military attaché is doing."

"I don't really think it's relevant. You and I both have our informants and sources. Unfortunately, you in the west are often too trusting of others."

Kleet made a mental note to talk to an MI-6 friend and let him know they had a leak in their Rome embassy, although knowing MI-6 they had likely turned the leak into a double agent. "Does that include me trusting you?"

"We are both taking a risk, but we are both professionals and know that is what we must do."

"I can get us to Palestine. Just don't talk too much to the pilot or the crew. Your English is good, but not that good."

"We should get going. I'll make a point to practice my English for future missions. You never know when it will come in handy."

# 71

Simon flew to Beirut on a French passenger flight. He had a brief reunion with his family before he was smuggled across the Lebanese border into Palestine. Once there he was able to easily make his way to Haifa, where he met up with Joshua, another of Avrum's operatives.

"Your friends have arrived at the British airbase. They are meeting with a consular official, who in actuality is a member of MI-6, but we have a problem," said Joshua.

"What?"

"There is someone coming who will explain it."

A few minutes later, there was a knock at the door. Joshua opened the door and greeted a thin be-speckled man who looked more like an accountant than one of the leaders of the Irgun, a militant and sometimes violent Jewish underground group.

Menachim Begin smiled, "Don't look so surprised Simon. Avrum has briefed me on your mission. Even though we have different approaches, Avrum has always been good at maximizing his options. Where our interests have been in common, we of the Irgun are happy to cooperate."

"And what would those interests be?"

"We would like to see justice done for our people. We, like you, want to find the war criminals who killed so many."

"Our versions of justice are different. I want to find Bormann and bring him before the world. I have a feeling you have a more expeditious end for him."

"Simply a matter of emphasis. We can discuss that when we find him. Of more importance is that your friends may be in imminent danger. We have informants among the Arabs. We think that the Mufti knows your friends are coming. We believe that there are people in the British occupying forces who have been bribed by the Arabs. They may have provided information to the Mufti about your friends."

"Then we need to get to them before he does."

"We are happy to help."

"I appreciate that. If we find Bormann, I want your word that you will turn him over to me," said Simon.

"If we find him and he will come peaceably, then you may have him. If he poses a threat, I can make no promises."

"Very well. What now? I am to meet them in Jerusalem."

"Both we and the British know where the Mufti has his headquarters," answered Begin. "They leave him alone as long as he leaves them alone. Your friends may be walking into a trap. The British will not help them. I suggest that you and some of my Irgun boys go to Jerusalem and try to intercept your friends before the Mufti does. I brought along some clothes more appropriate for blending in."

While Begin and Simon were meeting, Kleet and Dimitri landed on a small airstrip outside of Tel Aviv. They were met by a swarthy little man in a wrinkled suit who reminded Kleet of Peter Lorre in Casablanca. Dimitri turned to Kleet with a suspicious look. "Who is this?"

"Don't underestimate him. Even though he may have a suit that is worse than yours, he's a man of many skills. He worked with us during the war to help get supplies to people sympathetic to the Allied cause."

"So he's an arms dealer, a smuggler."

"I like to think of him as a contractor."

"Can we trust him?"

"We pay him very well. We also know where to find his family. His information has always been reliable. He calls me Colonel Smith. I know him as Emil. I think it best if I don't introduce you. Here he comes."

"Welcome, my dear Colonel. I am happy to be of service to you. I have gotten the information you need, at great personal risk I might add. Of course, there were expenses involved that I need to cover. And, who is your friend?"

"Who my friend is, is not your concern. You'll be paid well as usual. As to your risk, it will be much greater if your information is unreliable."

"Colonel, my information is always reliable. That is why you pay me so well."

"OK, get on with it."

"Your friends landed at a British airbase. I have an associate who informed me that they were driven to meet a British diplomat who we all know is MI-6. My source told me that there were others trying to get the same information. They are associated with much more dangerous people."

"Who?"

"The Grand Mufti of Jerusalem. He is a most disreputable character. Even I stay away from him and his followers."

"Where is the Mufti now?"

"In Jerusalem, but I can't tell you anymore."

"Can you get us there?"

"I am at your disposal. Of course there will be an extra charge to cover transportation."

"OK, another 10%. Now let's get going."

# 72

After landing at the British airbase, Monroe and Dionne were taken to a shed just off the runway where they were met by a contact of Morton's who worked at the British Embassy. There were only two chairs in the room, so Monroe stood. The room must have been rarely used, given the layer of dust everywhere. There was one window cracked open and no breeze. The agent was no nonsense. Monroe took an immediate dislike to him.

"Welcome to Palestine. Mr. Morton has asked me to help you find a German who goes by Schreiber. Of course you realize that the British mission has no official role in your business. I owe Mr. Morton a debt, which is now paid. Are we clear?"

Of course, Mr...," answered Monroe.

"My name is of no concern, nor are yours to me. Let's get on with it shall we?"

"May I have a word with my associate?"

"You stay here. I'll step out. Wouldn't want you two to be seen, would we?"

After the man left, Dionne asked, "Should we wait for Simon? We don't know anything about this guy."

"I don't think he will wait for Simon. Let's see what he has to say. I don't like him either, but if Morton trusts him he's probably OK. He may be our best shot even if he is a putz."

"You sound like my uncle. He would hate the guy."

"He must be a very wise man. Let the guy back in."

"I hope the two of you are ready to move along."

They both nodded.

"We have an agent, Arab, who provides intelligence to us on the comings and goings of the Mufti and some of his thugs. A driver will take you to the old city to meet with him. Frankly, I don't think your Mr. Schreiber is anywhere in this area, and that all this is a red herring. I've done as I have been asked." He handed Dionne a hijab. "Best wear this. Sit in the back of the jeep and walk a little behind the men. Less suspicious. I doubt we will see each other again. Good luck." He walked out of the shack, said something to a waiting driver, got in his own car and left.

"I hate that guy," said Monroe under his breath.

Their driver said nothing as they headed toward the Old City.

"Where are you taking us?" asked Monroe.

"I am taking you to meet Mr Abadi. He is a hawaladar."

"A what?"

"Hawaladar. A banker of sorts. In our world money is transferred by them. They are a network. I give money to you, you give me a note that I take to another hawaladar who gives me the money on the note. The two hawaladar later settle up. It is a system based on trust and has been around for hundreds of years. I think you had similar systems in the West long ago as well."

"So it's banking without banks or governments looking over your shoulder."

Dionne leaned forward and whispered into Monroe's ear, " Between the Swiss and this, Bormann could move his money and never be traced."

"I have a feeling Mr. Abadi may not be forthcoming with information. We'll check it out. We may need to get Simon to use his powers of persuasion."

Abadi's "bank" was a coffee shop that opened onto an alley. "How do you think we should do this?" asked Dionne.

"Hopefully they don't know we're coming.  I think that we tell him a friend of ours needs money and we would like to transfer it through him.   We use Bormann's alias and see how he responds.  If he allows us to proceed, we follow the money to Bormann.  If he won't do business, that will tell us something as well.  Then we come back with Simon and see if we can persuade him to give us the information we need.  In either case we should be able to get closer to Bormann."

"What if they know we're coming?"

"The only way they would know would be an informant in the British delegation or someone who works there.  I can't see our British contact having a gin and tonic with a local at a club.  He would think it beneath him."

They entered the shop.  Dionne was careful to stay one step behind Monroe.  A middle-aged man in traditional Arab dress walked out from behind the counter.  "Welcome, how may I help you?  May I offer you some coffee?"

Monroe knew it would be impolite to refuse.  Abadi gave him a small cup and took one for himself.  Dionne was ignored.  Monroe was a coffee drinker but had never tasted anything this strong.  His expression must have shown it.

Abadi smiled.  "The coffee is from India and the spices are from Ethiopia."

"Thank you. It is very good." They made small talk for a few more minutes as was the custom before getting down to business.

"A friend of ours told us about you. He said that we could use you to get some money to him without going through a bank. His name is Schreiber. He said that he had done business with you and that you were very reliable and discreet."

"How much money do you want to transfer?"

Simon had given Monroe 5,000 pounds to use in Palestine. "We would like to send him 2,000 pounds."

"And where do I find this Mr. Schreiber?"

"I don't have his exact address. I know that he is in Palestine. He told me that he would come to you to get the money."

"Why not give it to him yourself?"

"He moves around quite a bit. He felt it would be easier to work through you."

"Do you have the money? There is also a service fee of 50 pounds."

Monroe took the bills out of an envelope that Simon had given him and gave them to Abadi, who counted them and gave Monroe a receipt. "I will hold this for 2 weeks. If your Mr. Schreiber does not claim it, then I will donate it to charity, minus a deposit fee of course."

"Of course," answered Monroe. They heard the call to prayer. Abadi opened the door, signaling their business was concluded.

When they were a few yards away from the shop Dionne said, "He didn't seem upset when we mentioned Schreiber's name. Now we wait and see if he tries to contact Schreiber."

"Now we wait," echoed Monroe.

"We should contact Simon. I have a number of one of Avrum's men who will know where he is."

"Let's head out to the market. There must be a phone somewhere."

As they turned toward the market their way was blocked by two Arab men. Monroe then felt the barrel of a gun in his back. One of them spoke, "Herr Schreiber has been expecting you. We are going to take you to him. Please do not try and run. My friend has a knife that will go into the girl's back."

"I knew there was something I didn't like about that British guy."

Monroe and Dionne were taken to a car and shoved into the backseat. One man sat across from them and another next to Dionne, no longer hiding his knife. Both of their hands were tied and hoods put over their heads. "I guess we found him," thought Monroe.

# 73

Kleet and Dimitri were in a cab headed toward the Old City. One of Dimitri's sources had told them to seek out Abadi as well. The source had confirmed that if anybody knew what was happening in the Old City, it would be him.

"How are we going to handle this?" asked Kleet. "This guy seems to be well connected and may have security."

"We can try the American way of being nice and hope that he will be nice in return, or we can try the Russian way and get an answer."

"I think you are painting Americans with a broad brush. We are running out of time and need answers. I will let you take the lead. Just don't kill too many people."

As the taxi drew near the hawaladar's shop, they both noticed two Arab men going in the same direction.

"If your doctor is in that shop they may be in danger. It looks like he was expected," said Dimitri. He told the taxi driver to pull over and let them out. "I will approach them from behind. You try and get in front of them from across

the street. We need to get to them before they get to the
shop and the doctor."

"Got it," said Kleet. He pulled out his 45 and checked it.
They left the taxi and tried to catch up with the two men
without being too obvious. The men did not expect any
pursuers so were unaware when Dimitri closed in. Dimitri
came up behind the trailing man and shoved his gun into his
back. "Don't make a sound, or I will kill you," he said. Just
as he spoke, the leader turned around and pulled his own
weapon. That move allowed Kleet to get behind him.

"Tell your men to drop their weapons or the two of you
are dead men." The men did as instructed. "Now turn
around slowly." As the man turned around Kleet muttered,
"Oh shit. It's you." By now Dimitri had pushed his man
closer.

"Do you two know each other?" Dimitri asked.

"This is the guy who works with the girl that we are
following. I assume he has been following them as well. So
who are you? You're not an American or Russian. Are you
working for the Brits?"

Simon answered, "Neither, I work with a Jewish
organization. I am trying to find Dionne and the doctor like
you are. I was hoping that they would lead us to Bormann,
but I am more worried about their own safety. We need to
move, now."

"OK, let's go. We'll sort out the politics later," said Kleet. He looked at Dimitri, "I think these guys are OK." Dimitri shrugged indicating his agreement. Kleet gave Simon his weapon back. Simon whistled and two more of his men appeared. "You knew we were following you?" said Kleet, somewhat chagrined.

"Let's just say we are always careful in this part of Jerusalem." As the two newcomers approached one pointed ahead of them and shouted, "Look, the car." They all turned and saw Monroe and Dionne shoved into a car that quickly sped off.

"We need to follow them," said Kleet.

"In this part of the city they will disappear in minutes," said Simon. He said something to his men in Hebrew. Two of them ran off. "They are going to get a car and to contact their superior who may have some idea where the two of them are being taken. While they are doing that, we will go speak to the hawaladar." He looked at Kleet and Dimitri. " You two go in through the front. I will go around back in case he runs."

Kleet and Dimitri went in to the store. No one seemed to be around. "Anybody here?" yelled Kleet, raising his gun. They heard a noise in the back of the store and rushed back. They ran into Simon, who shoved Abadi back into the store at gunpoint and threw him down into a chair.

"Where are they taking them," demanded Simon. Abadi spit at him. "I will not tell you, Jew. The Mufti will take care of you and your kind." Simon was about to strike him when Kleet intervened.

"Well, Mr Abadi. I am not one of his kind nor do I care about your Holy War. I care about the two people that you just had taken away. So, here's what's going to happen. I'm going to burn up all these little papers of yours which I imagine will piss off the Mufti, but that will be later. He pulled out his gun and stuck it at Abadi's knee. "Right now, if you don't start talking, I'm going to make sure you don't walk right again, then I'm going to turn you over to my Russian friend here who won't be as kind."

Abadi looked at Kleet and Dimitri who shot him in the knee. "He was taking too long. You can do the other one."

"You are animals," screamed Abadi.

"You have no idea," said Kleet as he raised his gun.

"They are going to take them to the Mufti," said Abadi.

"Where?" said Simon in Arabic. Abadi answered back. Simon nodded his head. "I know the place. It is not far. We will get there at dark which should help us." He then spoke to his men in Hebrew. He turned back to Abadi. "You will show these two men where the Mufti's hawalah are. After they are satisfied, they will get you a doctor. If you hurry, you may not lose your leg."

"Why not just burn them all? It will be much easier," said Dimitri.

"Most of the people who use hawala are not criminals. We have no quarrel with them."

"Your nobility is admirable but will not win you any friends. A little fear will go a longer way," said Dimitri. He turned to Abadi. "Do as they say or I will come back and no doctor will save you then."

Just then one of Simon's men came in and whispered something to him in Hebrew, "The cars are here. We must go now."

# 74

Monroe and Dionne were taken inside a building and tied to chairs next to each other. There was an armed guard behind each one of them. Their hoods were removed. The room was more like a living room than the dimly lit rooms portrayed in spy movies.

The door opened. Two men came in. One was an Arab dressed in Western clothes who sat down on a cloth chair with ornate wooden arms. Behind him came a Western man in civilian clothing who, from the pictures Monroe had seen was Martin Bormann. He was middle height, overweight, and balding. He had no truly distinguishing features and wore a linen suit. For some reason, Monroe noticed that he had manicured nails. The perfect functionary, someone no one would remember. It would be easy to underestimate the position and power Bormann once held. The Arab spoke first. "You are here because you have interfered with our affairs. I wanted to deal with you as I dealt with the others. You eluded my men in London and Paris and later in Switzerland. I could have disposed of you here in the city, but Herr Schreiber insisted I bring you here. He has questions for you. Answering them may make your end less painful, especially for the girl. My men will have their way with her. You will watch, unless you cooperate."

Monroe was sure that they were going to die no matter what he said. He needed to stall. Maybe Simon would find them. "Let the girl go and I will cooperate. She knows nothing."

"Very gallant of you. She was in Germany. She knows something. We will keep her here. If we are satisfied with your answers. She will die quickly. Herr Schreiber has some questions."

Bormann sat down next to the Arab and turned to Monroe. "I think we can dispense with formalities as I think the good doctor knows who I am. Am I correct doctor?"

"You look like Martin Bormann, but we all know he's dead," answered Monroe. Bormann nodded and the guard struck Monroe across the face. He could taste the blood.

"I have no time for your impertinence. Yes, I am alive, no thanks to you," sneered Bormann.

"Excuse me?" said Monroe. "What do I have to do with it? I would have preferred it had been you on that table, then I wouldn't be here."

"Stalin was to protect me. Instead he thinks me a traitor and sent you to assassinate me," accused Bormann.

Monroe was totally confused now. He needed to keep Bormann talking. "I'm not a Russian and I certainly don't know Stalin."

"So you are not Russian, but you are one of us, one of the many infiltrators Stalin sent to the west before the war. "

"If you kill me, others will come," lied Monroe.

"And they will fail, too. Eventually, I will disappear and Stalin will give up."

Now even the Arab was interested. "What are you talking about, Bormann? You worked for Herr Hitler. I helped you escape."

"For which you were well paid," said Bormann. "I helped you and your fellow Arabs get the arms you needed to cause turmoil for the British and to kill Jews as well. You also made a nice profit for yourself from the Mufti's accounts. I found out from the Swiss banker early on. The money didn't add up. I didn't care because I got what I was promised. The arrangement worked for me. I knew if the Mufti found you out, it would end.

Bormann continued, "Now, I may as well tell you the whole story. We each will have something on the other. The arrangement can continue as before. I was an agent of the Soviet Union. I was sent to Germany in the 30's to help stir up revolutionary movements using Communist groups in Germany, one of many who were sent to Western Europe and the United States to infiltrate political parties and governments. I met Hitler and joined the Nazi Party. I was able to get close to Hitler. I became his right hand. As Hitler became more powerful, my mission was to influence him to make decisions that would help the Soviet Union. I was to nudge him toward defeat, all the while letting him and his generals think that they had made the decisions."

Monroe was incredulous. Bormann, a Russian spy? He interrupted, trying to sound confident, "And then you screwed up."

Bormann lashed out. "Hitler became too confident of his successes against the British and the French. He started to think about attacking Russia. I persuaded him to finish the British first to buy time so the Red Army could be built up, maybe even invade Germany. England didn't break, so Hitler moved up the invasion of Russia. I couldn't dissuade him. No one could. Hitler and I were flown to his East Prussian headquarters before the attack. I had no way to warn Stalin. Russia lost millions of people. I was sure Stalin would blame me. Since it looked like Hitler was actually going to win, I just switched sides to the Germans. Then came Stalingrad. I knew I was now going to be on the losing side, so I joined forces with the Mufti. He helped me get money out of Germany, and we developed a plan to make it look like I had been killed. Then Stalin ordered you, one of his American agents, to find me."

Monroe decided to raise the ante. "Let me go. I can get word to Comrade Stalin that you were loyal, that it was beyond your control. You might still be useful to us."

"You know as well as I do that Stalin makes up his mind and never turns back. If Stalin saw you here begging for your life, he would have you killed as well. At least I will accomplish that end for him."

The Arab stood. "I have heard enough. Take them out and shoot them. We have more important things to do."

Monroe looked at Dionne. "Sorry," he mouthed. With tears in her eyes, she smiled, "Je t'aime."

As the Arab stood, there was commotion outside. There were other Arabs attacking. Shooting started. Both of the guards holding Monroe and Dionne went down. Monroe felt a searing pain in his right arm but managed to tip his chair and knock Dionne out of the line of fire. The Arab with Bormann pulled out a revolver and pointed it at Monroe. The Arab's head then exploded. When Monroe looked up, he could see it was Simon dressed as an Arab who had fired the shot. All the guards were neutralized. Bormann raised his hands in surrender when another man walked up to him, said something in Russian, and shot him three times in the chest and once to the head. Then Dimitri was gone. Someone grabbed Monroe and untied him. "Doc you are one pain in the ass." It was Kleet. He helped Monroe to a waiting vehicle. Monroe saw Simon taking Dionne with him. They sped off in opposite directions.

Monroe and Kleet were taken to a clinic where Monroe's wound was found to be superficial and sutured closed. Soon after, Simon arrived.

"What's going on? Where's Dionne?" asked Monroe.

"She is all right. We are getting her out of the country and back home."

"I need to see her."

"Sorry, Doc, no can do," answered Kleet. "We're not even supposed to be here."

"What about what just happened back there? What about Bormann and his Arab friend?"

Simon answered, "Well, Bormann is dead. You signed a report to that effect in Germany. The Mufti's assistant was killed by another Arab, or that's what the story will be. We will get word to the Mufti that his assistant was stealing from him. He will not dispute the public story. It would make him look bad in the eyes of his supporters."

"Wait, I have more questions."

"That's the problem with you doc. Always more questions. Let's go now. We'll talk on the way home."

# 75

Home turned out to be just that. Monroe and Kleet were flown to England and put on a plane to the US. Monroe was exhausted and fell asleep after takeoff. He awoke when they were halfway over the Atlantic. Kleet was sitting across from him nursing a drink. "Need anything, Doc?"

"Answers."

"I'm not sure you're entitled to any. You left your duty station under suspicious circumstances, met with the former head of a foreign power, then went off on a mission of your own without orders or approval. The people you went with aren't recognized as legitimate by any power."

"So let me understand this. You, with the help of the very same people that I was working with, and some guy who spoke with a Russian accent, were on a sanctioned mission to rescue me? It's a great story. I'm sure the New York Times would love it."

"I would advise not making any real or implied threats. We can make sure that the New York Times is not interested in your story. However, I know you won't give up. I'll tell you what I can now. You'll learn more when we get to DC. My job was to keep you out of trouble. You made it extremely difficult, requiring me to take measures that I would otherwise not have taken. The Russian and I needed to find you but had different goals. I wanted to get you the hell out of there and avoid embarrassment for the United States. He, for whatever reason, wanted Bormann dead. We both accomplished our mission."

"I think I know why he wanted Bormann dead. Bormann himself told me." Monroe then told Kleet about Bormann's mission as a Soviet agent in the Third Reich. "Bormann made it sound like he was a patriot for Russia. In the end, he was nothing more than a self-centered opportunist."

"Well, then, I guess Dimitri did us a favor."

Monroe didn't know whether he should tell Kleet about Bormann bragging about Russian agents in the United States government. After all, Kleet might be one of them. But Kleet had saved his life when he very easily could have eliminated him. He just didn't look like a traitor. Monroe decided to trust him. "There's more. Bormann said that there were others like him in influential positions in other countries, including ours. At first he actually thought I was a Russian agent sent to kill him."

Kleet actually started to laugh at that. "Doc, you are many things, but you're just not devious or cynical enough to be a spy."

"You mean a spy like you."

"My reasons for doing what I do are not that simple. I will tell you that I am first a soldier. This is the way I know how to serve."

"This whole thing has gotten me thinking back to the beginning. Why was I chosen for this mission? I knew that I did not have the professional credentials for the job. I was told it was because of the Senator that I got the job. I know the Senator. I would not be the first person on his list for any kind of a mission. Someone put the bug in his ear. Whoever that is may be a Russian agent."

"Doc, I may be wrong about you. You are devious enough to be a spy. I'll look into it when we land."

"Thanks. How soon after we land can I see Dionne?"

"I knew you'd be asking about her. I can tell you that she's safe. I imagine that she is on her way to Canada. Given what you've just told me you both may be in danger. When we land they're going to want to keep you in protective custody and debrief you. Should only be a few days."

Monroe went on to tell Kleet about the British diplomat who had betrayed him and Dionne. "We figured something like that was going on. I'll handle it." They spent the rest of the flight in silence.

A few days turned out to be over two weeks. Monroe was under virtual house arrest. He was able to call his mother to tell her that he was all right but knew all of his calls were being monitored.

One day, Kleet returned with a civilian. "Doc, this gentleman is going to bring you up-to-date about what you and I talked about on the airplane. He works for a government agency that has been investigating Soviet espionage in the United States."

"Good morning doctor. I work for the FBI. My name is not important. We looked into your theory about a Russian agent influencing the Senator. It turns out that his aide on the intelligence committee was being blackmailed by the Russians because he was a homosexual. He reported the activities of the committee to his Russian handler. When Bormann's name came up, it must have spiked interest in Moscow. He somehow knew about your connection to the Senator and used that to get you assigned to the mission. When we confronted the aide, he confessed to his activities. He even told us who his handler was. Unfortunately, the handler has diplomatic privilege and is on his way back to Moscow to face the consequences of failure."

"And the aide?"

"Hung himself."

"What about me? Are the Russians going to be hunting me?"

"We don't think so. They know that you are not an agent. With Bormann dead and their network temporarily disabled here, we think that you are no longer a priority for them."

"Can I get out of here then?"

"Given your help on this matter, however irregular, your country is grateful to you. We have arranged for you to be honorably discharged from the army a few months early. I am sure that Colonel Kleet will personally walk your papers through."

Kleet actually looked happy. "I'll get right on it."

"One more thing, can I use the phone?"

Monroe desperately wanted to contact Dionne, but had no way of doing so. He knew that she lived in Montreal, but that was really about all. He remembered one of their conversations. He made a call to Kemp at the hospital.

"Kemp?"

"Doc, it's great to hear your voice. I thought you were dead."

"I'm OK. It's great to talk to you."

"What do you need? You didn't call to socialize."

"Remember that British WAVE you were seeing? I need to know the whereabouts of a Canadian who served in the British 8th army. Maybe she would help if she is still speaking to you. His name is Harry Gruber. I think he was a captain."

"We are still on good terms. However, it will cost you a bottle of French perfume. I won't ask why you want the information, but I bet it involves a girl. I'm on it."

"I'm stateside now but I'll get it to you somehow."

"Not to worry. I have a buddy who keeps it in stock. I'll send you the bill."

"Thanks, I owe you."

"Again."

"Again."

# 76

As usual, Kemp came through, sending Monroe Harry's address and telephone number in Montreal. Since Monroe was now a civilian with no real ties, he thought it would be best to go to Montreal and meet Harry directly. Dionne had been through a lot and he knew her family would be protective. He hoped after weeks of no contact that she still felt the same way about him as he did about her.

He waited outside Harry's home until he returned from work. He was opening the door. Monroe approached. "Captain Gruber, Harry, I am a friend of Dionne. She told me if I needed to get in touch with her to find you, my name is Jack..."

"Monroe. I had a feeling you would show up. Dionne told me about the two of you."

"I assure you my intentions are strictly honorable."

"I certainly hope so. Dionne is like a sister to me and as much as I want to keep her from getting hurt, I'm nothing compared to my father and her father."

"When can I see her?"

"Well, she is not in Montreal. Both the Israelis and our family thought it best that she lay low for a while. "

"That's what happened to me. My government wouldn't let me contact her. They think we are safe now."

"Like you, I was in the war. Forgive my skepticism when I hear that a government says I am safe."

"Then let me speak to her father."

"Of course. I could tell by the way Dionne talked about you that she cared very much for you."

Dionne's father and uncle met them the next day at Schwartz's Delicatessen. Harry brought Monroe. "Not exactly neutral ground," thought Monroe.

After introductions they decided to order lunch. Monroe was a veteran of New York delicatessens. He ordered a Reuben sandwich. He added poutine, even though he had never tasted it, to demonstrate his knowledge of Canadian cuisine. A pitcher of beer was ordered for the four of them. By the way his companions drank it, he expected it was only the first.

Her father spoke first. "Tell me about yourself." Monroe started to say something, but Harry interrupted. "He's a doctor."

"Yeah, so what else can he do?"

"If it really makes a difference, I ran track in college. I also played hockey in high school. Around my house we had to learn to fix everything. I'm a very handy guy," he answered, clearly trying to impress.

"Not bad, and not afraid to toot your own horn either," said her father, not overwhelmed.

"The point is sir, I love Dionne and I think she loves me. What I've learned about her is that what you and Harry and her uncle say won't mean a whole lot if she's made her mind up. I know, though, when we weren't sure if we would make it out of Europe, she thought only of her family. She would want your blessing."

Uncle Morty finally spoke. "Bernie, tell him where she is. He seems to be a good lad. More importantly, he's not a putz."

"While my brother-in-law can be somewhat blunt, he's also a good judge of character. Dionne is not in Montreal. She is at a cottage in northern Ontario that belongs to a client of ours. She was urged to stay there until everyone thought it was safe for her to return. Is it?"

"I'm sworn to secrecy about everything that took place. I have been assured that it's safe. If you don't believe me, ask your friend Avrum. Yes, I know Avrum and Simon too. They wouldn't lie to you. I'll go get her myself."

"Your word is good enough for me. Avrum and Simon need not be involved unless harm comes to Dionne."

Monroe thought that he had won over Dionne's family, but her father's remark left him a bit uneasy.

Harry broke the silence. "Would you two cut this poor bastard a break?" Bernie and Morty started laughing at Monroe's expense. Now he was sure he was in.

"OK it's done. Then I will tell Jack how to get to Temagami. Now, let's have some dessert."

# 77

Harry wrote directions for Monroe to get from Montreal to Lake Temagami in northern Ontario. In a surprise move, Uncle Morty loaned Monroe his car, a new model Chrysler. It took Monroe a couple of days to get there. He followed the Rideau River to Ottawa where he stayed overnight. He then headed toward North Bay and then followed the main route north. Harry had told him to go into the town of Temagami. Someone at the bait store would know where "PJ's cottage" was and take him over to it as it was on an island in the lake. Harry had also explained that PJ was a lumber man who had done business with his father and uncle for years, shipping his lumber from Montreal to the East Coast of the United States.

Their business relationship had evolved into a close friendship between a pillar of the Presbyterian Church and two Jewish guys from Montreal. They had done each other favors on many occasions. "If you ever meet PJ and ask him about his Jewish friends, he'll just say, 'They don't eat ham or some damn thing,'" laughed Harry.

The road to Temagami was winding and narrow. It was bordered on both sides by trees. It was one of the most peaceful areas that Monroe had ever been to. He saw many lumber trucks with the name of PJ's company on them. He also saw a couple of signs warning of moose crossing the road at night. There was also no shortage of mosquitoes.

He got to the bait shop at around 7 PM, though this far north the sun would not set until well after nine. The bait shop owner knew exactly where PJ's cottage was. He had a young boy in the store take Monroe over to it. The trip lasted about 10 minutes. The lake was spectacular. The water was crystal clear. The boy, Hughie, told him that the lake was spring fed and that there were hundreds of islands, most of which had cottages on them. "People come up here in the summer from Southern Ontario. We even have some Americans that come up." Monroe now understood what Dionne meant when she said that someone could forget what day it was staying up here. It was indeed a good place for Dionne to relax and hide.

Hughie docked the boat. Monroe got out and gave him some money. "Do you want me to wait? If it gets dark you're stuck here till tomorrow." Monroe hoped he would be stuck until tomorrow. "No thanks, Hughie. I see there's a boat here. I'll be able to get back."

Monroe walked up the steps to the cottage. It was probably the most anxious he had ever been. He knocked on the door and wiped his sweaty palms on his pants. Dionne answered.

"I wonder if you could help me. A guy named Harry told me they needed a doctor up here."

Then the smile appeared, the one that made him breathless.

"Took you long enough."

# EPILOGUE

Dimitri was ushered into Stalin's Kremlin office. Beria was there as well. They waited for Stalin to speak. "Comrade Dimitri, I have reviewed your reports. I am happy to say that you accomplished your mission. You have rid us of a traitor. While I was not happy that an American was involved, it sounds like he knew nothing of who Bormann really was."

"Yes, Comrade. The American colonel was only concerned about rescuing the doctor."

"And the girl?"

"Of no consequence, Comrade."

"We shall keep an eye on them anyway. Now, I have another job for you. One of our operatives in the United States failed. He recruited an unstable American. Fortunately the American is dead. Our agent has returned home and is staying outside of Moscow. It would be very unfortunate if he were to have an accident."

"Yes Comrade, I understand," he answered and left.

Beria turned to Stalin. "Unfortunate business, Koba. I thought our agent would do a better job."

"Not to worry, Lavrentiy, there are many others in America.

# AFTERWORD

This is a work of fiction.  The fictional characters are a creation of the author's imagination and experiences.

The historical figures all existed.  The events in which they participate in this book are completely fictional.  They never made any of the remarks herein, though the author would like to think they could have.  In addition, the timing of events only approximates the historical timeline.

Stalin, Churchill, Roosevelt  and Hitler are well known historical figures.  Their lives are well chronicled in multiple works about their lives and specifically about events that are adapted to this book.   Only Churchill left a memoir  - *The History of The Second World War*.   It is a valuable tool for anyone interested in World War II and Sir Winston Churchill.

Martin Bormann was  the head of Hitler's Chancellery.  He controlled access to Hitler and was present for many of the decisions made during the war.  His skeleton was unearthed in 1972 in Berlin and his identity verified by dental records.

Schwartz's is a Montreal landmark.  The author highly recommends the smoked meat.

Lake Temagami is in northern Ontario, where the author has spent many summers with family and friends.   It is a beautiful spring fed lake where you truly can lose track of time.

The author would like to thank his wife, Wendy, for going through all the versions of this book. Her help and support were invaluable. He would also like to thank his daughter, Elizabeth, for her careful proofreading of the manuscript. Any typographical or grammatical errors are the author's responsibility.

*Kirkwood, Missouri June, 2024*

# ABOUT THE AUTHOR

Michael Berk is a physician in St. Louis, Missouri. He has always had an interest in history, specifically that of the two World Wars and the American Cvil War, both non-fictional and fictional. He is a fan of the St. Louis Blues and Cardinals and enjoys cycling.

Made in the USA
Coppell, TX
11 October 2024